"Is it true?

We hear that floozy who ran off to Hollywood spent the night with you." The deacon's wife had decided to stop beating around the bush.

Not for the first time, Howard Blake was amazed at the speed and accuracy of Crystal Creek's grapevine. "What floozy would that be?"

"Eva Carmichael." She spat out the name as if it were distasteful.

"Eva did stay here last night, yes."

"Very incautious of you, Reverend," the deacon said. "*Very* incautious. I don't need to tell you that your actions have been under scrutiny since you took over your father's position...."

"Howard! Can you do up my zipper?" Eva's voice preceded her into the room by milliseconds. She almost ran through the door. She was wearing nothing but a strapless bra and a half-slip, and, with one arm through the armhole of her dress, she stopped dead in her tracks.

The deacon's wife leapt to her tiny feet and thrust out her impressive bosom, clinging to her purse as if it were a lifeline. "I refuse to stay in the same room with this shameless Jezebel!" Like a frigate cresting a tidal wave, she started across the room.

"Come, now," Howard said, in a voice designed to soothe ruffled feathers...or stormy seas. "Let's not be quick to judge."

"Judging has little to do with it. What's happened here is pretty clear, Reverend."

"Obviously not," Howard replied. Smiling benignly, he said, "Ladies, gentlmen, I'd like you to meet my wife."

Penny Richards is acknowledged as the author of this work.

Special thanks and acknowledgment to Sutton Press Inc.
for its contribution to the concept for the
Crystal Creek series.

ISBN 0-373-82533-1

UNANSWERED PRAYERS

Penny Richards

UNANSWERED PRAYERS

Harlequin Books

TORONTO • NEW YORK • LONDON
AMSTERDAM • PARIS • SYDNEY • HAMBURG
STOCKHOLM • ATHENS • TOKYO • MILAN
MADRID • WARSAW • BUDAPEST • AUCKLAND

Dear Reader,

Romantic Times greeted *Passionate Kisses*, Penny Richards's first foray into Crystal Creek, with a ringing endorsement, saying she "wonderfully blends the past and the present, and will entertain readers with a glimpse at a less confident but no less cocky young J.T."

Now, prepare for a return engagement! Ms. Richards catapults us once more down memory lane. When the new marriage of Rio and Maggie Langley takes a heart-stopping, unexpected turn, the author uses the opportunity to share with the reader the surprisingly poignant story of the courtship and marriage of Maggie's parents, Crystal Creek mainstays Eva and Howard Blake. It's an eye-opening, soul-wrenching revelation to their daughter. The drama of Maggie's and Rio's present-day difficulties is more than matched by the unexpected emergence of Eva's long-buried, startling secret.

Next month, author Sandy Steen returns to Crystal Creek with an intriguing, harrowing tale centered around Lynn McKinney and her new family, Sam Russell and his daughters. It's almost Christmas, and the extended McKinney clan should be returning to the Double C, not haphazardly disappearing from it!

Watch for *Somewhere Other Than the Night*, available wherever Harlequin books are sold. And stick around in Crystal Creek—home of sultry Texas drawls, smooth Texas charm and tall, sexy Texans!

Marsha Zinberg,
Senior Editor and Editorial Coordinator,
Crystal Creek

A Note from the Author

When I first began to acquaint myself with the people and the town of Crystal Creek, I was mildly surprised to learn that Howard Blake, the Baptist preacher, was married to a former actress. I didn't think much more about it—after all, Howard was a secondary character in the series and *way* past the age of being a hero.

Then, when several of us Crystal Creek authors got together to come up with new story ideas, and to tour the Hill Country, my good friend Sandy Steen mentioned that she, too, was fascinated by the idea that the preacher had married an actress.

As is apt to happen when writers get together, someone had the great idea to "go back in time" and create the lives of some of the characters in their youth. J.T. and Pauline, Hank Travis, and yes, Howard and Eva! Now some lucky author had the perfect opportunity to explore just how it could be that a nice, upstanding young preacher got ensnared by a woman with a —gasp!—*past!* I immediately volunteered!

As with J.T. and Pauline's story, I loved going back and flavoring the story with tidbits from an earlier time. It was fun writing about two such dissimilar people and exploring the different ways they approached life's problems. I learned a lot of details about the fifties, and gained a lot of insight about faith and perseverance and the many faces of love while writing this book. I hope you will, too.

Penny Richards

Who's Who in Crystal Creek

Have you missed the story of one of your favorite Crystal Creek characters? Here's a quick guide to help you easily locate the titles and story lines:

Available at your local bookseller, or see the Crystal Creek back-page ad for reorder information.

CHAPTER ONE

"THERE'S Miss High and Mighty, herself."

The feminine, sibilant whisper carried down the aisle, transmitted on the deodorized air. Maggie Langley, who had stopped her supermarket buggy in front of the ice cream section, was too engrossed in planning the impromptu celebration of her two-month-old marriage to Rio Langley to pay the comment any mind.

She and Rio had been so busy since they got married, they hadn't had much time for fun. Even sex had been rushed...except for the day Rio had led her up into the hayloft and they'd made out like kids sneaking around behind their parents' backs.

A naughty smile curved her mouth. If anything could take her mind off the upcoming appointment with her gynecologist in Austin the following day, it was a night of wild, decadent sex with the man she loved....

"Just look at her! Don't she think she's somethin' in that fancy outfit!"

Outfit. Hmm. She'd wear the scandalous black wisp of a thing Amanda had given her that was supposed to be a nightie and that she'd never had the courage to put on. Forget the ice cream. This was turning into an all-out seduction. She'd buy champagne and have candles—lots of candles. And music. "Shush. She'll hear."

"Don't *shush* me. She ain't no better'n the rest of us. Why, she practically shacked up with that half-breed! Can you imagine a shameless hussy like that tryin' to tell the rest of us how to raise our kids? That's a hoot, now idn't it?"

Hearing the word *half-breed* alerted Maggie to the fact that the woman was talking about her. She froze, as stiff and unyielding as the container of ice cream in her hands.

"I said shush up," cautioned the other voice. "She'll hear, and besides, he did marry her."

"Well, whoop-de-dang-do!" the harpy said, in a voice that dripped sarcasm. "That broke-down, bas-tard rodeo rider ain't no prize."

Maggie was too shocked to realize that her hands were stinging with cold. Hot color scalded her face, but it wasn't the heat of shame or embarrassment. It was anger. Fury, in fact.

Having grown up with a preacher father, in a family whose very cornerstone was love, it was hard for her to imagine how anyone could be so self-righteous, not to mention bigoted. Every time she confronted either attitude, she grew angry—and more than a little sad. Gossip was as much a part of Crystal Creek as its small-town friendliness, but Maggie wasn't sure she'd

ever get used to it. Didn't these women have any idea
how much potential pain their comments carried?

She wondered if she should confront the spiteful
woman or pretend she hadn't heard the unkind comments. She didn't care what was said about her, but
Rio had suffered enough during his life for being a
"bastard half-breed."

Maggie swallowed hard and gripped the cardboard
container tighter, a silent war raging inside her. She
wanted to march over to the woman and inform her
that whatever Rio Langley's heritage might be, he was
a good man, one who didn't have to boost his self es-
teem by hurting other people. He was kind and generous, with a heart as big as the state they lived in.

Drawing in another quivering breath, Maggie cast
a sideways look at the two women. A gasp of shock
escaped her. Fran Dunbarr and Ada Farmer! Why,
they were both women she saw often in her capacity as
a social worker.

Fran's daughter, Chrissie, who was marginally re-
tarded from an oxygen depletion at birth, had two il-
legitimate children herself, and Ada's husband, Bull,
was a drunk who battered his family on a regular basis.

Like many abused women, Ada refused to press
charges, and her unwillingness to get help was affect-
ing her children. Her seventeen-year-old son, Rick,
had experienced several minor brushes with the law the
past year. Most recently, he and his buddies had
gained notoriety with Crystal Creek residents and

Claro County sheriff Wayne Jackson for taking turns shooting at a neighbor's dog with a .22 rifle.

Though he denied pulling the trigger, Rick was now on six months' probation. Feeling he needed something to occupy his time and keep him away from the negative influence of the boys he hung out with, Maggie and the county psychologist had suggested an after-school job.

Unfortunately, even if Bull Farmer's reputation as a no-good drunk hadn't extended to his son, news of the dog shooting made prospective employers wary. When no one would hire the boy, Rio had seen Maggie's dilemma and offered Rick a job at the ranch, assuring her that he and his brother, Jeremy, could always use another hand with the stock. Since Rick didn't have transportation, Rio even hauled the boy back and forth to work.

And this was the thanks he got. Slurs and name calling. The urge to reciprocate rose in Maggie on a dark wave of indignation. Angry words trembled on her tongue. Her hands shook; the cooler of ice cream wavered through the sheen of her tears.

Be not overcome of evil, but overcome evil with good. The familiar passage from Romans came to her so clearly, her father might have been standing next to her. *Heap coals of fire. Turn the other cheek. Pray for your enemies.* All avenues of behavior she'd grown up hearing and done her best to incorporate into her life.

A staunch belief in God and his word was Howard Blake's answer to everything, which, Maggie supposed, was the good and right way to deal with life's problems. But her husband Greg's senseless death had weakened her faith in God's wisdom, and finding Rio's love was the only thing that had given it back.

Maybe she was just more like her mama than she was her daddy—not that Eva Blake was anything but the perfect minister's wife. But, as her mother often said, Howard had been born good; she had to work at it. The same way Maggie did.

Maggie set the ice cream down as carefully as if it were a vial of nitroglycerin. She uttered a little prayer, lifted her chin and, plastering a bright, false smile on her face, turned and gripped the handle of her grocery cart.

"Fran! Ada!" she exclaimed, heading toward the women as if she'd just noticed them. "How are you?"

She had the satisfaction of seeing Fran's narrow face pale and the brief flickering of shame in Ada's dark, birdlike eyes.

"I'm fine, Miz Langley, and you?" Ada said, careful to keep her gaze averted.

"Very well, thanks. How's Rick?"

Ada looked as if the question surprised her. "Why, uh, he's fine."

Overcome evil with good, Maggie, remember?

"That's great," she said with a gentle smile. "My husband says he's a conscientious worker. He doesn't know much about animals, but he's willing to learn."

The few words of praise brought a flush of pleasure and pride to Ada's sallow face. Maggie was suddenly glad she'd reacted to the situation the way she had. She wondered how long it had been since Ada had heard anything good about her son, and realized what a shame it was that Rick was branded a loser simply because of his father. The stereotyping was no more fair than the stigma Rio had carried on his shoulders while growing up in Crystal Creek.

"Ain't you gonna ask about Chrissie?" Fran said with a sniff and a look of disapproval down her narrow nose.

Maggie smiled politely. "I was just about to. How is she?"

"Pukin' up her guts."

"Oh," Maggie said in concern. "Don't tell me she's picked up that virus that's going around."

Fran shook her head. "Nope. She's pregnant agin."

Maggie couldn't disguise her horror—or her dismay. Chrissie's baby was only five months old.

"Oh, Fran! Why didn't she use the birth control pills the health clinic provided?"

"'Cause Delbert was sick and Billy Don was workin' over't the quarry. She didn't have no way to get there."

Billy Don was generally presumed to be the father of Chrissie's daughter, though by her own admission she couldn't be sure.

"She could have called me," Maggie said. "I'd have been glad to take her."

"I'll 'member that next time," Fran said.

Next time. When would that be? Maggie wondered. Seven or so months from now? "Is there anything I can do?" she offered, feeling somehow responsible. Even though she knew that she and the system could only do so much, and that there came a time a person had to help himself, Maggie felt as if she'd failed the Dunbarrs.

"You might bring her some of them candies she likes so well," Fran said. "Can't get them with food stamps, you know, and she's been cravin' them something terrible. Them candies and Co'-Colas."

Candy and Cokes. Maggie started to tell Fran that Chrissie needed well-balanced meals, but realized that the advice would be not only resented but ignored.

"I'll see what I can do," she said. Fighting a feeling of futility, she glanced at her watch. "Gosh!" She feigned surprise. "It's later than I thought! I've got to run. I'll see you in a couple of weeks, ladies, okay?"

Without waiting for their answer, Maggie wheeled her grocery buggy around and started back down the aisle. She'd get her flowers and, as her Uncle Bud often said, get the heck out of Dodge.

RIO, JEREMY AND RICK were moving a pen full of broncs from one pasture to another. Rio sat the saddle easily as the horses meandered down the wide aisle between pens; his younger brother and Rick less so. Babydoll, Rio's blue heeler, a recent gift from Maggie, trotted along by his gelding's side, veering off to nip at a straggler's heels at Rio's command.

While Rio watched, a particularly ornery mare whirled and kicked at the dog. Just what happened after that was anyone's guess. There was the staccato sound of barking, a shrill whinny and a sudden dusty burst of speed from the pack of horses. Rio saw Rick's horse rear up and heard the boy's startled cry as he tumbled off and landed in a heap on the ground.

Before Rio could do more than wonder if the kid had been hurt—and how badly—Rick leaped to his feet. Rio gave a relieved sigh, but then, to his stunned disbelief, Rick screamed a blistering curse and aimed a vicious kick at the dog's ribs. Babydoll yelped and ran, cowering from the attack.

Muttering an epithet of his own, Rio slung a denim-clad leg over the buckskin's neck and slid from his broad back, stalking toward his young charge. Before he got to Rick, the boy had whipped off his belt and begun to flail Babydoll, punctuating each stroke of the belt with another curse.

Rio cursed, too. Falling off a horse was no excuse for abusing the dog. Radiating fury, he snatched the leather strap from Rick's hands.

The sudden action caught Rick off guard. Confronted with the rage on Rio's face, he stumbled back a step. Rio folded the belt and took a step toward Rick, who raised his arms and ducked his head in a protective gesture that said more than words ever could.

Rio stopped dead still, his anger at the boy draining away like the waters of the Claro River when

The dumbfounded look on the boy's face was comical. "What?"

"You heard me. Come over here and pet Babydoll and tell her you're sorry."

"B-but she's just a dumb dog. She won't know what I'm doing."

"She's a lot smarter than a lot of people I know, and she'll know, all right. Now get your butt over here."

Rick took one slow step and then two. He stopped an arm's length from Rio and stretched out a tentative hand toward the dog. The instant Rick's fingers made contact with her nose, Rio said a soft "Boo!" Rick jumped back so fast he lost his footing and fell onto the ground with another curse.

Seeing Rio's slow, unrepentant smile, Rick pushed himself to his feet and thrust out his chin. "You're a sick man, you know that?"

"Maybe so, but you deserved that one. You ought to be glad Babydoll didn't bite your damned finger off. Now tell her you're sorry."

Rick glared at Rio. "No more funny stuff. I'm on to you."

"No more funny stuff," Rio promised.

Cautiously, Rick approached the dog once more. Babydoll looked up at Rio as if to ask if everything was all right. He murmured comforting words to her. Her baleful brown gaze slewed back to Rick, who riffled the hair of her neck in a tentative way. Babydoll's tail moved in a single, halfhearted wag.

"Tell her," Rio prompted.

Rick gave Rio a look that could kill. "I'm sorry," he growled.

Babydoll looked at Rio.

"She doesn't believe it," Rio said, "and frankly, neither do I. Dogs are like women, son. You've got to be nice to them. Sweet-talk them, and they're yours forever." Rio followed the sexist statement with a sheepish grin. "'Course, don't ever tell my wife I said that. She'll have my hide."

The irritation in Rick's eyes softened the slightest bit. It might have been a trick of the dying light, but Rio thought he saw one corner of the boy's mouth twitch.

"I'm sorry, Babydoll," Rick crooned, scratching the dog's hide harder. "I won't ever hurt you again."

"Don't say it if you don't mean it," Rio said.

Rick met his employer's unrelenting gaze without flinching. "I mean it."

The dog must have sensed that he was telling the truth, because she turned her head into his palm and began to lick it. Little kids and dogs were so forgiving it was downright sad, Rio thought. Maybe mankind in general ought to take a few lessons.

"She forgives you," Rio said. "And she believes you."

Rick looked at him, suspicion gleaming in his eyes. "How do you know?"

"Communicating with animals is an old Indian trick," Rio said, straight-faced.

The kid bought it. "Oh."

"See that you don't let her—or me—down," Rio charged, putting the dog to the ground, where she stood wagging her tail and grinning up at them.

"Yes, sir. I mean, no, sir. I won't."

"We won't talk about this again," Rio said. "It's forgotten." He gave Rick a hearty slap on the back.

Rick gave an anguished cry, and his knees buckled.

"What is it?" Rio asked, but even as he asked the question, he knew.

Rick squared his shoulders. "Nothing," he said through gritted teeth. "I'm just body sore from all this manual labor."

"And I'm your friendly Avon lady," Rio quipped, his voice laced with sarcasm. "Take off your shirt."

"What?"

"You heard me. Take off your damn shirt."

Rick clenched his fists and shook his head. Moisture glimmered in his eyes. "You can't make me."

Rio's voice was as gentle to Rick as it had been to the dog a few minutes earlier. "You're dead wrong there, boy, but I'm not up to proving it, and neither are you. I know what I'll find under that shirt...."

A single tear slithered down Rick's pale cheek with its end-of-the-day stubble that somehow made him look younger.

"And I know your life is hell. I know that you get so mad you want to do to the whole world what he does to you, but there's a better way."

"Yeah, what's that?" Rick asked in an angry, sarcastic voice.

"Don't get mad—get even."

Rick looked surprised. "How?"

"By being a bigger man than he is and not lowering yourself to his standards. By taking all that frustration and anger inside you and channeling it into something constructive." Rio thought he saw a glimmer of hope in Rick's dark eyes. "You do it by standing beside your mom and giving her the strength to press charges. You do it by making good grades and going to college so that you can walk away from this life to something better."

A single sob racked Rick's wiry body. He crossed his arms and hugged himself tightly, regarding Rio from eyes that had seen far too much. "How do I do all that?"

"I'll help you," Rio said. "Maggie and I will help you. If you'll let us."

For long moments Rick just stood there, looking into Rio's steady gaze as if he were trying to figure out whether or not he was telling the truth. Finally, he swiped at his face with his shirtsleeve and gave a sharp nod.

Rio felt his body relax. "And you won't show me your back?"

Rick shook his head.

"Probably just as well," Rio said. "If I saw what he'd done, I'd just have to go beat the hell out of him.

He'd press charges, *I'd* wind up in jail, and Maggie'd be madder 'n hell."

Rick gave him a quick, sideways glance. "I thought you didn't hold with violence."

Rio rubbed at his eyebrow with his thumb. His smile bordered on sheepish. "I don't believe in abusing animals, but then, I like them a lot better than most men I've met. Usually when an animal hurts you, it doesn't mean any harm. Can't say the same for most of mankind, though. They seem to like to brood on other people's misdeeds and plot their own little revenges."

A frown creased Rick's forehead as he thought about that. "I guess you're right," he said at last. "It doesn't say much for us, does it?"

"No, son, it doesn't," Rio said, his heart heavy. "Come on. I'll take you home."

BULL FARMER'S battered truck sat in the front yard, angled as close to the porch as he could get. Probably so he wouldn't have to crawl very far to the front door when he came home so stinking drunk he couldn't walk, Rio thought with rare uncharitableness.

When he recalled Rick's tortured features and the tears of shame in his eyes, Rio's jaw knotted in a fresh surge of anger. Come what might, he had to say something to the sorry outfit who'd sired Rick, just a little something to take him down a peg or two.

Rio could picture Maggie telling him it wasn't his place to interfere, to let the law do its job, but dammit, without Ada's cooperation, the law's hands were tied. Besides, it *was* his place in a way. Rick was his employee, and Bull's actions indirectly affected the boy's work performance.

Rio stifled a sarcastic grin and shut off the truck's engine. Hell, the reasoning sounded good, anyway, he thought, getting out of the truck.

"What are you doing?" Rick asked.

"I need to have a few words with your dad."

Rick's face turned chalky. "I wouldn't do that if I were you, Mr. Langley."

"If you're worried about him taking it out on you, you can bunk at my place until he gets over it."

Rick looked Rio straight in the eye. "Only thing left he can do to me is kill me, and that might be a blessing. It's you I'm worried about."

Rio reached out and clasped the kid's shoulder. "Don't worry about me. I'm a big boy. And don't you ever let me hear you say anything like that again, Rick Farmer. Life is a gift. Granted, yours might be rougher than most, but you can't ever give up hoping and working toward something better."

"That's easy for you to say."

"You could be right. I don't know exactly where you're comin' from. Nobody ever beat me, but my life hasn't been a bed of roses, believe me. I had a pretty sorry life myself until I met Maggie. Now I realize that everything I experienced was preparing me for her and our life together now."

Rick just looked at him uncomprehendingly.

Rio shook his head. "Look, I don't know how to explain it. All I know is that if you don't ever have any bad in your life, you can't really appreciate the good when it comes along." He offered Rick an embarrassed smile. "Let's go in. Or would you rather wait out here?"

"No. I'm coming in, too," Rick said, falling into step beside Rio. They crossed the yard to the small frame house. Rick wiped his feet on the mat outside the door and went inside. Rio followed suit, taking off his Stetson when he stepped through the entrance.

The first thing he noticed was that the Farmer house was scrupulously clean. Furnishings were minimal, and the decor was Early Flea Market with a little Chip and Scratch thrown in, but what possessions the Farmers had were spotless.

An uninspired gray, Formica-topped bar separated the living room from the kitchen, where Ada stood tending a skillet of frying pork chops.

Bull, who spent most of his time on the road driving an eighteen-wheeler, was the perfect stereotype of every redneck joke ever conceived. He wallowed in an oversize brown plaid recliner, his Western shirt unsnapped and his belly hanging over a gigantic silver-and-turquoise belt buckle. The pointed toes of his cheap boots were tipped in some faux silver metal, and the fancy-stitched tops disappeared beneath the flared legs of his tan stretch jeans.

His neck was thick, and so were his lips, which were partly hidden by a waxed handlebar mustache. His bulbous, red-veined nose looked as if it had been broken a time or two. The fat of his cheeks almost hid his eyes when he smiled, which he was doing at that moment... maliciously.

"Well, well, well. Look who's here," he said, reaching for a glass of whiskey sitting on the Spanish-style end table at his side.

Ada whirled, the turning fork in her hand. When she caught sight of Rio, the haggard look on her face became one of apprehension. "Mr. Langley!"

"Ada," Rio acknowledged with a nod.

"What can we do for you?" she asked.

"I'd like to speak to Mr. Farmer, if I might." Rio paused and added, "Alone."

Ada's anxious gaze darted to Bull, who scratched lazily at his crotch.

"Whatever you got to say, you can say in front of my wife."

Rio's smile was as taut as the emotions in the room. "I like that even better. That way there won't be any misunderstandings later."

Bull's pelletlike eyes narrowed. He quaffed another generous mouthful of the liquor. With a growling shudder, he shook his head and clenched his teeth against the Wild Turkey's bite. Then he wiped the back of his hand over his fleshy mouth.

Rio shifted his weight to one leg and slapped his hat against his thigh in a slow, mesmerizing movement. "I'm not going to say this but once, so I'll try to make myself clear."

"By all means," Bull said, waving his beefy arm in a magnanimous display of false cordiality.

"I know what's going on here with Ada and Rick and probably the girls. It's gonna stop, Bull," Rio said in a gentle, almost weary voice. "And it's gonna stop right now."

Bull thrust his chin out to a pugnacious angle. "I don't know what you think it is that I do to my family," he said. "And I don't really care. Now get the hell out of my house, before I call the law."

Rio swept his hat toward the phone that hung on the far wall. "Don't let my bein' here stop you. I'd love Wayne Jackson to get a gander of the boy's back."

Bull shot a murderous look at Rick, who stumbled backward as if he'd received a physical blow. Rio's heart throbbed like the ache of a sore tooth.

"What you been doin', boy? Spillin' your guts?" Bull yelled, the veins in his neck standing out.

"No sir," Rick answered. "I didn't say a thing."

"He didn't have to tell me," Rio said, going to stand directly in front of the man. "It's common knowledge that you beat your family, Bull. My wife has seen the evidence plenty of times."

Bull's face turned livid. He gripped the arms of the chair to heave himself up.

Rio placed his hand squarely in Bull's chest. "Sit down, shut up and listen," he commanded, giving a mighty shove.

Ada gave a little cry of surprise as her husband toppled back into the chair, knocking over his glass of liquor in the process. "You're way outta line, In-jun," Bull blustered, pointing a sausagelike finger at Rio. "How I discipline my family is none of your damn business—or your snotty bitch of a wife's."

For a man his size, Rio could move exceptionally fast. Before anyone realized what he was doing, his hat was on the floor. The fingers of his right hand closed around Bull's thick throat in a grip that had grown strong from years of clenching the leather rigging on bulls and broncs, a grip that had been all that stood between a broke and desperate cowboy and the hard, unforgiving ground of a rodeo arena and the final in-dignity of failure.

Bull gagged and glared up at Rio with so much malice, he could feel the hate emanating upward in invisible waves.

Thrusting his face close to Bull's, he said, "Don't ever call my wife a name again, you sorry excuse for a human being. As a matter of fact, don't call her any-thing except Mrs. Langley, ma'am, and then only if you're spoken to."

Rio released his hold on Bull and bent to pick up his hat. When he straightened, Bull's glare was still fixed unwaveringly on him, while he massaged his throat with a hand that trembled the slightest bit. Rio combed his fingers through his dark hair and settled his Stetson on his head.

"I've got an even better idea," he said in a thoughtful tone. "If you just happen to be home when she stops by, why don't you just make it a point to disappear? You're not fit to breathe the same air she does. Is that clear enough?''

''You're gonna be sorry you did this, breed,'' Bull croaked through aching vocal cords.

''Yeah, well, we all do things we're sorry for, and we all make mistakes, Bull,'' Rio said, heading for the door. ''But if I were you, I'd be real careful about making any more. I think your luck just ran out.''

He turned and headed for the door. ''I'll pick you up tomorrow afternoon,'' he said to Rick. ''Same time.''

Nodding, Rick followed Rio out the door, a combination of awe, admiration and fear in his eyes.

''You step a foot on this place again, and I'll kill you,'' Bull screamed after him. ''Damn you to hell, I may kill you anyway.'' The sound of the whiskey bottle shattering against the door punctuated the threat.

Rio hardly heard. A final rush of adrenaline carried him to his truck. He felt better getting that off his chest. He just hoped he hadn't made things worse for Rick and Ada.

''You better not come tomorrow,'' Rick said as Rio climbed into the truck's cab.

Rio paused, his hand on the door handle. ''You don't want to work for me anymore?''

''I do!'' Rick said. He shook his head. ''You don't know him. He gets crazy out of his mind when he gets really drunk. Does all kinds of terrible things. Then when he sobers up, he doesn't remember half of it.''

''What are you trying to say, Rick?''

"I'll meet you in front of the mailbox on the highway. If you come here, he'll be primed and ready for you, and there's no use asking for trouble."

Rio nodded. "Will you and your mom be all right, or did I just buy you another beating?"

"You rattled his cage pretty good," Rick said. "He doesn't know what you'll really do." He shrugged. "I imagine he'll just drink and worry on it a while. We'll be fine."

Rio nodded. "If you need me, you know where I am."

CHAPTER TWO

DURING THE RIDE HOME, Rio's thoughts were filled with his confrontation with Bull Farmer. He prayed he hadn't made things worse for Rick, but if ever a kid needed some guidance and someone to stand up for him, Rick Farmer was that kid.

Rio rubbed a hand over his whisker-stubbled cheek and expelled a harsh sigh. Now he understood why Maggie was so down some evenings. He was always telling her to leave her work at the office, but after today, he could see how much easier that was said than done. The amazing thing was that she was able to stay as objective as she did.

Rio's heart lifted when he saw her car in the driveway, but he had a few more chores to do before he could call it a night. He stopped by the trailer to visit with Tess and Emily and check with Jeremy to see how the broncs had settled in, but Tess said his brother had driven in to Crystal Creek to pick up some hamburgers for supper.

Having his recently discovered younger brother and his family on the ranch was a pleasure Rio was glad he hadn't missed. As he did often of late, he wondered if the man who'd fathered them both was lonely, and if he was sorry for the world of distortion he'd built now that it had collapsed on him.

He knew Jeremy missed his dad—and probably the easy life-style he'd grown up with. But he was a stubborn kid, and he was still mad and hurt to the bone by John Hardin Westlake's scheme to separate him from Tess and their unborn baby. Tess's father and Westlake had constructed a web of lies that put the two young people's love to the test. Only a miracle had brought them all together. A miracle and a woman named Maggie, who'd been willing to put her job on the line.

As Rio played with six-and-a-half-month-old Emily, he tried to imagine what his life had been like before he'd found her on his front doorstep. Lonely. Empty. But Emily's appearance had brought Maggie back into his life, and eventually Jeremy and Tess had come too. And suddenly Rio had found himself with a real family. It was nice, he thought. Real nice.

After giving Emily the attention she considered her due each evening, Rio checked Babydoll again and gave his gelding a rubdown and a handful of sugar cubes. Something about the mundane tasks was calming. It didn't occur to him that the small everyday chores were a validation—maybe even a celebration—of his own life and happiness.

When he stepped through the door of the house he shared with Maggie an hour and a half later, the aroma of baking apples wafted through the air to tickle his nostrils. He smiled. She had baked him an apple pie. He wondered what he'd done to deserve it. He wondered what he'd done to deserve his sweet, sweet Maggie. The sheer rightness of his life banished the last lingering thoughts of Bull Farmer from his mind.

He hung his Stetson on the antique hall tree and took off his boots in the entryway. Maggie got a little testy if he tracked up her floors. Considering the time she spent keeping the place clean, he couldn't say he blamed her.

"Maggie!" he called, padding toward the living room in his stocking feet.

"In here!"

Rio made his way through the house toward the sound of her voice. He stopped just inside the bed-room door. The room was dark, except for the flames of literally dozens of candles—tall, squat, thin, fat— a recreation that was poignantly reminiscent of their wedding night.

Maggie lay on the bed, the hair that tumbled over her bare, fair shoulders as bright as the copper kettle her Aunt Hattie had given them at their kitchen shower. A crystal bowl filled with grapes sat in front of her. She held a wineglass in her hand and swirled dark red liquid with a lazy motion. She was wearing a sultry, sexy smile and a pristine white sheet.

"Hi." She raised the glass to her lips, her green eyes twinkling over its rim, as if she had a secret too deli-cious to keep.

"Hi."

She reached out a hand toward him, and the sheet slipped heart-stoppingly low. Dazed, Rio headed toward the bed, his movements as slow and careful as those of a man under the influence. He eased onto the edge, feeling, as he always did in her presence, big and clumsy and unworthy of a woman like her.

She raised the glass to his lips, but Rio relegated the glass to the bedside table and tasted her mouth instead. The kiss was long, slow...luxurious. When she drew away, his heart was galloping in his chest.

"My sweet, sweet Maggie," he said in a husky voice as he rubbed his thumb over her bottom lip in a gentle caress. "What's all this for?"

Maggie captured his hand. "I know how hard you and Cal and Ken have been working at getting those rodeos lined up lately, and how uptight you've been about getting your business started. I got to thinking that it would be nice if I helped you unwind."

She untucked the corner of the sheet and closed his hand around the softly scented fabric. "You can start here."

AFTER MAGGIE had helped Rio unwind to the point of feeling like a wrung-out dishrag, they shared a candlelight bath in water dotted with slices of orange and lemon. A seductive saxophone cried softly in the background, and they sipped at the wine from a single glass. Rio wasn't crazy about the stuff, but he'd have downed arsenic to preserve the mood.

Maggie sat astride him in the water, her breasts crushed against his wide chest, her face pressed into the hollow of his neck while his soapy hands slid up and down her back. Her tongue traced a lazy pattern on his throat.

"You're beautiful," he said thickly, his hands moving around to capture her breasts.

"So are you," she countered on a sigh.

"Yeah, right." He hugged her tighter and gave a deep, satisfied sigh. "I don't know what I did to deserve this kind of treatment, but if you'll tell me, I'll make sure to do it more often."

Maggie's laughter was a low gurgle of pleasure. She lifted her head from his chest to look at him. "Dangerous, Langley. Very dangerous. We might die of that dreaded condition—sexual satiation."

"Yeah?" he said with a lift of his eyebrows. "Well, I can think of worse ways to go."

Their innocent comments unwittingly and morbidly reminded Maggie of her upcoming doctor's appointment the next day. Something was wrong with her, and it was more than the fact that she was tired and overworked; there wasn't one social worker on the face of the earth who didn't have a bigger caseload than she could handle.

No, something was out of kilter—probably some hormone imbalance. About six weeks ago, she'd skipped a period and thought she was pregnant. Secretly thrilled, she'd gone so far as to buy an in-home pregnancy test. Ironically, she'd started her period on the way home from the drugstore.

A bit disappointed, she'd blamed the whole incident on the combined stress of work and being a new wife. The irregularity had reminded her that she was overdue for her annual checkup, something she'd neglected due to the hectic pace of her life-style.

"Penny for them."

The softly rumbled words brought Maggie's thoughts back to the present and the man who was looking at her with a surfeit of love in his eyes. It was almost frightening to think that she might have missed him, if fate hadn't dealt her an unexpected hand in the form of Tess Holloway.

Maggie smiled and cradled his whisker-rough cheek with her palm, thoughts of her problems almost forgotten. Tomorrow she would have her fears allayed. In the meantime, she planned on having a heck of a time tonight.

"I was thinking about how lucky I am to have you," she said in a trembling voice.

He dipped his head to kiss her. Their mouths had just touched when the phone rang, shattering the feelings building between them.

"Don't answer it," he said as the phone rang again.

"It might be Cal calling from Calgary," Maggie said, reminding him of the trip Cal McKinney had made to see about providing the stock for the annual Stampede. The phone shrilled the third time.

"Damn."

"You don't want to miss it, do you?" she asked as the fourth ring pealed out.

Reluctantly, Rio hauled himself from the tub and stalked to the bedroom, leaving a trail of wet footprints in the silver-gray carpet. He grabbed the phone on the fifth ring and barked a short "Hello" into the receiver. Nothing but buzzing sounded in his ear.

Great. Whoever it was had hung up. He was just starting back to the bathroom when the doorbell rang. What was this? he wondered. Some sort of conspiracy? Muttering a curse, he reached for the jeans he'd left draped over the foot of the bed and, pulling them on over his damp legs, went to see who was at the door.

MAGGIE WATCHED Rio leave the room, a look of admiration in her eyes, a self-satisfied smile on her lips. Her husband was quite a man...in many ways. The music on the CD player had changed to an instrumental Christmas medley. Humming along with the soft strains of a violin, she reached for the bar of expensive soap she'd bought and sank against the back of the tub, closing her eyes in complete contentment. She rubbed the bar over her tummy and breasts with slow, erotic movements, imagining it was Rio's hand. She sighed in contentment. How had she gotten so lucky as to find him?

Her thoughts were scattered by the sudden unexpected roar of a gunshot from the front of the house. The noise drowned out the lilting melody of the

Christmas song and shattered Maggie's mood in a single thundering beat of her heart. Instant and inexplicable fear exploded inside her. Her brain kicked into overdrive, computing the information at hand and coming up with a horrifying answer.

Rio!

With her heart pounding in sudden terror, Maggie clawed her way out of the tub and grabbed the terry-cloth robe from the back of the bathroom door. Fighting an escalating panic, she dragged it over her wet body, tying the sash as she ran headlong through the house, screaming his name.

She careened to a stop just inside the living room. In the light that spilled through the open doorway from the front porch, she saw Rio lying sprawled on his back. Rick Farmer stood framed in the open doorway, a look of fearful disbelief on his face, a revolver clutched in his white-knuckled fist as he stared at Rio helplessly. Maggie's hand crept to her mouth to hold back the anguished cry that emanated from the depths of her soul.

"I'm sorry."

The sound of Rick's voice broke the spell of immobility that held Maggie rooted to the floor. With a high, keening wail, she launched herself across the room and dropped to her knees beside Rio's still, bleeding body, trying her best to rouse him, wanting, needing, to hear him say he was all right. But there was no sign of life, except a horrible sucking noise that came from his chest with every shallow breath he took.

Swaying from a growing light-headedness, Maggie was marginally aware of Jeremy arriving, his shotgun in tow, demanding that Rick put down his weapon, which he did, while chanting a litany that he was sorry.

"Call an ambulance, Maggie," Jeremy commanded.

Maggie's dazed gaze moved from Rick's white face to Jeremy's. "What?"

"Call an ambulance, dammit!" Jeremy yelled.

Shocked by the unaccustomed violence in his manner, Maggie scrambled to her feet and dialed 911, telling the operator in a strangely detached tone what had happened. Assured that the ambulance and the police were on their way, she went back and knelt beside Rio, wiping at the fine spray of blood on his face with the edge of her robe and watching in helpless surprise when more reappeared.

"He's bleeding to death," Jeremy said in a tear-thickened voice. "For God's sake, Maggie, do something besides sit there and watch him die."

Once again, the harsh criticism in his voice jolted her from the dreamlike passivity enshrouding her. Rio dying? She looked up at Jeremy with the idea of giving him a piece of her mind and encountered the anguish on his face. It was like the slap of a wet washrag. Jeremy thought Rio was dying.

She looked down at Rio, really seeing him for the first time. He was pale and still. Too still, except for the noise rattling in his chest. Too still, she thought on a fresh rush of panic, but alive.

Bits and pieces from the first-aid classes she'd taken in college came rushing back. Nothing was obstructing his breathing. But he was bleeding from the wound that misted his chest with a fine spray of blood with every breath he expelled.

The term for the type of wound emerged from somewhere in the back of her mind, probably all the thrillers she read. It was a sucking chest wound.

Petroleum jelly and gauze. That tidbit, too, came from nowhere . . . somewhere. It was worth a try, better than watching blood being pumped from him with every beat of his heart. Running to the bathroom, Maggie located some gauze bandages and a jar of Vaseline.

She got back to the living room in time to see Wayne Jackson's car screech to a sliding stop in the driveway, his siren blaring, the red-and-blue lights on top of the county vehicle slashing the darkness with metronomic frenzy.

Fully aware of the danger of the situation, Maggie was too busy trying to stanch the flow of blood to concern herself with what Wayne was doing. She knew that Jeremy relinquished his guard to a deputy while Wayne handcuffed Rick. As the sheriff herded his prisoner toward the squad car, Maggie heard him reciting the Miranda code over the harsh sounds of Jeremy's crying and the scream of the approaching ambulance.

But the thing that she would always remember was Rick's quivering young voice saying brokenly, "I didn't do it, Sheriff. Swear to God, I didn't do it."

Maggie closed her eyes. It was the same thing he'd said about the dog.

EVA BLAKE LOOKED UP from the delicate square she was crocheting, one of many that would comprise the bedspread she was making for Maggie and Rio. She laid down her handwork and gazed tenderly at her husband. At sixty-five, he was still a fine-looking man, tall and trim and fit from his twice-weekly tennis games, the craggy lines in his face only adding to his good looks.

As it always did when she looked at Howard, her heart swelled with a wave of love so strong it hurt. How many times during the past forty-three years had she looked across a room and fallen in love with him all over again? His head, mostly gray now, was buried between pages of newsprint, as it was most evenings. He preferred to digest the news along with his breakfast, but it was seldom that he made it through his morning meal without someone calling about this crisis and the next, needing his advice, his help, his steadfastness.

In all the years they'd been together, Eva had never known him to put his own wishes ahead of those of his flock. His selflessness was just one of the reasons she loved him. Howard would be the first to tell her not to put him on any pedestal, that he wasn't perfect by a long shot, but he was so close to perfection—at least in her mind—that it wasn't worth splitting hairs over.

She knew she was getting sentimental, but what if she was? She couldn't help being sentimental any more than she could help that her hair was more gray now than auburn or that she cried when she heard the "Star-Spangled Banner" or that she liked country line dancing—which she often practiced in the living room when Howard was at the church building. She shot Howard a sideways glance and bit her bottom lip to hold back a giggle. What would Howard say if he knew?

A Christmas commercial filled the television screen and Eva sighed. The McKinneys' big party was coming up soon.

"What should I wear to the McKinneys' Christmas party?" she asked, lifting her gaze to Howard again.

"Whatever you want," he said without looking up.

Eva smiled. He was on automatic pilot. "I was thinking of getting something new."

"That's fine."

"I saw a cute little number in Fredrick's of Hollywood the other day," she said with feigned nonchalance.

Did she imagine it, or was there the slightest pause before he answered? "That's nice."

Eva moved her crocheting from her lap to the coffee table and hugged a throw pillow to her ample breasts. "Howard," she said in a serious tone.

"Mmm?"

"I'm having an affair." It was a credit to her acting ability that she delivered the line straight-faced.

His eyes never left the paper. "Uh-huh."

Her eyes widened and her mouth fell open. "Is that all you have to say?"

Howard turned another page of his paper. "Lucky guy," he said, deadpan.

"Oh, you!" Eva fumed.

His blue eyes alight with merriment, Howard looked up in time to catch the pillow that came flying through the air at him.

"I had you going there for a while, didn't I?" he said with a chuckle.

She pretended to pout. "I'm not talking to you."

"Come on, Evie, talk." He wiggled his eyebrows. "Tell me about the Fredrick's outfit."

"You're incorrigible!" she said, but she was doing her best to hide a smile.

"But you love me."

She leveled an accusing look and pointed a finger at him. "And prideful."

Howard winked at her. "But not boring."

She tried to hold back a smile and failed. She shook her auburn curls, which were preserved from the ravages of time by Suzi over at the Curl Up and Dye beauty salon, who touched up Eva's roots the third Tuesday of every month. "No one could ever accuse you of that."

"Not even back in high school?"

Eva cocked her head to the side and pretended to consider the question. "Well . . ."

Howard pushed himself up from the chair and held out his hand to her. "Come on. Let's go make some popcorn."

"Honestly, Howard," Eva said, as he drew her to her feet. "You're so helpless. Just put the bag in the microwave, press the popcorn button and three minutes later it's ready."

Howard slid his arm around her shoulders. "I know, but I'll miss you."

Eva dimpled up at him. "What a sweet thing to say."

"And besides," he said, giving her a light squeeze, "I thought if I sweet-talked you a little you might make us up a batch of real hot chocolate instead of that packaged stuff."

"I've been had!" Eva said indignantly.

Howard's smile was angelic. The look in his eyes was devilish. "That's after the popcorn."

The shrill ringing of the phone interrupted their lighthearted banter. Howard bent and reached for the receiver, offering the caller a hearty "Hello."

Eva saw his eyes close and the color drain from his face. An icy, unaccountable fear swept through her like a cold Panhandle wind.

"Of course," she heard him say. "We're on our way." He hung up the receiver and met Eva's worried eyes with a bleak gaze.

"What?" she cried softly.

"That was Maggie. Rick Farmer just shot Rio."

LESS THAN thirty minutes later, Maggie found herself pacing the waiting room of Crystal Creek's small hospital, wiping periodically at the tears she couldn't stop, praying incessantly and waiting for some word about Rio's condition. Jeremy, Tess and Elena, Rio's housekeeper and friend, were all out in the hallway, wild with grief and coping with their sorrow and worry in their own way. Jeremy had called Ken Slattery, who was on his way. Serena McKinney was trying to get in touch with Cal.

Dr. Purdy had called in Dr. Dekker, the new Indonesian doctor, who, having just put in a fair share of time in one of Austin's busy emergency rooms during his residency, had more skill with gunshots than the country doctor did. There was a faction in town that was prejudiced against the young doctor, but Nate said Sonny Dekker was "damned sharp," and the old doctor's stamp of approval was all Maggie needed. She'd have welcomed help from the devil himself if she thought he could keep Rio alive.

Dear God! she asked herself again. How could something like this have happened? How could she have been making love with Rio one minute and the next find him laid out on the living room floor from a gunshot?

She pressed her knuckles to her mouth to hold back a sob. Why had Rick done it?

He'd said he hadn't.

But he was holding the gun, and he'd apologized over and over.

"Oh, Rio!" she cried aloud.

"Are you all right?"

With tears running unchecked down her face, Maggie whirled. Jeremy stood in the doorway, red-eyed and disheveled. Funny. She'd never noticed before how much alike the two brothers looked. She felt another rush of tears and did her best to blink them away. "I don't know," she said truthfully.

Jeremy drew her into his arms. As Maggie clung to him for comfort, it occurred to her that he'd matured a lot in the past few months, growing into a strong, dependable man, just like his brother.

"Why, Jeremy?" she asked, choking on a sob. "Why would Rick hurt Rio after all he's done to try and help?"

"They quarreled this afternoon." Jeremy's voice was heavy with finality.

Maggie drew back and looked at Jeremy with tear-drenched eyes. "Quarreled? About what?"

"We were moving that pen full of broncs, and Babydoll got the horses riled up. Rick got thrown. He was pretty mad and took it out on the dog."

"Oh, God!"

"Rio wasn't too happy," Jeremy said.

Knowing how attached Rio was to the dog and how much he loved animals in general, Maggie figured Jeremy's comment was an understatement.

"When I rode up to see what was going on, Rio was giving Rick a pretty good tongue-lashing. He took him home a little while later."

Maggie should have been furious with Rick. She should be hating him for what he'd done. Instead, she was confused by his behavior.

"But would Rick shoot Rio because he chewed him out? That seems so...I don't know...drastic. Like the punishment didn't fit the crime."

"In the environment Rick's grown up in, I imagine that's a way of life."

"Probably," Maggie conceded, but even with the picture so vivid in her mind of him standing there with the gun in hand, she still had difficulty reconciling the action. "It's just hard for me to imagine Rick hurting the only person in Crystal Creek who was willing to give him a chance."

Jeremy took her hands in a firm grip. "It's a crying shame the way people make judgments about a person based on hearsay and heredity instead of taking the time to see what that person is really like."

The gleam of sorrow in his eyes told Maggie that Jeremy was thinking about Rio. Fortunately, Rio had enough strength of character to rise above those who condemned him. If only Rick could have found that same strength, instead of sinking to the depths everyone expected of him.

"I know it's hard to believe Rick did it, but we can't overlook the fact that he was holding the gun and saying he was sorry," Jeremy said.

"I know," Maggie said. "But, it's such a waste. It isn't like Rick is a real loser or anything. Mama remembers him from school. She says he's very smart, but that his dad sabotages his schooling every chance he gets." She shook her head. "I'm afraid if he doesn't get an education, he'll wind up another statistic."

"I hate to break it to you, Maggie," Jeremy said, "but he already is."

The gentle reminder brought a picture of Rio lying on the floor, his blood covering them both. "I guess so."

Wearing a sad smile, Jeremy gave her a quick hug. "It's just like you to be as worried about Rick as you are about Rio."

"Not quite as worried," Maggie said with a wry twist of her lips. "But it does bother me. And I'm disappointed, I guess. I grew up under the old 'do unto others' dictum, and it's always a disappointment to me when it doesn't work the way it should."

Jeremy's smile was edged with bitterness. "Problem is that a lot of people today figure it's 'do unto others' *before* they do unto you."

Maggie wondered if Jeremy was thinking about his father. "It isn't a very good testimony for the human race, is it?"

"Margaret?"

At the sound of the deep, mellifluous voice, Maggie looked up and saw her parents standing in the doorway of the waiting room. Her mother's plump, still-beautiful face wore a frown, and her father's beloved features held the peaceful, steadfast look they always did... as if he'd figured out the answers to all life's problems, and was satisfied with the solutions.

Maggie felt a twinge of envy that she squelched immediately. He'd be the first to tell her that if she'd just turn things over to God she would have that same attitude, that same contentment. Young people, he was fond of saying, were always trying to do it themselves instead of asking for help from the one source that would never let them down. All Maggie knew was that even when she wasn't sure God was listening, she'd always been able to count on her dad.

"Daddy!" she cried, flying into Howard Blake's arms. The familiarity of his embrace gave her a sense of security, a feeling that now everything would be all right.

Howard hugged her for a long moment and, pressing a kiss to her forehead, relinquished her to her mother's gentle, floral-scented embrace.

"How is he?" Eva said, brushing Maggie's hair— still damp from the bath she'd shared with Rio—away from her pale cheeks.

Maggie shrugged. "You know how doctors are. They tell you as little as possible. Dr. Purdy called in that new doctor...Dr. Dekker."

"I've heard he's very good," Eva said. "I guess there's nothing we can do but wait and pray, then, is there?"

"Do you think that will help?" Maggie asked a bit acerbically.

"Margaret Langley!" Eva chided in a shocked voice. "How can you ask such a thing?"

Tears pooled in Maggie's eyes. "Because I loved Greg, and I asked God to spare his life and he died, anyway." She swiped at her eyes almost angrily. "I still remember how I felt after Greg died. Empty... and lost. Like I was in limbo, just waiting for something to happen."

Eva's agonized gaze sought Howard's. He closed his eyes, feeling his daughter's pain as if it were his own.

"I tried to remember you and Daddy reminding me that the Bible says everything works for good to those who love God, and when Emily was left on Rio's doorstep, I thought that finding happiness with Rio was what God really wanted for me."

"I believed that, too," Eva said. "I still believe it."

"Then why did Rio get punished for doing good?" Maggie railed. "Why is he in surgery about to die? What kind of loving God would put a person through this hell twice?"

"A God who knows what's best for us, Maggie," Howard interjected in a soothing tone. "One who won't put more on us than we can bear."

"Spare me, Daddy!" Maggie said, her face contorted with anger. "I've heard it all before, and let me tell you... I'm not so sure I believe it anymore."

Without waiting for her father to reply, Maggie swept past her parents and Jeremy into the hallway, where Elena stood talking quietly to Ken Slattery, who'd just arrived.

Eva's tortured gaze followed her daughter's retreating form and then moved from Jeremy's pale features to Howard. Mumbling something about checking on Maggie, Jeremy slipped from the room.

AN HOUR LATER, Nate Purdy entered the waiting room accompanied by Dr. Sunarjo Dekker. Dr. Purdy's craggy face was lined with fatigue. Even the younger doctor's face held weariness, Maggie thought.

Nate made the introductions, and let the younger man do the talking.

"How is he?" Maggie asked, clutching her mother's hand.

"He's stable," Sonny Dekker said. "The bullet passed through your husband's lung and exited his back. What we had was pneumothorax of the left lung, caused by what we call a sucking chest wound."

"What's pneumothorax?" Jeremy asked.

"Collapsed lung. What happens when there's a tear in the lung is that the vacuum that normally surrounds the lung fills with air and causes collapse. With a sucking chest wound, air is drawn into the lung with every indrawn breath and foamy blood and air are sprayed out with exhalation. Whoever thought to use the gauze and petroleum jelly may have saved his life."

"It was Maggie," Jeremy said.

"What do you do with a collapsed lung?" Maggie asked.

"We insert a chest tube into the pleural space between the chest wall and the lung. The tube is hooked to suction that removes the air and blood trapped inside. Once that's removed, the lung can reexpand. Considering the amount of blood he lost, I have to say that he came through the surgery pretty well. We'll be keeping him in ICU for the time being."

"But he's going to be all right?" Maggie demanded.

"Rio's condition is serious, Maggie," Nate Purdy said. "But he's strong as a bull and he's a fighter." He gave her an awkward pat on the shoulder. "Why don't you go home and try to get some rest?"

"Can I see him?"

Nate looked at Dr. Dekker, who nodded. "Just you for now, Maggie. And only for a couple of minutes. In the morning two at a time can go in for five minutes every three hours while he's in ICU."

"Then I'm staying the night," Maggie said, her voice brooking no argument. "I have to be here to see him."

"Somehow I thought you might say that," Nate said with a smile. "I'll have one of the nurses round up some pillows and blankets. You'll need them before morning."

WHILE MAGGIE WAS being ushered into the Intensive Care Unit, Eva went looking for her husband. It didn't take a sleuth to figure out where she'd find him. He was seated in the hospital's small chapel, his hands clasped together between his legs, his head bent as if he were staring at the floor. Anyone else might think he was deep in thought; Eva knew he was deep in prayer.

She stopped just inside the door, unwilling to interrupt whatever conversation her husband might be having with God. In a matter of seconds, almost as if he sensed her presence, he lifted his head, pushed himself to his feet and turned to face her. He looked older than he had earlier in the evening, when they'd joked about her Fredrick's of Hollywood outfit.

Eva fought the sudden urge to give in to the tears that had threatened ever since she'd heard the news about Rio. The only thing that had kept her dry-eyed was the knowledge that Maggie needed her strength.

"Hello, love," Howard said with a crooked quirk of his lips as he motioned for Eva to join him. "How's Rio?"

Eva negotiated the narrow aisle. "Out of surgery and in ICU. He has a collapsed lung, but he's doing as well as can be expected."

Howard nodded and patted the padded cushion beside him. They sat down, and Howard circled her shoulders with his arm, leaning his cheek against her hair. "How's Margaret?"

"Honestly?"

"Honestly."

"I'm worried about her."

"So am I," he confessed.

"It's almost as if she blames God for what's happened instead of Rick."

"I know," Howard said. "I heard."

Eva drew back and looked into Howard's beloved
face. Tears glistened in her eyes as she whispered, ''I
have the strangest feeling of déjà vu, Howard. Like
history is repeating itself.''

Howard nodded, his eyes mirroring the pain he felt
at knowing that Maggie's circumstances had resur-
rected old sorrows, old heartaches for Eva.

''That could be me in there,'' she said, her voice
breaking. ''It *is* me…in a way. It would take a fool not
to see how similar her situation is to mine back before
we got married.''

''I know.''

Neither spoke for long moments. Eva was the first
to break the silence. ''We've got to tell her, Howard.
She's in so much pain.''

Though he'd suspected as much, Howard's eyes
filled with alarm. ''Evie … We promised we'd never
tell.''

''I *have* to!'' Eva cried in a soft, desperate voice.
''Didn't you hear her say how she felt in limbo after
Greg died … as if she was waiting for something and
didn't know what it was? I know exactly how she feels.
I was going through the same thing the day you came
knocking on my door.'' In spite of her pain, a tremu-
lous smile curved her lips. ''It took me a long time to
realize that what I was waiting for was you.''

Howard's fingertips caressed her cheek with infi-
nite tenderness. Eva took his hand in both of hers.
Their fingers meshed tightly.

"Don't you see, Howard? I have to tell Maggie not to give up and not to lose faith. Telling her about me—about us—will help her to understand that despite what's happened to Rio, something wonderful might be just around the corner."

Howard's troubled eyes clung to his wife's. "It might change how she feels about us."

"It might," she agreed. "But I'm willing to take that chance. If it helps get her through this, and strengthens her faith, it'll be worth the risk."

Howard shook his head and gave her a wry smile. "If you want to convince her not to give up, can't you just tell her the story of Job?"

In spite of the seriousness of the situation, a glimmer of humor twinkled in Eva's eyes. "I don't think it would be the same, honey."

He carried her hand to his lips and pressed a soft kiss to her knuckles. His eyes were troubled. "I just don't want you to be hurt. God knows you've had enough hurt to last a lifetime."

"I want to do this, Howard."

He closed his eyes. Finally, he spoke. "Sing to me, Evie."

"*Sing* to you?" she asked, stunned by the request.

He nodded. "Sing 'It Is Well with My Soul.'"

"How can you want me to sing when our daughter is in so much pain and Rio is lying in there...." Her voice broke again, and she swallowed hard.

"I've been praying nonstop since Jeremy called. God knows what's in my heart. Sing. You sing like an angel."

Eva smiled around her tears and began to sing about peace like a river and sorrows rolling like sea billows, her clear soprano voice echoing sweetly throughout the room. When she got to the part about all being well with her soul, no matter what came her way, a look of peace came over Howard's features.

Eva clung to his hand and prayed with all her heart that it would be so with Maggie.

WHEN EVA LEFT HOWARD, she went in search of her daughter. Ken, his wife Nora, and Elena were still there, but Jeremy had taken Tess home. Maggie was walking the hallway, examining the framed pictures on the wall as if they were some sort of costly art. Though she appeared to be engrossed, Eva knew her daughter's thoughts were far away.

"Are you all right?" she asked, putting her arm around Maggie's shoulders. Maggie nodded. "How's Rio?"

Maggie turned her tortured gaze to her mother's. "He's so pale and still," she said in a strained voice. "And he won't answer me when I talk to him."

"I imagine the anesthesia still has him out cold."

"I guess."

Eva sighed. In some ways, Maggie's lifelessness was more disturbing than her earlier anger. Anger could be channeled into something constructive. Passivity left nowhere to go.

"Maggie," Eva began, "I'm worried about you."

"I'm fine!" Maggie said in a sudden spurt of irritation. "It's Rio you should be worried about."

"I am worried about Rio, but I can't help worrying about you, too. It isn't like you to be so negative about everything you've been brought up to believe."

Maggie looked at Eva, her eyes sparking with renewed anger. "How do you know whether it's like me or not?" she challenged. "I haven't been your innocent little Maggie in a long time. Face it, Mama, you don't know me anymore."

The words stung, but Eva was determined not to let on how much. "Maybe I don't," she said, "but contrary to the impression you give to others, you aren't the kind of person who just lies down and lets life run over her. You're a fighter, Maggie. You always were in your own quiet way. So why are you giving up now?"

"I'm not!"

"Well, it looks that way to me. Instead of looking for the best, you're anticipating the worst. Instead of putting your trust in God, you're turning your back on him and the strength he can give you."

"I haven't seen much of his loving care lately," Maggie said.

Eva thought of the happiness Maggie and Rio had shared the past few months, of Rio's slow but steady success in getting his business going, of his new relationship with Jeremy and Tess and little Emily...of

Maggie's success in her work and the community's gradual acceptance of Rio. How could she not believe in God's loving care when her life was a walking testimony to his love?

Eva's patience with her daughter snapped. "Oh, stop wallowing in self-pity, Margaret! You're behaving as if you're the only one in the world with a tragedy in her life."

Maggie looked as if Eva had slapped her. Memories of their many battles during Maggie's high school days rushed through Eva's mind. As much as she loved her only daughter, they'd butted heads often in the past.

"What's the old Indian saying about not judging a man until you've walked a mile in his moccasins?" Maggie said sarcastically. "It's easy to be holier-than-thou when you have a nice cushy life-style, a wonderful husband who's crazy about you and two healthy children who never gave you a moment's worry. You've never lost a man you love, so don't come preaching to me when you don't have the slightest idea what I'm going through."

At the end of her speech and her temper, Maggie turned away, intent on leaving. Eva grabbed her daughter's arm in a tight grip. Maggie glared at her, her eyes bright with tears and fury.

"I do know what you're going through," Eva said.

"Oh, really?" Maggie's face wore a look of patent disbelief.

"Really."

"Did you and Daddy have a few little spats those early years, is that it?"

Eva's lips tightened. "Sit down, Margaret," she commanded in a firm voice. "There are some things we need to talk about—woman to woman. Some things you should have been told long ago."

Even through her outrage and distress, Maggie heard the serious note underlying her mother's voice. Her irritation fled. "What sort of things?" she asked, her voice wary... almost fearful.

"Things about me and your father and a baby I had before you and Ronald came along...."

PERHAPS THIRTY MINUTES had passed since Howard's talk with his wife. He stood staring out of the waiting room window at the light-flooded parking lot, wondering how things were going with Eva and Maggie, and whether Eva's confession and story of regained faith would make any difference to how Maggie dealt with her situation.

He drew a deep breath. Even if it made no difference in Maggie's feelings, he supposed she should be told the truth. She had a right to know what her parents were like in their youth. She *should* know that he had loved Eva for as long as he could remember.

And, he conceded, it might help ease some of the concerns about her own marriage to know that her parents hadn't always seen eye to eye... that the young aspiring actress he'd married hadn't always been the perfect preacher's wife, and that their vastly different upbringings and ways of approaching life had caused some problems during their life together. Problems they'd overcome with love and God's help.

Howard sighed. He knew he was fooling himself. There was no doubt the stories could help Maggie. His real concern was how breaking a forty-three-year-old silence would affect his wife.

Bowing his head, Howard prayed that Eva's decision was the right one, that she would find the right words to tell Maggie the truth. That Maggie would forgive.

God answers prayers in three ways, Howard. Yes, no and wait a while.

Howard recalled his father's words from his childhood. He realized all too well that people often questioned God's wisdom and sometimes turned their backs on him when the answer to their prayers was a "no" and they so desperately wanted it to be "yes."

Maggie had a right to know the truth so that she could see that God was in control, and that sometimes unanswered prayers were blessings in disguise.

CHAPTER THREE

April 1951

DALLAS WAS WAY TOO BIG, Howard Blake thought as he surveyed the bustling traffic and the towering buildings whose windows flung the day's last rays of sunshine into his eyes. As the old adage went, it was a nice place to visit, but he wouldn't want to live there. A three-day National Baptist Convention was plenty long enough for a country boy like him.

Howard had graduated from Baylor at midterm, just in time to step into his retiring father's shoes as minister of the First Baptist Church in Crystal Creek. It was a position he'd always aspired to, even though it had necessitated his leaving home for four years. Growing up in the small Hill Country town, he had been predisposed to attend Baylor, located in Waco, instead of the modest Bishop College in the large city of Dallas. Howard could contend with the larger university better than he could handle the chaos of big-city life.

Still, when he was urged by his new congregation to attend the convention, there had been no way he could decline without making waves. Following in his father's footsteps was no easy task, and Howard was

well aware that while he was still in the "honey-
moon" period with church members, both he and his
actions were under constant scrutiny.

Just twenty-two himself, he knew the younger folk
liked him. High school and college students could
identify with him better than with his father, whom
they considered ancient at sixty-three. The younger
Blake represented exciting new ideas, a fresh ap-
proach, a more modern outlook—within the confines
of church doctrine, of course.

The elderly members weren't so sure. They liked the
old, familiar ways and had grown accustomed to the
tenor and content of Thaddeus Blake's sermons. There
was also a small contingent who looked down on
Howard because he hadn't joined up to fight in Korea, even though, as an only son—an only child—he'd
been deferred from active duty.

The over-forty members regarded Howard warily,
as if they expected him to suddenly denounce all they
considered holy and run off with the church secretary...and the weekly contribution. After almost four
months, Howard still felt as if he were living under
some gigantic microscope, his every move monitored
and judged by some unseen jury...which was why he'd
smiled and assured the deacons that he'd be thrilled to
attend the convention in Dallas.

He supposed the endeavor had been a success, but
being cooped up for three days and contributing even
a small part to the decision making that would shape
his life and that of others was serious business. How-

ard was past ready for some quiet time . . . and a nice
Texas-size steak in a good restaurant.

He planned to follow his meal with an early night
and be ready to head back to the Hill Country at day-
break . . . unless he decided to look up Evalyn Carmichael, who was back in Texas—more specifically,
Dallas—after spending the past two years in Hollywood, where she'd sought a career as an actress.

Though he was unaware of it, the thought of Eva—
her shapely Marilyn Monroe-like body and her Botti-
celli Venus-like face—made Howard's heart beat a
little faster. He told himself that looking her up while
he was in town would be a good deed. He could check
and see how she was doing and give her parents a
firsthand report when he got back home. As the minister of her former congregation, he could consider the
visit his Christian duty.

He sighed. It seemed he'd loved Eva Carmichael
most of his life . . . at the very least since the day he'd
looked up into the choir loft and seen her standing
there in her pristine white robe, singing her heart out.
She'd looked like an angel . . . her roundish face aglow,
her eyes alight with pure pleasure while the Sunday
morning sun filtered through the stained-glass window and shot fiery sparks off her auburn hair.

With his heart fluttering in his chest like a caged
bird, Howard was sure he'd never seen anything or
anyone so beautiful. He'd lost his heart to her that
day, and unbeknownst to her, she'd had it ever since.
He was twelve; Eva was only ten.

Not surprisingly, Eva had grown into the most gorgeous creature Howard had ever seen, with masses of naturally wavy auburn hair and a face and figure that caused no little stir in the small town. He heard whispers—even from girls her age, who said she dressed like a floozy with her too-tight skirts and sweaters and her full-blown, movie-star makeup.

Even Howard's mother had shaken her head in dismay. She knew that Eva, an aspiring actress, was in love with Hollywood and that she was just looking for glamour, but feared the young woman's tendency to go to extremes would cause her heartbreak some day.

Howard, who fell more and more in love with Eva every day, had listened with half an ear. Her glamorous persona represented a world that was as far removed from his day to day existence as Mars, and even though he carried the torch for her all through high school, he knew she was as out of his reach as that faraway planet.

She never once looked his way during that time—not that he really expected her to. He'd been a tall, skinny "square" back then—complete with a fairly serious case of acne and horn-rimmed glasses. It was no wonder Eva had overlooked him in favor of Nate Purdy, who was not only her own age but tall and good-looking, with aspirations of becoming a doctor like his father.

Eva and Nate had dated their senior year, and then by mutual consent they had broken up—Nate to pursue his medical degree, Eva to reach for the stars . . . a

serious journey for the daughter of Sally and Pete
Carmichael, lifelong residents of Crystal Creek.

Pete owned and ran the local grain co-op, and ru-
mor had it that Sally ran Pete, as well as her three girls,
with an iron fist. What a scandal it had been when Eva
graduated and, with blatant disregard for her parents' warnings, set out for California with five hundred dollars of baby-sitting money in her purse and a
pocketful of dreams.

Howard found himself wondering what had happened to those dreams and why, since she was back in
Texas, she hadn't returned to Crystal Creek to visit her
family and friends . . . a question that brought his
thoughts full circle. Should he contact her or not? He
reached into his pocket and pulled out a crumpled envelope that bore her return address.

Howard tipped back his head and looked up at the
sky, as if he hoped to see some sort of sign from God
there. Nothing. No star to lead the way. No pillar of
cloud, no pillar of smoke.

He reached into his pocket and took out a quarter.
Heads, he'd call. Tails, he wouldn't. He flipped the
coin, caught it and turned it over on the back of his
hand. Tails. He frowned. Maybe he'd take the best
two out of three, he thought, even as he slipped the
coin back into his pocket. He paced in front of a shop,
whose shining plate-glass window reflected his con-
servative slacks and jacket.

If he called, she might say she was too busy to see
him. On the other hand, if he just dropped by and she

did have plans, he'd at least get a brief glimpse of her that might tide him over until the next time their paths crossed. Of course, she might not be at home, and the trip would be wasted....

Howard stopped pacing abruptly. All this rationalizing and analyzing was ridiculous. It was what made him such a boring guy. Women liked men who were fun...spontaneous, impulsive. Men who were full of compliments and could make them laugh, men who thought up entertaining things to do on the spur of the moment. Howard's mouth twisted in a wry grin. He couldn't recall doing a single impulsive thing in twenty-two years.

Drawing a determined breath, he turned and marched down the block to where he'd parked his car. With a determined gleam in his eyes, he pulled out a city map and located Eva's street on it. He needed to get to her apartment as fast as possible...before he talked himself out of seeing her at all.

EVA SAT at her red, Formica-topped kitchen table stroking blood-red polish onto her long nails in an effort to lift her flagging spirits, even though she was certain that she'd never feel young or happy again. Early April sunshine streamed through the west windows, undimmed by the worn lace curtains, turning the small, one-room apartment into a veritable oven. The sun's brightness maximized the shabbiness of the sofa and sought out the worn places in the kitchen linoleum with its violent pink cabbage roses.

Her wet hair was bound up in a terry towel, turban style, and she wore the black satin robe Denny had sent her from Korea. She'd just gotten out of the worn claw-foot bathtub, having sat in the tepid water longer than she really wanted to in an effort to cool off. The unseasonable heat had been unbearable the past few days. She dreaded to think what it would be like in August...or in September...when her baby would be born.

Thoughts of the baby sent a ripple of fear through her. The fear was quickly followed by guilt and shame. She was going to have a baby. Denny's baby. A baby that would be born out of wedlock. She hated to think of what her parents would say when they learned the news.

Eva pushed away the troubling thoughts. She wouldn't consider that now. She'd just take one day at a time. A wave of homesickness washed over her. More and more lately, she found herself longing for the hometown she'd been hell-bent on leaving. It had taken her two years, but she'd found that even though the grass might be greener on the other side of the fence, it was still unpalatable sometimes.

She wished she could make peace with her mother, who was still harping about how she'd disgraced them by going out to Hollywood—that sinful place where girls who hoped to become movie stars were led down the primrose path by men in power. They were lured by empty promises of stardom into the webs of sin, she'd warned, only to be dumped when someone newer, fresher, prettier or more interesting came along.

A weary, reminiscent smile curved Eva's mouth as she recapped the bottle of fingernail polish. It had taken only a couple of wrestling matches with the so-called men in power for her to realize that the casting couch route wasn't for her.

She might have longed for glamour, but her strong Baptist upbringing and vivid memory of Reverend Blake's hellfire-and-brimstone sermons had stood her in good stead, which was why, even though she managed to get a few bit parts, she'd never landed a big role.

One executive had told her straight out that even though she was no Elizabeth Taylor, he could still do great things for her...if she'd do a little something for him in return.

"You can sing like a nightingale, baby, but if you want to know the truth, your acting is average at best."

Eva—who preferred to go by the name Eve Michaels—let him know quickly that she wasn't interested. She had thanked him for his time and left his office, her head high, her heart broken. She thought about what he'd told her often in the following months, while she worked waiting tables and selling tickets at a nearby movie theater. As hard as it was to admit, she'd known he was right. Her acting ability, which had seemed so incredible to the townsfolk of Crystal Creek, was no better and no worse than that of hundreds of girls who came looking for fame and fortune.

Disillusioned and feeling very much a failure, she'd considered packing her things and going home. After a year and a half, homesickness was a constant knot in her breast, but going back to Crystal Creek without any real movie credits seemed like an admission of failure, so she'd stayed in California. She'd never been good at admitting she was wrong.

Eva wasn't sure she'd ever been so low as that night early in December, when she'd agreed to go with her friend Maria to a Knights of Columbus dance. It was there she'd met Private First Class Denny Talbot of the United States Army and fallen head over heels in love.

Denny was home on furlough for the Christmas holidays. His family—his parents and two sisters—who lived just outside Fort Worth on a small cattle operation, had driven out to California to be with him, a sort of combined vacation and family reunion.

From the instant she and Denny had met, they'd both known that this was IT. Every moment she wasn't working at her two jobs, Eva spent with Denny and his family.

Well, not every moment... There were those evenings when his parents claimed weariness and his sisters were sent to bed to rest up for the next day's outing that the young lovers were granted time alone. They talked well into the night, telling each other of their hopes and dreams, confessing their disappointments and faults, professing their growing love for each other, and kissing and petting until the feelings building inside them threatened to rage out of control.

After just a week, Denny bought her an engagement ring, three small diamonds—not much more than chips in a fancy setting—that Eva wore proudly. They made plans. She would go back to Texas with his parents so that she could be close to both his family and hers. She would get a job, and he'd send her his checks so they could save up. As soon as his hitch was over—maybe before—they would be married.

Denny's family was less than pleased over his decision to marry Eva. After all, they argued, while she seemed like a nice girl, he hardly knew her. Stubbornly, Denny maintained he knew enough.

Eva and Denny were delirious with happiness, and even though her conscience threatened to get the best of her, Eva gave in to the cravings of her young body and let Denny make love to her. While the act wasn't what she'd imagined it would be, he was so sweet and loving and apologetic for hurting her that she decided it was worth it. The next time was easier—both physically, and on her conscience.

Denny shipped out on December 27, and Eva cried for hours. Once his plane left, she followed their plans to the letter, scrunching into the back seat of the Talbots' Chevy with his sisters, her belongings packed in cardboard boxes and loaded onto a Greyhound bus to be delivered to her home state later. It didn't take her long to find her small apartment and a full-time job in a Dallas department store.

Eva wrote to Denny daily, and he answered as often as he could, trying to make light of the war and bemoaning the heavy losses the Allies had encountered.

For the most part, war was far from Eva's mind. She was in love, soon to be married, and life was as close to a fairy tale as it was ever likely to get. She prayed for Denny at all hours of the day; she had no doubts that God would answer her prayers.

Then, one day in February when she woke up with a queasy stomach, she realized that she hadn't had a period since the first part of December—the fourth. She remembered the exact day because it was the day the Allies had begun to retreat from Pyongyang, bested by the battering they'd been taking since the Chinese Communist attack that had begun November 26.

Pregnant. She had absorbed the truth in stunned disbelief. Things like this didn't happen to girls like her. She'd been good and chaste...until Denny, and surely he didn't count. They were in love and engaged to be married. It wasn't as if she was loose or anything.

Afraid for her future for the first time in her life, afraid Denny might abandon her and the baby, Eva wrote him a panicked letter, telling him about her condition and seeking assurance that he still loved her. His reply arrived early in March.

Gallantly, Denny maintained that it was wonderful about the baby and that of course, he still loved her and that he was doing his best to get an emergency leave so he could come home and marry her as soon as possible. He wasn't sure when that might be, though, because the Allied forces were pressing the advantage of the successful northward march that had taken them to the outskirts of Seoul. The U.N. troops had been inflicting staggering casualties to the Chinese army, and Denny believed that they would be successful in retaking the city.

Don't worry, he had written. *I'll be home as soon as I can, and I'll take care of you, I promise. I love you. Forever yours, Denny.*

His reassurances eased her mind, and she counted the days until he came back home. She didn't tell either set of parents about the baby. She wanted to wait for Denny so that they could present a united front. She needed his support.

Operation Ripper began on March 7, and Eva, like the rest of the country, sat by her radio, listening for every tidbit of news she could glean about the battle raging in Seoul. When she heard of the Communist evacuation of the city on the night of March 14, she had cried tears of thankfulness. Maybe now that the U.N. forces seemed to have things under control, Denny could come home.

Three days later, she had opened the door of her apartment and found his parents standing there with red eyes and long faces. Tears streamed unashamedly down Denny's father's cheeks as he told her that they had been notified by the War Department that Denny had been killed during the retaking of Seoul.

Eva had fainted, and when she came around, she'd cried so long and so hard that Denny's mother wanted to take her to the hospital. Later, when Eva calmed down, Mrs. Talbot had smoothed her hair and suggested in a gentle tone that maybe Eva should go back to Crystal Creek for a while...just until the edge wore off her grief.

Eva had thanked the Talbots for coming and sent them on their way. She needed to be alone, to ponder her future, a preoccupation that had taken up a lot of her time since she'd learned of Denny's death. Days of thinking brought her to two conclusions: She had no real future without Denny. And more important, the idea of spending the rest of her life as an unwed mother was unbearable.

She had debated—was still debating—whether or not she should tell the Talbots about the baby. If she did, she'd have to tell *her* parents, and they would insist that she move back to Crystal Creek. They would never let her live down her mistake, and the people of Crystal Creek...well, she was pretty sure she knew what their reaction would be. She would be an outcast. A scarlet woman, unfit to associate with the "respectable" people of the small town.

Three weeks had passed since she'd heard about Denny, and the pain of her loss still nagged like a sharp stone in her shoe. She missed him—his smile, his

gentleness. His common sense. She was lost and rud-
derless, unable to make the simplest decision.

Even after three weeks of careful consideration, she
wasn't sure she could go back and face the people
she'd known all her life. She'd been so full of pride
and confidence when she left, so sure that when she
returned, she would be a success—a star.

Eva felt the familiar sting of tears in her eyes. As
Reverend Blake had often preached, pride went before a fall. Her success hadn't materialized, and not
only had she lost the only man she'd ever love, she'd
"got caught," the price her mother had warned her
that "bad girls" often paid for "letting a man do it"
to them.

Eva shuddered at the memory of her mother's frequent, scathing lectures. She couldn't go back to
Crystal Creek. Going back home a failure was one
thing. Going back a pregnant failure was something
else altogether.

What to do about the situation was something she
thought about daily...while she worked, while she sat
whiling away the hours until bedtime. She was now
almost four months pregnant; luckily she'd been so ill
that she'd lost a lot of weight, and so far she didn't
show at all.

She knew she couldn't keep the baby a secret forever, and she didn't know how she could work near the
end of her pregnancy. And even if she didn't lose her
job at the department store, it didn't pay much. How

could she support herself and a child when just taking care of herself was all she could do?

She'd tried praying for guidance, but she was convinced God no longer heard her prayers. The faith instilled in her by years of faithful church attendance wavered. She'd prayed for success as an actress and found herself inadequate, and she'd prayed for Denny's safety, and God had allowed him to be killed. Maybe God wasn't listening because he was angry with her for sleeping with Denny.

Unmindful of her manicure, Eva buried her face in her hands and fought back the threat of more tears. She'd cried enough tears the past three weeks to fill the Gulf, even though she knew her crying wouldn't change a thing.

Pushing aside her troubling thoughts, she got up from the small table and went to the window that was open to let in whatever wayward breeze might be lurking between the buildings. She braced her palms on the windowsill and leaned her forehead against the rusty screen. She felt in limbo, uncertain about what to do with her life, almost as if she were waiting…though she had no idea what on earth she might be waiting for.

In spite of her determination not to cry, she felt a thick knot of emotion gathering in her throat and the moisture pooling in her eyes. One by one, the tears trickled down cheeks that had grown too thin in the past few weeks. Too tired to wipe them away, weary to her very soul, she let them fall.

HOWARD STOOD outside the door of Eva's apartment for long moments, debating whether or not he should knock. The trip hadn't been in vain. He knew she was there because he could hear the sound of her radio.

What could he say? That he was in the neighborhood and thought he'd drop by? That her parents, who were upset and worried because she hadn't made any effort to see them since she'd come back to Texas four months ago, wanted him to check up on her? That he'd wanted to get a glimpse of her beautiful face so that he'd have something to think about during the long lonely nights he lay sleepless in his solitary bed?

Another, sobering thought struck him. What if she had someone in there with her—another man? His stomach churned at the thought of her having a boyfriend. *Of course she'll have a boyfriend, Howard. Beautiful women like Eva always have boyfriends.* Even though his intelligence told him that he'd be a fool not to believe otherwise, his heart ached.

Howard willed away his ridiculous feelings and told himself to act like a man, not a mouse. Regardless of whether Eva had a male friend, he still had a favor to carry out for her parents. He was an adult, not an untried kid. He was a man who had grown accustomed to speaking to large crowds, a man who had attained a certain poise during his college years—not that she'd probably notice. Drat it all! This indecision wasn't like him. What was it about Eva that made him feel like a pimply-faced jerk again?

Don't think about it, Howard, he told himself. *Just do it. Be impulsive, remember?* Without giving himself time to back out, he squared his shoulders and rapped his knuckles sharply against the door.

"Just a minute!"

He bit back an involuntary smile of pleasure. He'd have recognized that voice anywhere.

The door swung open, and she stood there, looking like the sum total of every good—and every erotic—dream he'd ever had. Speechless, Howard could only stare. She wore a robe of black satin, whose lapels were stitched with embroidered flowers and fire-breathing dragons.

He tried not to notice that the short robe exposed a generous portion of creamy thighs, or that the peaks of her breasts thrust against the shiny fabric with a heart-stopping impudence.

A towel was wrapped around her head like a turban; she must have just washed her hair. Bright tendrils straggled along her neck and clung to one cheek. Her face was naked of artifice, and her eyes were red-rimmed, as if she'd been crying. He noted with a bit of surprise that her face was no longer the face of a teenager. It was the face of a woman.

Howard felt the love he'd harbored for so long clench his heart in a painful grip. Dear God, it wasn't fair for any woman to be so gorgeous.

When he just stood there without speaking, a wary look crept into her blue eyes, and her eyebrows drew together in a frown. She reached up with slender crimson-tipped fingers and clutched the lapels of the robe together in a protective gesture.

That was when he saw the ring on her left hand. She was engaged. His heart plummeted to the pit of his very soul.

"Is there something I can do for you?" she asked.

Howard was too shocked by the sight of the ring to realize that she didn't recognize him.

"Look, mister," she said in a voice filled with irritation. "I don't know who you are, or what you want, but—"

"It's me, Eva," Howard ventured, finding his voice at last. "Howard."

He understood why she didn't recognize him. Physically, he'd changed a lot the past four years. Boxing and tennis had improved his physique considerably. Time had taken care of his skin problems. He still wore glasses, but there were plenty of girls who had no problem at all with them, except to say that it was a shame they hid his eyes.

He watched as her eyes—gorgeous blue eyes—widened with incredulity, and her beautiful mouth with its full lower lip fell open in surprise. "Howard? Howard *Blake?*"

He nodded.

She shook her head. "I'd never have recognized you! You've changed, put on some weight...and some muscle."

Muscle. That was good, wasn't it? Howard's mouth quirked in a quick, nervous smile, and he shoved his hands into the pockets of his slacks, feeling a fool. "I was on the boxing team at school."

"What! Not the debate team?" Eva asked, with a hint of a smile.

He gave a small shrug. "That, too."

She laughed, and the sound that fell on his ears was as soft as an angel's song. "What are you doing in Dallas?"

"I came to attend the National Baptist Convention."

Her smile faded. "The convention! Then you did it? You're preaching?"

He nodded. "I took over from my dad the first of the year."

"Is it what you expected?"

Talking about his calling was something Howard felt more comfortable with. His smile held a hint of chagrin, and he rubbed the side of his nose with his forefinger. "I'm not sure what I expected, but it's what I've always wanted to do."

Eva nodded. Everyone had known Howard intended to follow in Thaddeus Blake's footsteps. "How did you find me?" she asked.

"Your mother gave me your address." Was it his imagination, or did her face grow pale suddenly? "I promised her I'd look you up if I had time. The last meeting broke up a couple of hours ago, and I thought I'd see if I could talk you into going out to dinner or something."

"That's awfully sweet of you, but—"

"If your fiancé doesn't object, of course," he tacked on belatedly.

This time, there was no doubt about it. Not only did her face turn ashen, but she actually swayed. Howard reached out to steady her in an automatic gesture. The bones of her shoulder felt fragile beneath his steadying grip.

"Are you all right?"

Eva nodded and raised tear-filled eyes to his. "My fiancé won't object," she said in a quivering voice. "He's dead. He was killed when the Allies retook Seoul last month...."

"YOU WERE ENGAGED to some other man before you married Daddy?" Maggie asked, her shock apparent from her pale face and her disbelieving eyes. "You were *pregnant* by him?"

Eva nodded; a residual shame lingered in her eyes.

"Did you love him—this...Denny?"

Eva clenched her hands together in her lap. "With all my heart."

"But what about Daddy?"

"If you're asking if I love him, I think you know the answer to that," Eva said with a tender smile. "I adore Howard Blake. How could I not? Denny was my first real love. A young, innocent kind of love—regardless of my getting pregnant. With all the things kids are exposed to today, I don't think that kind of innocence even exists anymore—not that what I did was right," she hastened to add.

"Why haven't you and Daddy ever told me and Ronald about any of this before?"

"When I agreed to marry your father, he made me promise not to tell anyone about Denny and the baby, and I never did."

"Not even your parents—or his?"

Eva shook her head. "Howard may have told his parents, but I was too embarrassed back then to want to talk about it. I wanted to forget it."

"Why are you telling me now?"

"Because I see how much you're hurting, and how alone you feel. When you said you felt in limbo, I knew exactly what you meant. I'd been there. I know what it's like to feel as if God has turned his back on you. And I want you to learn from my experiences, if you can."

"That which does not kill you makes you stronger, huh?" Maggie paraphrased.

"Exactly. We make choices in life, Maggie. You know that. We can either place blame, or we can take what we're handed and make something good happen from it. It's the same premise you deal with every day in your social work, and I'll bet you always encourage your people to pick up and go on."

Maggie nodded.

"That was a lesson your father taught me. I could wallow in my misery, or I could build a new life. I could blame God and let my bitterness eat away at my soul, or I could look for the good things he gave me and start over."

Maggie's face wore a whimsical smile. "Daddy always makes it sound so easy...so logical, doesn't he?"

Eva nodded. "But it wasn't easy, Maggie. Once I made the decision to marry him, I thought the hard part was over. I wasn't a fallen woman anymore. My baby wouldn't be born out of wedlock. But when we came home and told people we were married, it didn't take but a few days to see that the hard part was just starting. Those first few months of our marriage were hell on earth. I felt as if the whole town was against me.

"It was months before I saw what his marrying me and our silly agreement really meant to your father. And it took me a long time to realize just how much he must have loved me to jeopardize his whole future by bringing a pregnant woman back to Crystal Creek as his bride."

CHAPTER FOUR

April 1951

"I LOVED HIM so much." The knuckles of the hand gripping the lapels of Eva's robe were taut and white. "I loved him, and your God took him away from me."

Howard wasn't sure if it was the shock of her accusation or the depth of pain he saw in her eyes, but something inside him clicked. His concern for her overrode his own feelings. In the blink of an eye, he made the transformation from a gauche young man who'd been worried about knocking on Eva's door to the man he'd spent years studying to be.

"I'd like to listen, if you'd like to talk about it."

"Why would you want to listen to a sad story like that?" she asked with a shake of her head.

"Because that's part of what I do."

Eva wasn't impressed. "You turn people's lives around, huh?"

"No," Howard said with a shake of his head. "Mostly, I just listen. People can usually figure out how to turn their lives around all by themselves."

Instead of answering, Eva studied him for a long moment. "How are my parents?" she asked at last.

"Fine. They miss you, and they wonder why you haven't been to see them since you moved back to Texas."

"I was busy working, and then Denny...died. I haven't been able to think of much else."

"Surely your parents could be a big support for you right now."

"I doubt that," she said with a shake of her head. "Mama's still mad at me for going off to California."

It was plain to see that the rift between Eva and her mother was a painful subject. "My offer still stands," he said. "For dinner and a talk. I'm a good listener."

"You always were a glutton for punishment," she said with a listless smile. She gave a sigh of acquiescence and stepped aside to let him in. "All right, we'll go to dinner, but I don't want to talk about Denny."

"Fine," Howard said with a nod.

Still holding the edges of her robe together, she backed toward the bathroom door, scooping up an armful of clothes from the back of the sofa as she went.

"I'll just change and be right out. Make yourself at home."

The door closed behind her. Howard expelled a deep sigh and thrust his hands into the pockets of his slacks once more, absorbing the news that Eva had lost her fiancé in the war, reconciling himself to the news that she'd even had a fiancé...a man she loved. He wondered why Sally Carmichael hadn't mentioned her daughter's engagement.

Forcing the questions from his mind—Eva would provide the answers soon enough—Howard let his curious gaze roam the one-room apartment. The kitchen was nothing but a refrigerator, apartment-size stove and porcelain sink. A small square table completed the kitchen furnishings.

A worn green velvet sofa done in a high-low pattern was set parallel to the table, its length separating the kitchen and living areas. A crocheted afghan lay across the sofa's back. The vibrant hues of the yarn scraps that made up the covering reminded Howard of Joseph's many-colored coat. Since there appeared to be no bedroom, the sofa no doubt did double duty as Eva's bed.

Starched, crocheted doilies covered mismatched tables that gleamed with furniture polish. A bulky radio stood in the corner. A Currier and Ives reproduction graced the far wall, and colorful throw pillows and various whatnots scattered around the room added splashes of color and lent an air of homeyness to the otherwise shabby furnishings.

Howard went to the window. Shadows from the nearby buildings rushed the end of day. Soon the streetlights would come on, and night would fall. He wondered how Eva would have spent her night if he hadn't come. He had a sneaking suspicion that the answer was the same as how he would have spent his: alone.

EVA COULDN'T HELP feeling a little lift in her spirits as she painted her lips with True Red lipstick. Her days were so filled with the business of survival that she had little time for fun, and even if time was available, there wouldn't have been enough money. Her last outing to dinner had been in Los Angeles with Denny and his family.

She blotted her lips on a square of toilet tissue. Howard Blake. Whoever would have imagined that he of all people would look her up? Of course, it was just like him. He'd always been kindhearted, if a bit conventional. The kids at school always said if you looked up the word *boring* in Webster's, you'd find a picture of Howard Blake there. Well, she wasn't looking for excitement. All she wanted was a decent meal and a chance to get out, and Howard could provide that without any of the hassle she could expect from most men.

If anyone had told her a year ago that she'd be going out with Howard Blake, she'd have said they were crazy. Actually, she wasn't going *out* with him; it wasn't a date or anything, so she didn't have to worry about feeling guilty about Denny. They were just two acquaintances from the same town who would share a meal and bring each other up-to-date on what had been happening in their lives.

Eva turned to see if the seams of her stockings were straight and reached for her dress. Howard had certainly changed. She would never have recognized him if she'd run into him on the street. She had to admit that he looked far better than she'd ever expected.

She wriggled into the silky garment and smoothed the red-and-purple-splashed fabric over her hips. She reached for the side zipper, noting that the dress, a scoop-necked, cap-sleeved sheath, was tighter than the last time she'd worn it, even though she'd been plagued with her fair share of morning sickness. Of their own volition, her hands moved to her abdomen. Was it rounder than normal? Would Howard notice? Eva closed her eyes and gripped the edge of the basin in a sudden rush of despair. How much longer could she keep her secret?

Don't think about it. Not tonight.

Forcing her mind away from her disruptive thoughts, she regarded her reflection in the spotted mirror and wondered if she'd changed as much as Howard. Dabbing her wrists with some Tabu cologne, she straightened her shoulders, an action that thrust out her full breasts, and opened the door.

Howard was standing at the window, his hands in his pockets in a stance that was rapidly becoming familiar. He turned at the sound of the door opening, his eyes making a slow examination of her—from the toes of her recently polished black high heels to the top of her gleaming head.

Eva felt her face growing hot. Was he seeing her tummy? Or the extra fullness of her breasts caused by the pregnancy? And her hair! It must be a mess, she thought, tucking a strand behind her ear in a feminine move that betrayed her self-consciousness. She hadn't had time to coax out the curl with a hard brushing, and it was drying in the loose waves she despised.

"Your hair is beautiful."

"Thank you." Uncomfortable with the unexpected compliment, Eva went to the kitchen table to retrieve her purse. "Where are we going?"

"I'm not sure," Howard said. "I have a craving for a good steak. How does that sound?"

After weeks of bologna sandwiches and ground beef, it sounded like the closest thing to heaven Eva had had in ages, and she told him so.

Howard laughed. His teeth—one in front was a little crooked—flashed, and two deep grooves appeared in his lean cheeks. The deep, warm sound of his laughter wrapped itself around Eva's heart like a cozy blanket. She smiled in return.

As he offered her his arm and ushered her out the door, she was suddenly very glad that Howard Blake had appeared on her doorstep.

THE RESTAURANT WAS SMALL and crowded, and if the number of patrons was any indication, the food promised to be excellent. Howard placed their order with a waitress who assured them she'd have their salads in a jiffy.

While they waited for their steaks to arrive, Eva and Howard devoured their salads and Howard filled her in on what had happened in Crystal Creek over the past two years.

He told her about his parents' extensive traveling since his dad's retirement, and what a big job it was stepping into Thaddeus Blake's shoes.

He divulged the little-known news that Nate Purdy had given Rose Montgomery an engagement ring, even though his parents thought he should at least wait to marry until he finished his premed. Rose's parents weren't too thrilled, either, and the families were feuding somewhat over what was best for their respective offspring.

Howard told her that some new people named MacBride from Fort Worth had bought some property smack-dab in the middle of town and were in the process of building a motel and café that would face Main Street. Having a motel was a big deal to the people of Crystal Creek.

With a grin and a shake of his head, he also told her that the biggest cause for concern recently was that Bubba Gibson had talked Flynn MacGregor into buying him a case of beer, which he proceeded to distribute among his friends—including J. T. McKinney, who'd gone home and thrown up on his mother's new rug. Calvin, J.T.'s dad, had threatened to flay the boy alive if he ever did anything like that again.

"Which one?" Eva asked, her eyes dancing with merriment. "Bubba or J.T.?"

"Both, I think," Howard confided, his rich baritone melding with her tinkling soprano. Their laughter faded away, and the waitress brought their steaks and French fries, leaving them with the directive to enjoy their meals.

"Bubba always was a ring-tailed toot," Eva said, her lips still curved at the memory of Howard's story. Though she'd missed her family, she hadn't realized just how much she missed the people she'd grown up with until Howard had shown up on her doorstep. Homesickness was an ache that throbbed deep inside her.

"Bubba is just Bubba." Howard reached for his glass of iced tea. "It's good to see you laugh, Eva," he said, his blue eyes crinkling at the corners. "Your smile is one of the things I always remembered about you."

Eva felt the smile fade from her lips. Her hand trembled the slightest bit as she picked up her steak knife. "There hasn't been much to laugh about lately."

"I can see that. But time has a way of easing pain when nothing else can."

For some reason she couldn't fathom, the statement fueled the ready anger that simmered just below the surface of the calm demeanor she presented to the world. Howard had always been a dreamer, she thought in exasperation, such a believer in "happily ever after." She wondered what he would do if he was ever involved in a real-life situation, something beyond his control, something that couldn't be dismissed with a Bible verse and the unconditional faith he believed could answer any problem.

"A biblical truism, Howard?" she asked with a hint of sarcasm.

Frowning, Howard shook his head. "One of my psych professors. I do think he's right, though. If you cling to that hope, it might make the next few months easier to get through."

"Maybe," she said, but her disbelief was apparent.

"So tell me about Hollywood," he coaxed in a voice that tried too hard to exude cheer. "I've been doing all the talking. It's your turn."

"There isn't much to tell. Obviously, I didn't set the town on fire with my tremendous acting ability." The bitterness in her voice surprised even her. "As much as I hate to admit it, my mother was right. It's a hard place to get noticed unless you're willing to play the game. I wasn't."

"Surely you have some good memories. Friends? The place itself?"

"Oh, California is pretty—what little I got to see. A girlfriend and I took the bus to Palm Springs one weekend. I liked the desert. But the only good thing that happened to me in California was meeting Denny."

As soon as she said the words, she wished she could call them back. Her animosity faded. Her throat tightened and she bit her lip to still its trembling.

"No crying," Howard ordered, looking at her over the top of his glasses. "Not until you finish eating."

She swallowed hard and nodded. Throughout the remainder of the meal, Howard kept up a steady flow of conversation, that, in spite of herself, Eva found herself responding to. She'd always enjoyed lively discussions about any arts-related field.

They talked about the books they'd read—or planned to read. Howard had finished John Hersey's *The Wall*, a book about the Warsaw Ghetto, and *A Man Called Peter* by Catherine Marshall. Mamie Lucas was holding him a copy of *The Catcher in the Rye* at the Claro County Library.

Eva's taste ran to James Jones's *From Here to Eternity*—a powerful book, he agreed—and *The Roman Spring of Mrs. Stone* by Tennessee Williams, which Howard confessed he'd read but hadn't liked.

The diversity of their tastes spilled over into their preference for movies: Howard wanted to see *An American in Paris,* and Eva was dying to see Marlon Brando in *A Streetcar Named Desire.*

Obviously, Howard said, she was a staunch Tennessee Williams fan. Her dimples flashing, Eva confessed to being a Marlon Brando fan.

They did agree that Johnnie Ray's "Cry" and the tender "Kisses Sweeter Than Wine" were two of the best songs ever recorded.

Over dessert, which Eva declined because her stomach was acting up a bit, Howard asked her which jazz player she liked the best—"Jersey" Joe Walcott or Ezzard Charles. Eva drew a blank.

"I've never heard of either one of them," she confessed, "but then, I don't listen to much jazz."

Unholy glee glinted in Howard's blue eyes.

"What?" she said, her eyes narrowing in suspicion.

"I was just testing your sports IQ," he said with a typical masculine shrug of unrepentance. "Those guys aren't jazz players. They're boxers."

"Boxers!" Eva tossed her wadded-up napkin at Howard. "What is it about me, anyway?" she asked, putting her elbow on the table and resting her chin in her palm. "Denny liked to tease me, too."

"He sounds like a nice guy," Howard said truthfully. "How did you meet him?"

Caught up in the sweetness of a memory, Eva said, "I went with a friend to a Knights of Columbus dance. Denny was back in the States on furlough."

With skillful and seemingly innocuous questions, and despite Eva's reluctance to talk about her past, Howard gleaned the highlights of Eva and Denny's courtship. At the end of twenty minutes, she realized that she had related the past five months of her life, including the trip back to Texas with Denny's parents. Her voice was husky with emotion as she recounted the Talbots' visit to break the news about Denny's death at Seoul.

"You're an easy person to talk to, Howard," she said, rummaging in her purse for a handkerchief. "I didn't mean to bore you with my life story."

"I wasn't bored," he told her. "And talking about it can only help. I've never lost someone that close to me. It must be hard."

With a nod, she caught her bottom lip with her teeth and dabbed at the corners of her eyes with the floral-patterned, lace-edged hankie.

"Would you like to go?" he asked.

"Please."

Howard called for the check, and in a matter of minutes, he was helping her into his car, a green Ford sedan that had seen better days. Eva was unusually quiet during the drive to her apartment. She was tired, a condition that seemed more and more common as her pregnancy progressed. To make matters worse, her queasy stomach was getting worse—probably the steak sauce she'd used. Though her morning nausea had passed for the most part, there were still times when some food or other just didn't agree with her. She swallowed back the sick feeling and prayed for light traffic.

As soon as Howard pulled the car to a stop in front of her building, Eva grabbed the door handle, turning to him with a smile. "Thanks for the dinner," she said in all sincerity, even though it wasn't sitting well at the moment.

"My pleasure. Hold on. I'll walk you up."

"You don't have to do that."

"I insist," he said, opening his own door. "My mother would consider all her teachings a failure if she knew I hadn't seen you safely inside."

Eva sighed. There was nothing to do but let Howard escort her to the door of the building.

"Give me your key," he said as they stepped inside the foyer.

Eva's foot was already on the bottom step that led to the second floor. "What?"

"Your apartment key," he said, holding out his hand. "I'll walk you up."

She licked her dry lips and groped frantically in her purse for her key. Darn it! Why wouldn't he go away and leave her alone? If she could just get inside and lie down with a wet washcloth on her forehead, maybe the nausea would pass.

Her fingers closed around the key, but instead of handing it to him, she raced up the stairs as fast as her tight skirt and heels would permit.

"Evie! What's the hurry?" Howard asked from behind her.

Without slacking her pace, she called over her shoulder, "I have to get to the bathroom."

"Oh," he said. No doubt her admission of something so personal had struck him dumb. At that particular moment she could not have cared less about offending Howard's sensibilities.

One hand clamped over her mouth, she rammed the skeleton key into the lock, flung the door open and raced to the bathroom. With tears streaming down her cheeks, she fell to her knees and embraced the cold porcelain of the toilet bowl like a long lost lover.

When she stepped through the bathroom door some ten minutes later—after indulging in a storm of weeping—she was surprised to see Howard standing at the window in the exact position he had been in earlier...his head bowed as if he were looking down onto the sidewalk, his hands in his pockets.

She hadn't expected him to still be there. Most men would have run as far and as fast as they could from a sick woman. Suddenly, she felt like crying again.

Her hand went to her hair. She looked a wreck. The medicine chest mirror had told her so. Her tears had caused her mascara to run, and wiping at the moisture had smudged the makeup. She was as pale a death warmed over, and her hair looked like a wild woman's. In fact, she resembled a sick raccoon who'd stuck his paw in an electric outlet.

As if he could sense her presence, Howard turned. She saw an exquisite tenderness in his eyes. Tenderness, and...was that pain? She saw something else too. A soft gasp escaped her. He knew what was wrong with her. Somehow, he *knew*.

The realization that her secret was out triggered another burst of the hostility that had plagued her ever since she'd learned of Denny's death and realized that she was alone in her predicament. Her chin lifted to a to-hell-with-it angle, and a defiant light entered her blue eyes. She crossed the room with a sexy, swivel hipped stride and took a cigarette from the case on the coffee table. Though she seldom smoked, Denny had and she kept the case as a reminder of him.

"So my parents wanted you to come spy on me, huh, Howard?" she said, spinning the wheel of the lighter and holding it to the tip of her Camel.

"They asked me to see if you were all right," he said, but if she heard, she chose not to comment.

She drew in a deep draft of smoke, choked and exhaled it toward the ceiling. Her eyes filled with tears, and her lips twisted into a grimace.

"Well, you can go home and give them an earful, can't you?" she taunted, leaning over and stubbing out the cigarette she'd just lighted. She straightened, meeting his eyes once more. Misery was rapidly overtaking her anger. "You can tell them they were right. Tell them I said that L.A. was everything they told me it would be—except worse."

Her shoulders slumped and she swiped at the two tears that trickled down her cheeks. "And you can tell them that I didn't let them down. I did just what they expected me to do. I got pregnant. Want to know a secret, Howard?" she jeered. "It didn't feel wrong. It felt good."

Howard made no comment, but she saw the muscle in his cheek knot. The confession robbed her of what little composure she had left. "Oh, God!" she cried raggedly.

Covering her eyes with her hands, she swayed like a sapling in a high wind. She heard Howard say her name and felt his arms go around her in a hard, comforting embrace.

It felt wonderful to get her shameful secret off her chest. It felt good to feel the strength of a man's arms around her, even if that man was the honorable, upstanding Reverend Howard Blake. It felt even better to lean on someone after trying to hold everything together alone for so long.

She let him ease her onto the sofa and felt him sit down beside her and cradle her close to his wide chest. She made no effort to halt the scalding tears that drenched the pristine whiteness of his shirt. She couldn't have stopped them if she'd tried . . .

PREGNANT!

Howard held her and let the truth wash over him. So Eva wasn't the angel he imagined her to be, after all. She was just a woman, a flesh-and-blood woman with a heart that could be touched by love and anger and . . . passion.

He felt as if he were submerged in sorrow, drowning in disappointment. Though he knew his feelings were ridiculous, he felt betrayed, somehow. How could Eva have turned her back on her upbringing and everything she'd been taught about right and wrong? His eyes burned with unshed tears; he squeezed them closed against the unmanly show of emotion.

His imagination conjured up a vivid picture of her with some faceless man, engaged in the act of love—of sex—and his gut clenched in an automatic, violent rejection.

The pedestal Howard had put Eva on ten years ago crumbled, the perfect image his mind had created of her shattering into a million pieces on the altar of his pain and disillusionment.

A single tear trickled down his cheek.

He wished he'd never come, wished he'd never told her parents he'd look her up. He wished he'd never seen the pain in her eyes and heard the sarcasm in her voice when she'd taunted him about *his* God letting Denny Talbot die. And he wished with all his heart that he hadn't heard the confession she'd just made.

But he *had* come to see her. He *had* seen the mockery in her eyes as she confessed her faults and heard the contempt in her voice as she'd scorned the God who guided every facet of his life, directed his every step.

He wanted to go back to his hotel room and cry for the loss of all his secret dreams, but instead, he held Eva until her tears were all cried out and she drew away with a shaky apology.

"It's all right," he assured her, even though his heart wailed that it wasn't all right at all.

Eva wiped her eyes with the handkerchief he offered her. "I shouldn't have been so...so...ugly about everything."

"It's never wrong to be truthful about your feelings, Evie, even when the truth hurts."

She stared into his steadfast blue eyes. "How do you do it?"

"Do what?"

She shrugged. "Handle everything with such... *aplomb* is the word, I guess. You never get ruffled. You always stay calm. You're always in control."

If only she knew, Howard thought with a sigh. "It's all done with smoke and mirrors," he said, hoping to elicit a smile. When it failed to appear, he opted for the truth.

" 'I can do all things through Christ who strengthens me,' " he quoted. "*He* helps me through. I can't do anything alone."

THROUGHOUT THE NIGHT, Howard's mind circled round and round Eva's predicament like a rat wandering in a maze...considering it from every angle. He pondered his raw feelings and vented his fury at Eva for doing what she'd done. He tossed and turned, sat up and lay down, raved, prayed and cried.

He took a long hard look at her bitterness and tried to put himself in her place by asking himself how he would feel if someone he loved had died. He took his consideration a step further by asking himself if he'd be able to control his carnal desires if he were faced with a strong emotional and physical attraction.

He tried to envision Eva as a mother, tried to picture a baby cradle in her small apartment, but the image wouldn't materialize.

At two a.m., his bed looked as if Ezzard Charles and "Jersey" Joe had gone a full fifteen rounds there and Howard had been the one who'd gotten KO'd.

It was dawn before he found any respite from his torment, and when it came, it was so simple he wondered how he'd managed to overlook it for so long. He—Howard Blake—had to practice what he'd preached. He couldn't solve Eva's problems alone. He couldn't do *anything* alone. He had to turn it over to God, who would provide the answers and the peace Howard longed for.

Howard prayed.

He prayed for knowledge of how he could best help Eva during her time of trouble. For strength to stand for what he knew was right in the face of her derision. For answers to her questions, answers that would help him set her on the right track. For forbearance of her weakened faith. For a greater faith of his own. For a greater love.

When the solution came, it stole his breath.

He would ask Eva to marry him.

With a husband, she could go back to Crystal Creek and start over without the stigma of having a baby born out of wedlock. He had a good, dependable position in town; he could provide for her and the baby far better than a lot of men.

It was the perfect solution, he thought with a slow smile...perhaps the opportunity of a lifetime. He had always loved Eva Carmichael, and he was sure that down deep inside him, he still did. Was his love so shallow that it could be killed because she'd loved another man and given herself to him? Was he so unforgiving? He hoped not.

A picture of Eva's voluptuous body in the tight dress and her heavily made-up face flashed through his mind and filled him with uneasiness. That negative thought was followed by the memory of her derision toward things he considered holy...things that were a part of his life. Maybe she wasn't cut from the right cloth to be a preacher's wife. Maybe he shouldn't act on this impulse without giving it more consideration.

He pushed the niggling doubts aside, reminding himself that the members of his congregation were Christians, people who sought to do good. Kind, forgiving people who would want to help Eva however they could. With time, he was sure Eva would return to the beliefs she'd grown up with.

As for the way she dressed and conducted herself...well, he could teach her the proper behavior for a minister's wife. His mother could show her how to dress more conservatively. There would have to be some understanding, though. He would have to make it very clear that she would be responsible for a fair amount of entertaining. He tried to picture her as dinner hostess to the deacons and their wives. Couldn't.

Again, he shook off the vague, uneasy feeling. It would be fine. He wanted to marry her. Not only was it a good work, deep down it was a dream he'd always cherished.

Somehow, he had to make it her dream, too.

IT WAS BARELY DAYLIGHT when Howard got into his car and drove to Eva's apartment. He had to bang on the door several times before he roused her.

"Who is it?" she called out in a voice heavy with sleep.

"Me. Howard."

"Howard?"

In a matter of seconds, he heard the dead bolt sliding back. The door swung open. Eva was wearing floral print pajamas and a frown.

"Howard! What are you doing here at this time of morning? I thought you were going back to Crystal Creek."

"I want you to go with me. I hardly slept all night, Evie," he said, the words pouring from him. "But I finally got it all figured out. It's a great idea, and it'll work just fine—you'll see."

Eva put a small hand on his chest, and Howard's heart took a sudden painful leap. "Whoa! Wait! What idea? What will work just fine?"

"I want to be the baby's father."

Involuntarily, Eva's hand tightened on his shirt. "You what?"

"I want to marry you, Eva. I want to take you back to Crystal Creek as my wife...."

"SERENA JUST CALLED," Ken Slattery said, poking his head into the waiting room and interrupting Eva's story. "She finally got hold of Cal. He's going to get a flight back home as soon as he can tie up a few things."

"Thanks, Ken," Maggie said. She glanced at the window where the darkness of the night was dissipating. "What time is it, anyway?"

He glanced at his watch. "Near six. I'm going home and have a shower. Can I get you ladies anything before I go?"

"No, thanks," Maggie said. "I appreciate your staying, Ken, but I know you have things to do at the ranch. You don't need to come back."

"Yeah, I do," Ken said. "Rio would do it for me."

Maggie gave a weary smile and a nod. Ken was right.

"I'll be back in an hour or so," he said, and disappeared.

"Rio has some wonderful friends," Maggie said.

"Yes, he does," Eva concurred.

Maggie shook her head. "I still can't believe you and Daddy kept this a secret all these years."

Eva lifted her plump shoulders in a little shrug. "Howard thought the fewer people who knew the truth, the better. Then, as time went on and we built our life together, it was easy to forget for long periods of time that any of it happened. But even after all these years I always get a little sad on March fifteenth."

Eva stood and stretched, glancing at her watch. "I could use a cup of coffee. How about you?"

"That sounds great. I'll go get us some, and when I come back you can tell me the rest. It sure beats reading outdated magazines."

Eva gave her a raised-eyebrows look. "When your father gets here, I'm taking you home to get a few hours' rest, young lady."

"I can't go home, Mama," Maggie said. "I need to be here."

"Your eyes look like two burnt holes in a blanket, Margaret. You're exhausted," Eva said in her best concerned-mother voice.

"Rio might need me."

Eva pursed her lips in the disapproving way Maggie remembered from her youth. "You're a grown woman. I can't make you go."

Maggie smiled and reached for her purse. "The coffee's on me." She stood, and when she did, the room took a sharp dip. She reached out a steadying hand toward the wall.

"Maggie! Honey, are you all right?" Eva asked, taking Maggie's arm in a firm grip.

Maggie put a hand to her forehead. "Yeah, I'm fine. Just a little woozy." She looked up at her mother. "I've had a couple of dizzy spells lately."

"Don't you think you should see a doctor?"

"I have an appointment in Austin tomorrow," Maggie told her. "Or is it today, now? I guess I should call and reschedule it for another time."

"Hi," Nate Purdy said from the doorway, "I'm glad to see you two are still here."

Howard, his gray hair mussed from the wind, followed the doctor into the room. Eva tilted up her face for her husband's kiss. "Hi, honey."

It gave Maggie a warm feeling to know that her parents were so devoted after so many years... especially now that she knew their marriage had gotten off to a less than auspicious beginning. She was too busy noticing how their eyes lighted up when they saw each other to see the troubled expression on Nate Purdy's face.

However, Eva was more in tune with Howard's body language. "Is something wrong?" she asked, her gaze slewing from Howard to the doctor.

Nate took in Maggie's pale face and the dark circles beneath her eyes. He ran a hand through his iron-gray hair. "The ICU nurse called me back a little while ago," he said in a heavy voice. "Rio has slipped into a coma."

"What! How?"

"It happens sometimes with a sudden, substantial blood loss."

Maggie's eyes moved from one person to the other and finally lighted on the aging doctor. She tried not to think of all the horror stories she'd heard. Stories where victims never came out of their comas. "A coma. What does that mean? How long will it last?"

"I can't say, Maggie. We've already given him some blood, and we're giving more."

"What can I do?"

He shook his head. "There's nothing we can do except monitor the situation. I think the best thing you can do is go home and get some rest."

Stunned, Maggie fixed her gaze on the doctor. She couldn't think. A coma. How could she leave Rio here in a coma? "I can't leave, Dr. Purdy. Even if I went home, I wouldn't be able to sleep."

"I can give you a mild sedative," he told her.

"Please, honey," Eva implored. "You haven't been feeling well. Let me take you home...just for a while. Daddy can stay here with Rio."

Maggie thought about Rio lying in ICU. Even before the coma, she hadn't been able to elicit any response from him. But she couldn't deny that she was numb with fatigue. The idea of a few hours' sleep sounded like heaven on earth. Still unconvinced, she looked from her parents to the doctor.

"Will it knock me out for hours?"

"No."

As she had so often in the past, Maggie looked to her father for advice. "What if something happens?"

"I'll call," Howard said. "Nate's right, Margaret. There's nothing you can do here, and you can't be here every minute. Let us help you."

Maggie exhaled harshly. She nodded. "All right. I'll go."

"I'll go with you," Eva said, rising. "I'll drive you right on home after Nate's finished with you." She turned her attention to the doctor. "I want you to

check her blood pressure when you give her the sedative. She's been having dizzy spells.''

"Mama," Maggie groaned.

"Better safe than sorry," Eva said, looping her arm
through her daughter's. "Isn't that right, Nate?''

"You bet," Nate said, following them into the hall.

Maggie let her mother guide her to the elevator. She
was too tired and worried to waste time arguing, even
though she figured that when Nate Purdy got finished with her she'd have the next best thing to the
checkup she'd intended to have in Austin that afternoon.

Now that she'd made the decision to get some rest,
she just wanted to go. The sooner she slept, the sooner
she could come back.

WHEN MAGGIE FIRST woke up, she felt fuzzy and dis-
oriented. Weak winter sunshine fought a losing battle
with the gray clouds that straggled across the dull sky.
She turned and reached for the clock, knocking a book
off the bedside stand in the process. It hit the car-
peted floor with a dull thud.

The hands of the old-fashioned, wind-up clock
pointed to ten to twelve. Twelve noon, obviously. Why
had she slept until noon? Why hadn't Rio awakened
her?

"You're awake!" came her mother's cheerful voice.
"I thought I heard something."

Seeing her mother brought the events of the past
fourteen hours back in a rush. Rio had been shot. He

was in the hospital. In a coma. Without replying to Eva's greeting, Maggie threw back the covers and leapt to her feet. Another wave of dizziness, this one more severe than the one at the hospital, swept through her. Holding her head, she sank back onto the bed.

Like a mother hen hurrying to the aid of her chick, Eva rushed to her side. "Are you all right?"

"I feel about half-looped," Maggie confessed, more than a little chagrined. "It must be Dr. Purdy's shot."

"Possibly," Eva said, smoothing back the tangled auburn hair that was so much like her own. "It might be that flu bug that's going around, though. A lot of people were out of church with it last Sunday." She smiled. "Maybe that blood test Nate took will tell us something."

Maggie sat up gingerly. "That wasn't necessary, Mama."

"Maybe not, but it can't hurt." Eva plumped the pillows behind Maggie's back. "Why don't you just lie here while I fix us a bite of breakfast? Then you can shower and we'll go back to the hospital."

"I need to clean up the living room floor," Maggie said, recalling the bloodstained carpet.

"Jeremy and Tess have already taken care of it," Eva said. "Now, how do you want your eggs?"

It dimly registered that she should thank her brother-in-law and his wife before Maggie responded, "I don't care. Anything is all right."

Eva was just disappearing through the doorway when Maggie called to her. She turned, a question in her eyes. "I'm going to call and check on Rio, but while we have breakfast will you tell me more about you and Daddy?"

With a slight smile, Eva nodded.

Maggie gave a sigh of relief. Hearing about her parents' problems would help keep thoughts of her own at bay.

CHAPTER FIVE

April 1951

"YOU WANT to *what*?" Eva exclaimed, her eyes wide with shock.

"Marry you."

Eva shook her head. "I can't marry you, Howard!"

"Why?"

"Why?" Eva cried. "Because we really don't know each other. Because I don't love you, that's why."

Howard shrugged. "Under the circumstances, that's not a problem. I think it's a great idea."

"It's a terrible idea," she cried, aghast.

"Just think about it."

"I don't have to think about it!" she shrieked. "The idea is preposterous!"

"Is everything all right, Eva?" The querulous question came from the ancient woman standing in an open doorway farther down the hall.

"Everything is fine, Mrs. Pittman," Eva said in a conciliatory tone. The old woman nodded, stooped and picked up her newspaper with gnarled, bony fingers and shuffled back inside.

"Look, it might be better if I came in so we can discuss this like two rational adults." Without waiting for Eva to agree, Howard brushed past her.

Too stunned to object, she closed the door behind them.

"Marrying me will solve all your problems," Howard said, his enthusiasm carrying him around the small apartment. "First, I can hear in your voice that you want to go home," he said, ticking off the valid points of his argument on his fingers. "It's understandable that you don't want to go back to Crystal Creek without a husband. Marrying me will solve that problem."

"It's not like a clogged pipe, Howard," Eva said. "It isn't that easy."

Howard ignored her. "Second," he said, "you'll be able to be with your family and friends again. Third, I have a good job, so you won't have to work. You can stay home with the baby. Fourth, the baby will have a father."

Though she wore a dazed look, he could see that he had her full attention, whether she liked the idea or not. He came to a stop in front of her and took her cold hands in his. His eyes glowed with sincerity and determination. "I'll be a good husband, Evie, and a good father to your baby. I promise you that I'll love it like it's my own."

"But why, Howard?" she asked, her fair brow furrowed in puzzlement.

"Why?"

She nodded. "Why would you want to saddle yourself with a...a...pregnant woman and a baby that isn't yours?"

Howard's gaze shifted from hers. He released her hands and turned away.

"Is it because deep down inside your puritanical little heart, you secretly want what I gave Denny and think marriage is a way to get it?" she ventured.

He whirled, disbelief and anger contorting his features. "No!" he cried, though deep inside, on some level neither was prepared to take too close a look at, they both knew it was a lie.

"Then what's in this noble gesture for you?"

"I'd have a chance to do something worthwhile by helping you put your life back in order."

"You want to marry me because you want to do something worthwhile?" Eva shook her head. "Don't you think that's taking the Good Samaritan bit a little too far?"

"It has nothing to do with my being noble or a Good Samaritan," Howard asserted in a voice that straddled the fence between anger and hurt.

"Then what does it have to do with, Howard? Help me understand," she begged in a soft, earnest voice.

Howard glanced around the room, as if he hoped to pull an answer from some nook or cranny. He scrubbed a hand down a cheek stubbled with twenty-four hours' growth of whiskers.

"Okay," he said at last. "You want the truth? It has to do with selfishness."

"Selfishness?"

"Yeah." He stuck his fists into the pockets of his slacks, gathered his resolve and lifted his eyes to hers. "I'm offering to marry you because I love you."

"You what!"

"I love you. I have for a long time."

Dumbfounded, Eva sat down hard on the edge of the sofa, which was tumbled with blankets. Minutes ticked by. Neither spoke. Finally, she lifted her head and dragged her gaze back to his. "I suppose it's safe to assume, then, that you would want this to be a real marriage—not one in name only."

Howard pondered the question, searching for words that would sway her to his way of thinking. "I believe that marriage is forever, and I'd like children of my own someday, so, yes...I guess that means that I'd like our marriage to become a real one at some point. But not now. Only when you come to care for me...only when you're ready."

"What if I never learn to care? What if I'm never ready?" she asked.

The look in his eyes held acceptance. "Then that's the way it will be."

"This is crazy," she said again, leaping to her feet. "I still love Denny. I can't marry you."

"I promise I'll do my best to make you happy."

"Stop!" She put her hands over her ears to block out whatever else he had to say and shook her head, as if to rid herself of the entire conversation. When she opened her eyes there was finality in them. "I don't want to hear any more, Howard, so you'd better go."

Howard nodded and crossed the room. "I'll be back to take you to lunch."

"I don't want to go to lunch with you."

He opened the door and stepped into the corridor. "Eleven-thirty."

"Howard!"

"Think about it," he said, and closed the door behind him.

HOWARD SHOWED UP FOR LUNCH. Eva was ready, but she told him that just because she'd given in about lunch didn't mean she would be as agreeable to his outrageous proposal.

Howard just smiled and asked her what she wanted to eat. Over hamburgers, fries and thick chocolate milk shakes, she asked when he was leaving for Crystal Creek. He responded by asking if she was packed yet.

Over the next four days, Eva learned that when Howard Blake got something into his head, he was immovable. He was outside her building when she left for work and insisted on driving her to the department store where she clerked. He met her each day for lunch and was waiting when she got off work to drive her back home. He usually had a sack of groceries in the seat between them, and when they got to her place, he insisted that she listen to the radio and prop up her feet while he cooked.

Eva admitted that it was nice being pampered. She hadn't felt so special, so cared for, since she'd first met Denny. She spent hours thinking about Howard's fantastic proposal and, even though the idea shocked her, there were moments when she admitted that his wild scheme held a certain appeal.

It would be wonderful not to have to get up and go to work when she was sick. Marvelous never needing to worry about having enough money to pay bills and buy groceries. Fantastic to put the past behind her and move into a new life, one with a secure future.

Never needing to explain her predicament to her parents—or the whole world—would be a dream come true, a genuine second chance. Never having to explain to a child why he was ridiculed and shunned would be the answer to her prayers...if she still prayed. But even though she would receive a lot by marrying Howard, the price he proposed was higher than she was willing to pay.

Thursday evening found Howard unusually quiet while they shared a meal of meat loaf and mashed potatoes.

"What's wrong?" she asked at last.

His frown deepened. "I called my secretary today. Everyone in Crystal Creek wants to know what's happened to me."

"Did you tell her why you stayed?"

He shook his head. "I said I had some personal business to tend to, but I have to go back soon—by

Saturday at the latest." His wide shoulders lifted in a shrug. "I have responsibilities."

The thought of his leaving filled Eva with a cold, empty dread. Howard's unexpected advent into her life had brought her a breath of hope and a measure of happiness. He was a stimulating conversationalist, surprisingly humorous and an unexpectedly interesting and complex person. He'd made her mad; he'd made her think; he'd made her laugh. Most important, he had the rare ability to laugh at himself, and he wasn't afraid to admit he was wrong. She'd been so lonely before he showed up on her doorstep. Imagining settling back into her dull routine was next to impossible.

"I...I'll miss you," she said, somewhat surprised to realize it was the truth.

Howard took her hand in his. "I was hoping I could convince you to take me up on my offer, but since I can't..." His voice trailed away. "Is there anything else I can do for you? A loan, maybe?"

"No!" she cried, horrified at the very idea of taking money from a man. "I mean, it's very kind of you, but I couldn't possibly."

Howard nodded and went back to his meal. The rest of the evening passed in a strained, quiet thoughtfulness. At nine, when he rose to leave, Eva waged a battle with the threat of tears.

"Take care of yourself," he said, leaning down to brush a soft kiss to her cheek.

"You, too."

"I will." Without another word, he turned and headed down the long hallway to the stairs. Eva watched him go, a lump the size of her fist in her throat. Loneliness enveloped her like a mummy's shroud. Had she felt so alone when Denny died?

She pictured herself waiting for the bus the next morning and eating a solitary lunch of cold cuts and Coke. Returning to the emptiness of her apartment and having another solitary meal. Spending countless nights with no one to talk to. Giving birth alone in a strange city and not having the faintest idea of what to do with a baby.

Another image took shape before her eyes. A picture of the church parsonage... of her fixing breakfast in the kitchen, of Howard holding a baby and of herself being surrounded by friends and family....

Without making any conscious decision, Eva found herself racing down the hall and heard her voice calling "Howard!"

He was nowhere to be seen on the stairs. Her feet skimmed the worn runner. Had she missed him? Had she missed a chance she should have taken?

Breathless, she reached the lower floor and pushed through the entrance. Howard was unlocking his car door. Thank God! she thought, her breath catching on a sob of relief. Thank God.

She skittered to a halt at the bottom of the steps outside the building and stood there, her hands clasped together against her heaving breasts, fear in her eyes and a frangible hope in her heart. He looked strong and solid, standing there in the glow of the streetlight. God forgive her, he looked safe.

Inadvertently, Howard glanced up and over the top of the car. To her it seemed as if her thoughts had somehow connected with his. When he saw her, his mouth curved in a smile so sweet, so full of prom- ise . . . so full of joy, that Eva felt the impact deep in- side her. He rounded the hood of the car slowly. Just as slowly, Eva started toward him.

HOWARD DID HIS BEST to let Eva know what she was getting into. He would expect her to be faithful in her church attendance and her Bible study. She would be required to attend and give showers and dinners and be in charge of many of the church activities that the ladies were involved in. He expected her to comport herself in a manner becoming his position at all times.

Giddy with relief at seeing the end to her self-im- posed exile, Eva paid scant attention to his list of re- quirements. All that mattered was that she was going home and that her baby would be born within the sanctity of marriage.

If Howard was concerned about the reception of his bride—and he was—he never let on to her. He didn't want to frighten her away, not when he finally had his fondest dream within reach. He wasn't so naive that he supposed people would just accept the situation without gossiping about her going off to Hollywood and speculating about the kind of life she'd lived out there. And when her pregnancy began to show, he knew rumors about them would fly. Nevertheless, Howard doubted that anyone would be brazen enough to say anything to his face.

In an effort to protect her to the best of his ability and to wipe the slate as clean as possible between them, he made Eva promise that no mention of her past would ever cross their lips. No one—not even their parents—was to know about the affair with Denny. It was over. Done with. Best forgotten.

If the citizens of Crystal Creek thought the baby was his, fine. He'd rather have them think ill of him than brand Eva as a woman of loose morals. Bearing the brunt of their whispers was little enough price for having Eva as his wife.

Eva agreed to his stipulations with no hesitation.

She quit her job on Friday, apologizing for not giving notice. Then she packed up her meager belongings while Howard phoned around trying to get the legalities of their marriage satisfied. Through some string pulling—Thaddeus Blake was a longtime friend of a Fort Worth judge—Howard was able to get the required three-day waiting period waived.

They argued over the ceremony. Howard wanted a preacher; Eva said that seemed too hypocritical. In the end, Howard bowed to her wishes, and on Saturday at noon, Eva Carmichael became Eva Blake. After saying their "I dos" in front of a justice of the peace, they climbed into Howard's Ford and headed for Crystal Creek.

Exhausted, Eva slept most of the way. When she awakened just outside Austin and got a look at the Hill Country for the first time in two years, tears sprang into her eyes. She drank in the familiar countryside during the forty-odd-mile drive from the capital to Crystal Creek, feeling more and more alive the closer she got to the town where she'd grown up.

She was smiling broadly when Howard pulled the car into the driveway of the parsonage, just as dusk was settling. Whoever said you could never go home again obviously didn't know what he was talking about.

Howard unlocked the front door, and she helped him carry in her things—though he wouldn't let her carry the heavy boxes. Once the car was unloaded, he gave her a tour of the house, which she'd visited several times during her youth. It was interesting to see how Howard had changed things, and as she peeked into each room, her smile of satisfaction grew wider and wider.

Besides the living room and kitchen, there was a formal dining room, three bedrooms—Howard had converted one into an office—and a bath and a half.

"You can take the master bedroom," he said. "I'll use the guest room."

"You don't have to do that."

He shrugged. "The half bath will be convenient for you while you're getting dressed...putting on your makeup and all."

The unselfishness of the gesture was touching. "Thank you, Howard."

He stood there uncertainly for a moment. "Why don't you unpack while I fix us something to eat?" he said at last. "I'll call you when it's ready."

FROM HER VANTAGE POINT across the street, Prudence Burns let the drape fall into place, put down her husband's hunting binoculars and hurried to the phone.

"Operator," was the familiar greeting of Polly Rafferty.

"Give me Harriet Meyers, Polly," Pru said, excitement making her breathless. "And hurry."

"You okay, Pru?" Polly asked. "You sound a little winded."

"I'm fine, Polly," Pru said in an acidic tone. "Just ring Harriet."

"Okeydoke."

Harriet answered on the third ring. "Reverend Blake just drove in," Prudence exclaimed without preamble.

"Pru?"

"Of course it's me!" Prudence snapped. "Did you hear me? Reverend Blake just got home, and he brought some redheaded woman with him."

"What!"

"Yep. And you'll never guess who it is in a hundred years."

"Who?"

"Looks an awful lot like Sally Carmichael's girl to me. And from the looks of all the stuff they took out of the car, she's staying a spell."

"You mean that . . . that floozy is planning to stay with Reverend Blake *overnight?*" Harriet said. "Unchaperoned?"

"Overnight and unchaperoned. If the number of boxes they carried in is any indication, I'd say she was moving in, lock, stock and barrel."

"Good grief!" Harriet said. "This is pretty serious. I'd better call Mama and tell her . . . and Deacon Miles, of course."

"I'll ring your mama for you," a third voice said.

"Polly Rafferty!" Harriet and Prudence cried in unison.

"Are you listening in to our conversation?" Pru demanded.

"Sorry. I didn't mean to."

"Humph!" Harriet said. "I'll bet. Well, go ahead, then. Call Mama for me."

"And connect me to Aunt Hazel," Pru said.

"Will do," Polly said cheerfully. When Crystal Creek's two biggest gossipmongers were connected to their parties—along with the two other women who were on the same party line and had been listening in— Polly, who was humming "God Is Calling the Prodigal" beneath her breath, plugged in another connection.

"Catherine?" she said when the woman answered the phone. "This is Polly. Guess who's back? Eva

Carmichael. You know? Pete and Sally's girl. And you'll never guess what I just heard about her and Reverend Blake...."

WHILE EVA TOOK a bath, Howard set about frying bacon and scrambling eggs for their dinner. He was setting the table when Eva walked into the room on a cloud of some oriental fragrance.

"It's almost ready," he said, folding a napkin and laying a fork on it. "You must have smelled it."

"I did. It smells wonderful."

Smiling, Howard looked up. The instant he set eyes on her, his smile died.

Eva had washed her hair, and fixed it in a Susan Hayward pageboy with a deep wave over her eye. Her makeup had been redone, complete with false eyelashes and red lipstick à la Joan Crawford. She wore a white, floor-length satin gown that plunged low in the front, revealing enough cleavage to raise his heart rate to a level he felt certain was lethal. Though the nightgown was topped by a voluminous robe of sheer chiffon edged with ostrich feathers, it was clear that she wasn't wearing anything underneath.

Desire rose in him on a devastating wave of embarrassment. If his new bride could read his thoughts, she wouldn't think him so noble now.

Eva caressed the soft feathers. "I've been saving this for a special occasion. Do you like it?" she asked, holding out her arms and pivoting in a slow three-hundred-sixty-degree circle on the toe of one matching, high-heeled slipper. "I had it on layaway forever, and the girls at the store just went wild over it."

Howard was too busy trying not to gawk at the tantalizing glimpse of firm, full breasts that were exposed by the low-cut armholes of the gown.

When he didn't respond, the pleasure in Eva's eyes faded. She lowered her arms. "You don't like it."

Witnessing her disappointment, Howard felt he was behaving like a bully who'd just snatched another kid's ice cream cone. "I do like it," he said quickly— too quickly. "I like it a lot. Uh...what's the special occasion?"

She looked surprised by the question. "This is our wedding night."

Howard's heart surged into an even faster rhythm. Despite himself, his hopes began to rise. "Have you...changed your mind about this being a real marriage, then?"

"No," she said with a confused shake of her head. "Why?"

Howard felt his face flame. "Then, uh...maybe you should go and change into something a little more...sedate."

"But this is all the rage in Hollywood. I saw one almost like it in a movie a couple of weeks ago."

"It may be the rage in Hollywood," Howard said, gathering what he could of his scattered senses and his dignity, "but I'm afraid it's a little showy for Crystal Creek. And a little too...revealing to wear around the house."

It was Eva's turn to blush. "But you're my husband. I should be able to dress like this in the privacy of our home."

"You're right," Howard said, striving for a placating tone. "You should. And if this were a normal marriage, I'd encourage it. But if you don't plan on consummating this marriage, I'd advise you to leave that hanging in the closet. In case you weren't aware of it, ministers have the same physical urges as other men when they're properly stimulated."

A stunned look entered Eva's eyes. The glimmer of tears followed. "Are you implying that I'm a tease?"

"I don't think that's your intention, but—"

"You think I'm cheap!" Eva cried, two tears trickling down her cheeks. "Just go ahead and say it!"

"I don't—" Howard began, but before he could finish, she gave a cry of anguish and fled from the room. Howard stared after her, wondering how he'd managed to mess things up so fast.

After a while, he followed to try and make amends. The sounds of her sobbing were heart-wrenching, even through the mahogany door. He pushed it open a crack.

"Get out of here!"

"I'm sorry," he said with a helpless shrug. "I never meant to hurt your feelings. Please come out and have your dinner."

To his surprise, she yanked off one of her slippers and sent it sailing toward his head. "Go to hell!"

Howard managed to get the door closed just in time to deflect the shoe. After five more minutes of pleading and cajoling, he gave up and returned to finish his meal, his heart as heavy and cold as the eggs.

After cleaning up the kitchen, he went into his study with full intentions of going over the sermon he'd prepared during the week in Austin while Eva was at work. But he soon realized that concentrating was an impossibility when all he could think about was his new bride and the sounds of her weeping that still emanated from the bedroom.

He looked in on her some time after midnight and saw that she had finally cried herself to sleep, still dressed in her seductive finery. He retrieved the alarm clock from the bedside table and, with an aching heart, left her to her rest. The sounds of her harsh crying lingered in the empty chambers of his heart. It wasn't a very auspicious beginning for their marriage. He reminded himself that they were both tired and on edge, and told himself that things would be better after they got a good night's sleep.

He was wrong.

WHEN HOWARD'S ALARM went off the next morning, his eyes felt as gritty as if someone had tossed a handful of sand into them. He rolled to his back and threw a brawny forearm over his face. He hadn't shut an eye until the "wee hours," as his mother had always called that predawn time when things seemed the darkest.

Wishing it were Monday, so he could sleep a while longer, he got up, slipped on his trousers and made coffee in the shiny new electric percolator that had been a housewarming gift from Calvin and Emily McKinney.

As per his usual morning routine, he went out and retrieved the newspaper from the flower bed, where Bobby Hancock insisted on throwing it. He waved at Alfred Burns, who just stood and stared at him. Howard gave a philosophical shrug. Al was a strange one.

The paper in hand, Howard went back inside and washed down two slices of toast and red plum jam with two cups of black coffee. He glanced at the kitchen clock. It was time to get ready, and Eva still wasn't awake.

Wondering what to do, he took a bath and pulled on his boxer shorts and a soft, sleeveless ribbed undershirt. When he finished shaving there was still no sign of Eva. He had no choice but to wake her up. They'd be late if he waited much longer.

Dreading the confrontation, Howard wiped the traces of soap from his face and started for the master bedroom. As he approached the bedside, he saw that Eva lay on her side, her hands beneath her cheek. She'd pulled the chenille bedspread up over her hips for warmth, but the light covering didn't cover her upper body at all. The white gown gaped, exposing all but the rosy crest of one breast.

Averting his gaze and uttering a silent prayer for strength, he reached out and took her by the shoulder, shaking her gently.

"Eva . . . time to get up."

"Hmm?"

"Come on. It's time to rise and shine." He did his best to inject cheerfulness into his voice.

Eva rolled over, and when she did, the front of the gown parted farther. There was nothing between her naked breast and Howard's lustful gaze except his willpower, which abandoned him like rats deserting a sinking ship.

His body responded in a purely masculine reaction that was startling in its intensity. Dear heaven, she was beautiful, he thought, as his hungry gaze roamed over her. Beautiful . . . and out of bounds.

The realization that he might never partake of the ripe bounty she'd given Denny Talbot acted like a dose of cold water to his passion. Irrationally, anger took its place. Anger at her for giving herself to Denny. Anger at himself for wanting her in spite of it.

He yanked the bedspread up over her. "Get up, Eva," he said, not bothering to hide his irritation. "We're going to be late."

Her eyelashes lifted a slit and she tried to focus her sleepy blue eyes on him. "Late for what?" she murmured.

"Sunday school and church."

"I don't go to church anymore," she said around a yawn.

"You do now, Mrs. Blake—remember? That was our deal. I sleep alone. You go to church."

Something in his voice must have gotten through to her. Her eyes widened in sudden remembrance. "Howard?"

"That's right. Your husband, the minister. Come on, up and at 'em."

"Can't I stay home?" she groaned. "I hardly slept all night."

"Me either, and no, you can't." Howard glanced at his watch. "You've got exactly twenty minutes to get ready."

Eva jackknifed into a sitting position. "Twenty minutes!"

"Twenty minutes," he said, granting her no quarter. "If you aren't ready in twenty minutes I'll haul you out of that bed myself."

With that, he strode from the room. He'd no more than stepped into the hallway when the doorbell rang. Howard was so furious with Eva and himself that he gave no thought to the fact that he was in his underwear. He crossed to the front door and jerked it open.

Three men—two deacons and another board member—and their wives stood on his doorstep. Howard would have been hard-pressed to say who was the most embarrassed.

"Morning, Reverend," Paul Dunn said. "Hope we didn't wake you."

"Not at all," Howard said, his stunned gaze moving from one face to the next. "Come in. If you'll...uh...excuse me, I'll just go grab a shirt...and some pants."

He beat a hasty retreat from the room, uncomfortably aware of the six sets of eyes that watched him go. Fearing he knew what the early Sunday morning visit was all about, he pulled on some dark socks, slipped into his starched white shirt and suit trousers, and hurried back to the living room, where the sextet sat on the edges of the sofa and various chairs. Only serious church concerns would bring out this bunch so early in the morning. Someone knew Eva was here.

"Would you care for some coffee?" Howard asked.

"That sounds goo—" A sharp poke from his wife's elbow silenced Paul Dunn's acceptance.

"No, thank you," Vera said in a frigid voice. "This isn't a social visit." She gave her husband a pointed look.

"We, uh..." Paul ran a finger around the collar of his shirt as if it were suddenly too tight. "We got a call last night, Reverend. Several calls in fact."

Howard rammed his hands in his pockets. "Oh?" he said in a bland voice.

"We were told that a, uh, young woman spent the night here, last night. Is that correct?"

"It is," Howard said, offering no further explanation. Being judged so readily on so little evidence piqued not only Howard's anger but his perverse sense of humor. It would be interesting to hear what they had to say and watch them hang themselves.

"Was it your sister?" Lloyd Miles asked.

"I don't have a sister." As if they didn't know.

"Oh, for heaven's sake, Paul!" Vera Dunn snapped. "Stop beating around the bush!" She turned her haughty, long-nosed gaze on Howard. "We hear that floozy who ran off to Hollywood spent the night with you last night. Is it true?"

Not for the first time, Howard was amazed at the speed and accuracy of Crystal Creek's grapevine. "What floozy would that be?"

"Eva Carmichael." Vera spat out the name as if it were distasteful.

"Eva did stay here last night, yes."

The three ladies exchanged horrified glances. One dabbed at her upper lip with a lacy hankie and looked ready to succumb to a fit of the vapors. The men cleared their throats and cast nervous glances at one another.

"Very incautious of you, Reverend," Fred Graves said. "*Very* incautious."

"I don't need to tell you that your actions have been under careful scrutiny since you took over your father's position," Deacon Miles said.

"I'm aware of that."

"As you well know, we have a sacred duty to keep the congregation free from any sin and worldliness we see creeping in."

Howard nodded.

"Then you'll understand if we have a problem with your preaching for us while you're harboring a—a painted woman under your roof."

"Howard! Can you do up my zipper?"

Eva's voice preceded her into the room by milliseconds. She almost ran through the door. To Howard's chagrin, she was wearing nothing but a strapless bra and a half slip—though to give her some credit, she was in the process of wriggling into a splashy rayon sundress.

A common gasp of surprise went up from the gathering. With one arm through the armhole of the dress, Eva stopped in her tracks. Her shocked gaze moved from one face to the other and then to Howard's.

Vera Dunn leapt to her tiny feet and thrust out her impressive bosom, clinging to her purse as if it were a lifeline. "I refuse to stay in the same room with this shameless Jezebel!" Like a frigate cresting a tidal wave, she started across the room. The other ladies rose to follow.

Eva's hand came up to her lips to stifle her anguished cry. In an automatic gesture of comfort, Howard moved to her side and slid his arm around her bare shoulders.

"Come, Vera," he said in a voice designed to soothe ruffled feathers ... or stormy seas. "Let's not be so quick to judge."

"Judging has little to do with it. What's happened here is pretty clear, Reverend," Paul Dunn said.

"Obviously not," Howard replied. Smiling a benign smile, he said, "Ladies, gentlemen, I'd like you to meet my wife."

ONCE THE CHURCH committee had revived Milli
Graves, who had fainted in the doorway at Howard'
announcement, they cleared out, but not before he'
wrung an apology from each and every one of his ac
cusers. Apology or not, the looks on their individua
faces said without words that, even though he hadn'
lost his religion, they thought he'd lost his mind.

Eva's occasional sniffle as they hurried to get to the
church building signaled that she was upset over he
first impression. So was Howard, but there wasn'
time to discuss what had happened. All he could do t
ease her distress was to tell her not to worry too much
about their visitors.

To his pleased surprise, Eva was ready in the allot
ted time. To his horror, she was wearing a too-tigh
dress in violent colors of purple, red, black and yel
low. Chunky bracelets circled her wrists and long ear
rings dangled from her ears. He supposed he should
be thankful that the short matching jacket covered he
bare shoulders.

He ground his teeth in irritation and prayed for pa
tience. There was nothing he could do about it now
Later today, he'd ask his mother to take Eva shop
ping for some clothes that were more in keeping with
her new station in life. Right now, they needed to ge
a move on. The congregation was waiting.

THE PARKING LOT was packed, and people were driv
ing up and down the street searching for an empty
parking spot. At first Howard was thrilled that his re

cent flurry of cards, phone calls and visits had paid off
so handsomely, but when he and Eva intercepted a few
pointed looks, he understood too well what was going
on.

He taught his Sunday school class with his customary thought-provoking intelligence but without his
usual enthusiasm. But it was only when he stood in the
pulpit, introduced Eva as his new bride and heard the
whispers run up and down the pews that he realized
just how wrong he'd been about the people of the
town.

Contrary to his earlier belief, a vast majority of
them didn't care about exercising their Christianity.
They'd shown up to take a gander at his new bride—
and not just to see her, but to judge her worth. And,
Howard thought, if the whispers and malicious looks
were anything to go by, he'd lay odds that they weren't
impressed with his choice.

"OH, MAMA!" Maggie said, setting down her coffee
cup, "I can't imagine anyone being ugly to you!"

Eva dumped a spoonful of sugar into her cup.
"When folks suspected their minister of having a sor-
did little affair with a woman who'd run off to California to become an actress, it caused quite a stir."

"I guess," Maggie said, "but it's hard for me to
believe they were so judgmental when everyone loves
you so much now."

"I'm not condoning my behavior, but you have to
remember that getting pregnant outside of marriage

wasn't as easily accepted back then," Eva said. "I've worked hard to earn their respect, but I think the passage of time had as much to do with my acceptance as anything I actually did. The old hardnoses who didn't come around eventually died out, and younger people tend to be more forgiving—not that they're any more likely today than they were back then to overlook their preacher bringing home a pregnant bride."

The doorbell rang, and Maggie jumped in surprise.

"Sit still, honey," Eva said, pushing back her chair. "I'll get it."

While Eva was gone, Maggie glanced at the clock. She'd become so engrossed in her mother's story that time had slipped away from her. Even though Howard had just assured her that there was no change in Rio's condition and that there was nothing she could do, she felt it was time they got back to the hospital.

When Eva returned to the kitchen, she was followed by Jeremy, whose young face looked as haggard as Maggie felt. But there was something besides weariness and worry in his eyes. There was determination.

"Did you get any sleep?" Maggie asked with a fond smile.

Jeremy shrugged. "A little, between Emily's feedings."

"Do you want some coffee, Jeremy?" Eva asked.

"Yes, ma'am, that sounds great," he said.

Jeremy stirred sugar and creamer into the coffee Eva provided. "What is it?" Maggie asked, acutely aware that something was on his mind.

Drawing in a deep breath, as if he needed to fortify himself in some way, Jeremy said, "I called and told Dad about Rio."

The confession left Maggie wordless. John Hardin Westlake, Rio's father, had never acknowledged him in any way, and Rio had never set eyes on the man until three months before, when he'd decided that the only way he could rid himself of the resentment eating at him was to confront the man who'd fathered him.

"You did the right thing," Maggie said, to Jeremy's profound relief.

Jeremy shook his head. "I don't know why I was so worried about telling you. I should have known you'd react the way you did. You're always fair."

"I don't know about that," Maggie said.

"I do." Jeremy downed one more sip of his coffee and rose. "Dad wants me to keep him posted on Rio's condition. I said I would."

"You do whatever you think you should, Jeremy," Maggie said.

"Thanks." He started to leave, and when Eva rose to see him to the door, he waved her back into her seat. "I know the way, Mrs. Blake."

Eva smiled, and Maggie watched him go, a thoughtful look on her face. Was it possible that John

Westlake had a heart after all? Was there some feeling for his older son hidden in the deepest recesses of that heart? And in spite of his denial, was it possible that he harbored regret for the way he'd denied Rio?

CHAPTER SIX

May 1951

"THIS SUDDEN MARRIAGE of yours is very unorthodox," Deacon Frizzel said at the Monday morning assemblage of deacons and board members that followed the impromptu meeting at Howard's the day before. "We had no idea you were... seeing anyone, much less that you were seeing Eve Mi—uh, Eva Carmichael."

"Am I wrong to believe that my private life is just that?" Howard asked.

"Your personal life is private only until or unless it reflects badly on your position here in Crystal Creek," Paul Dunn piped up.

"I believe my behavior has been exemplary."

"Until now, perhaps," Fred Graves said.

"How so?" Howard queried. He wasn't in the mood for another inquisition; he'd just been through one with his parents, who'd heard the news half a country away, on the East Coast.

"Let's just say your choice for a wife is not one we—" Fred's gesture included all the men in the room "—or the members of the congregation deem suitable."

"Fred . . ."

"Well, it's true, Calvin!" Fred said to Calvin Mc-Kinney, the board vice president. "Everyone knows what kind of woman she is."

Howard felt his face grow hot with anger. "With all due respect, gentlemen, going to California with aspirations of becoming an actress does not a scarlet woman make."

"She *looks* like a scarlet woman."

Howard kept his temper on a tight rein. He'd expected a few disgruntled members, but he'd had no idea that such judgmental, unforgiving attitudes were so pervasive within his flock.

"And looks can be deceiving," Cal McKinney said. "Howard is right. For all we know, Eva Carmichael might have spent every Sunday of the past two years singing in the choir."

"You mean Eve Michaels, don't you?" Paul Dunn asked with a smirk. "Isn't that her stage name?"

"Eva, Eve . . . what's it matter?" Cal challenged.

More worried than he had been since he'd proposed marriage to Eva, and disappointed over the degree of censure he was receiving, Howard rubbed the side of his nose. He shuddered to think of the board's reaction when they learned the Blakes were expecting a baby, which would be in the near future, because Eva was bound to start showing soon. Maybe he should just go ahead and tell them and get the unpleasantness out of the way. That way, he'd only have to face their ire once, and maybe he could take part of the blame the board seemed determined to lay at Eva's feet.

"Actually, her name is Eva Blake now," Howard reminded them in a gentle voice. "Look, I'm sorry if you don't approve, but the decision to get married was based on necessity."

Lon Frizzel's eyebrows snapped together in a frown. "What does that mean?"

"There's no use in trying to hide something that can't be hidden," Howard said, choosing his next words with extreme care. He had to word the explanation so that he was telling the truth—as far as he was willing to—without adding lying to his list of transgressions.

"Eva is expecting a baby," he said at last. "Marriage seemed like the acceptable, the only right thing to do."

Well phrased, Howard.

Pandemonium broke loose in the small room. Howard caught an occasional fragment like "disgrace," "terrible example," "just like Eve of old."

Witnessing just how eager the board was to condemn him for his supposed indiscretion was a revelation to Howard. If these were practicing Christians, God save him from the bad people of the world. Where was the brotherly kindness? Where was the love?

"I say we make him step down."

Howard raised his head sharply. Make him step down? That was the same thing as handing in his resignation, which was what they would ask him to do so they wouldn't have to fire him. Howard had never considered the possibility that he might lose his job.

There was nothing he could say in his defense, except to tell them that he hadn't fathered Eva's child, but he couldn't do that. She would suffer enough without bearing that burden alone. For the first time in his life, Howard's conviction that mankind was basically good wavered the slightest bit. If these men, men he'd looked up to all his life, were disappointed in him, Howard was even more so in them.

Like a dying man, he saw his short life as a minister flash before his eyes. What would he do if he was fired? he wondered in a rush of panic. How could he support Eva and her baby? Howard lowered his head into his palm and fought back the unmanly sting of tears.

"I say we vote on it right here and now," Paul Dunn cried over the roar of half a dozen conversations. "Everyone in favor of asking for Reverend Blake's resignation raise your hand."

"Just a minute!" Calvin McKinney said, surging to his feet. "Since Dale is out of town, I'm in charge of this meeting." He made a concerted effort to lower his voice. "Let's not be hasty, gentlemen. Let's think this through."

"We don't need to think about it! The situation speaks for itself. Howard Blake is a disgrace to his position," Fred Graves roared.

"Where is your compassion?" Cal asked, his gaze encompassing each man. "Your Christian love?"

"Compassion?" Paul Dunn cried. "Surely you don't condone the sin that's been committed?"

"I don't condone any sin," Cal said. "But let's not forget that Howard Blake is a man as well as a minister. He isn't perfect. He has the same weaknesses we all do."

The roar of dissatisfaction quieted to an occasional low mumble, and Howard raised grateful eyes to Calvin's empathetic gaze.

"Howard Blake comes from a good family," Cal continued. "One that has served the community well. He has done an excellent job since taking over from his father. Sunday school attendance is up twenty percent, and most of that in the youth classes. Should we forget the impact he's had in the community just because of one mistake?

"His marriage has proved that he is ready to accept the moral responsibility for his actions, that he has done his best to remedy the wrong in his life. He has just confessed that wrongdoing to us, as I'm sure he already has to God, who has promised to forgive him. Can we do less?"

Some shamefaced glances passed among the disgruntled group.

"What I'm saying, gentlemen," Cal drawled in a tone more disgusted that conciliatory, "is what Jesus might say if he were here. Let him who is without sin among us cast the first vote to rob this fine young man of his future." He sat down.

Fearful and wordless, Howard waited for the ax to fall.

Paul Dunn thought about the waitress back in his twenties that no one—not even Vera—had found out about.

Fred Graves mulled over the slightly shady real estate deal he'd been smack-dab in the middle of a few years ago that had netted enough money to ensure him and his wife a secure old age.

Lon Frizzel considered the business trips he took and how he tended to leave his religion at the boundaries of Crystal Creek.

The others must have had similar thoughts. No one said a word.

"It's still not right," someone grumbled, finally.

"No, it isn't," Cal agreed, "but Hank Travis has taught me a few things, and one of them is that two wrongs don't make a right. I think if we all do our best to make Howard's wife feel welcome, we'll feel better about ourselves and the situation in general." Cal smacked the gavel on the table. "Meeting's adjourned."

The men filed out, still muttering among themselves. Howard held out his hand. "Thanks, Mr. McKinney."

"Calvin."

"Thanks, Calvin. You don't know how much I appreciate your standing up for me that way."

"You'd have done the same for me." Cal shook his head. "I don't know what gets into people sometimes. You'd think they'd never made a mistake in their lives."

"Maybe they don't think they have."

"Bull." Cal smiled. "Hang in there, Howard. It'll all come out okay. Tell you what. Emily and I will have you and Eva out for supper one night real soon."

"Thanks, Calvin. We'd like that a lot."

"Good, then. See you later." Cal gave Howard a hearty slap on the back. Wearing a wide grin, he winked and said, "Go thy way and sin no more."

Howard watched his champion leave the building with a sigh of relief. He knew he hadn't heard the end of the matter, but he'd dodged the bullet for the moment. The McKinneys carried a lot of clout in town, and Howard considered himself pretty lucky to have Calvin on his side.

He knew there were plenty who might not like the situation, but they'd get used to it, in time. Until then, he and Eva would have to mind their p's and q's...whatever they were.

WHEN HOWARD WENT HOME for lunch, Eva was nowhere to be found. She must still be at her mother's, he thought, stripping off his wilted shirt and pitching it into the laundry basket. He was taking a fresh shirt from a hanger when he heard the faint, unmistakable sounds of weeping. Draping the shirt on the massive bedpost, he went to Eva's room, where he found her

huddled on the bed, sobbing her heart out. Memorie
of his recent harrowing meeting with the board va
ished beneath the crushing weight of concern.

"Eva... Evie, are you all right?" he asked, sittin
down next to her.

Eva rolled onto her back, tears and mascara ru
ning down her temples and into her hair. "Oh, Hov
ard!" she wailed, pushing herself up and flinging he
arms around his neck. "It was terrible... just terr
ble."

"What was terrible, sweetheart?" he asked, fram
ing her tear-ravaged face between his palms.

"M-Mama," Eva hiccuped. "I didn't see her
church yesterday, and I thought I'd drive out to th
house and surprise her. She wasn't surprise
and... and she wasn't glad to see me. Someone ha
called and told her I was back, and she didn't come t
church yesterday because she was *embarrassed.*"

Her sobs tore at Howard's heart.

"I asked her what she was embarrassed about, an
she said—" Eva swiped frantically at the tear
streaming down her cheeks "—she said that she'
spent two years living down my reputation, and sh
didn't need me coming back and stirring up the go:
sip again."

"I'm sorry, Evie," Howard said, smoothing he
damp hair away from her flushed face.

"I... I got mad, then, and I told her about th
baby—not about Denny, just that I was having a baby
I told her that now she'd have something to be em

barrassed about. I know I shouldn't have been so hateful, but I don't understand how she can be so mean. She's my *mother.*"

Howard held her and ran his hands up and down her back while she cried. He prayed that when he spoke he would say the right thing. "Your mother is hurt, Evie. When a child grows up and does something the parents don't approve of, they take it personally...like it's a reflection on how they brought up the child. And in some ways, in some cases, it is."

"But all I did was go to California and try to become an actress!" she cried, clutching at his bare shoulders. "I didn't do anything bad while I was there. Except for Denny." Succumbing to a fresh bout of tears, she lowered her head back to his shoulder.

"I'll drive out and talk to her," Howard promised, to soothe her.

"No!" The soft explosion of sound was accompanied by a warm burst of breath that he felt through the soft cotton of his sleeveless undershirt. Howard would have been hard-pressed to say what emotion was uppermost—his growing desire or his concern.

He tried to gather his scattered thoughts. "Sometimes it's hard for adults to remember what they did as young people. I imagine there are things in her past she isn't proud of, but as time passes, people tend to forget their own mistakes. She'll come around."

Eva leaned back and looked up at him, her eyes awash in tears. "Do you think so?"

"I'm sure of it."

"What about everyone else?"

"Who do you mean?" Howard asked, but he knew what she was talking about.

"I may be too trusting and a little naive, but I'm not stupid. I heard the whispers yesterday."

Howard struggled to find words to reassure her without telling her the ugly truth. It wasn't easy. "I think everyone was surprised when I showed up married," he hedged. "They had no idea there was any such plan in the works."

"I imagine they were more shocked by *whom* you married."

"Don't be silly. Your mother has exaggerated this Hollywood thing all out of proportion. Most people wouldn't think twice about your wanting to pursue a career. As you said, it doesn't make you a bad person, but there are always a few who feed on this sort of thing."

"What about when they find out about the baby? They'll think I'm terrible, then."

Howard blew out a deep breath. "There will be talk, Eva, there's no sense denying that, and it's going to start sooner than you imagined," he confessed in a hesitant voice. At her started look, he went on. "I couldn't see any sense in putting us through the wringer twice, so when I met with the board this morning, I told them about the baby."

Eva's face paled.

"Calvin McKinney helped smooth things out for us." There was no way Howard would tell her about the persecution he'd suffered that morning. "It'll be okay." He forced a smile he was far from feeling. "Calvin said he and Emily would have us out for dinner soon."

"Really?" Eva's eyes widened in surprise and pleasure. For the moment, her concerns were forgotten. "I always did admire Emily McKinney. She's such a classy lady."

Howard cupped her cheek with his palm in a comforting gesture. "I'm glad you like her. It will take a while," he said with as much confidence as he could muster, "but you'll soon have a circle of friends you're comfortable with."

EVA WAS TO RECALL those words often in the next few weeks. If she'd thought marrying Howard would end her problems, she'd been dead wrong. They'd just begun.

First, there were church services three times a week where she was subjected to whispers, sly glances and biblical questions she didn't know the answers to. There was Bible study daily with Howard. Considering that she felt God had let her down by not answering her prayer to keep Denny safe, Eva wasn't too keen on giving him so much of her time. But she'd struck a deal with Howard, and she'd stick to it.

It seemed to her that the congregation was divided into two factions: one that looked down on and condemned her for being the kind of loose woman who had trapped their preacher into marriage, and a second, much smaller, group that was willing to give her the benefit of the doubt. Not surprisingly, the more congenial of the members were the younger ones.

There were a couple of women Eva's age who had gone the extra mile to be nice to her, but when she pursued their overtures by going out shopping with them and exchanging daily coffee klatches, Howard cautioned her not to get too close to any one person or group, or it might be construed as "favoritism" by certain other members.

Friendly and outgoing by nature, Eva was disappointed to know she had to monitor her every action, her every word. Howard cautioned her about striking up lengthy conversations with the men, who might think she was flirting. He had advised her about laughing too much or too loudly and warned her not to say *anything* about *anyone* that might be mistaken for or twisted into gossip. The rules chafed, but she gritted her teeth and promised she'd do her best.

Then there was the small matter of living in the same house as a man...a man who was a virtual stranger. Eva hadn't given much thought to sharing a house with Howard; how could that be any big deal? After all, it was a large house. But even though they had three bedrooms and two bathrooms, there was a level of intimacy in just being under the same roof that she hadn't expected from her marriage of convenience.

If she happened to go to the kitchen for coffee wearing only her shorty pajamas and found Howard there, she recalled what he'd said that first night and hurried off to change. If he happened out of his bathroom shirtless, she was disturbingly aware of his broad shoulders, wide chest and the crisp hair that covered his pectorals and disappeared down his flat stomach into his trousers.

And, in a typical admiring and prideful way, she couldn't help noticing how wide his shoulders were beneath the starched plaid of his short-sleeved casual shirts, which he wore to his office to conduct his everyday tasks.

They accidentally brushed against each other a dozen times a week. Their hands touched as they passed bowls of vegetables. The vexing, masculine scent of Howard's after-shave lingered in the air long after he left in the mornings and kindled longings she couldn't—wouldn't—put into words.

Deep inside, in a place she refused to examine too closely or too often, she saw Howard less as the skinny boy he'd been in high school and more as a man who could fight her battles, a man whose nearness made her heart race.

Invariably, guilt followed those awkward moments of appreciation. Guilt and shame for being aware of another man while she was carrying Denny's child. It made her wonder if the people in Crystal Creek were right. What kind of woman was she, anyway?

IN AN EFFORT to show the world that they were just like any happily married young couple, Howard had asked Eva to meet him at MacBride's Café, for lunch.

The new eating establishment was celebrating its grand opening by offering a half-price menu the first five days.

Eva dressed with special care for the occasion, making certain her makeup would do Joan Crawford proud and fixing the deep wave over her eye just so. The early June days were already scorching, so she chose to wear a halter-top sundress with a voluminous skirt and petticoat that would hide her tummy...which, it seemed, was getting harder and harder to camouflage.

The sunshine-yellow dress had a wide white belt that she let out by poking another hole in it with the ice pick. It buttoned at her nape, and the low-cut sweetheart neckline had a notched white piqué collar that looked like lapels. The bodice fastened with large white covered buttons that marched primly down the length of the skirt. She wore big button earrings and a choker made of white grosgrain ribbon and a white fabric flower stiffened with sizing.

Though the dress was snug around the waist and the fullness of her breasts strained the top buttons the slightest bit, she looked pretty and she knew it. As she got into the old car Howard had bought for her to get around town in, she was humming the popular "Hello, Young Lovers" under her clove-scented breath.

When she reached MacBride's, she saw that the half-price meal offer had brought out a goodly porion of the Crystal Creek citizenry. A line had formed along the sidewalk, waiting for tables to be vacated.

Eva stood beneath the overhang of the building with the others, her clutch bag hugged to her breasts, scanning the street for Howard's car. She was careful to speak politely to the people she recognized from church, but no one offered to include her in their conversation. She longed for Howard to arrive and rescue her, something he seemed to do often.

She had moved away from the gathering and was looking down the street with one hand shielding her eyes, when she felt a hand on her bare shoulder. She turned, smiling, expecting to see Howard's clean-shaven countenance. Instead, she came face-to-face with the lecherous leer of a stranger with a dirty cowboy hat and a waxed mustache.

"Waitin' for me, sugar?"

His whiskey-scented breath washed over her in a sickening wave. Eva looked down at the hand on her shoulder and noted with disgust that his fingernails were ragged and dirty. She pulled away from his grasp with as much dignity as she could muster.

"I'm waiting for my husband." She turned her back, hoping the cowboy would take the hint.

"Too bad," he said. "Ol' Dan could show you a real good time...if you know what I mean."

Eva's first inclination was to lambaste the stranger with a few succinct words about cleanliness and manners, but she was all too aware that there were several members of the congregation standing nearby, just waiting to see what she would do. Howard would *die* if she didn't behave as a proper minister's wife should.

"You're wasting your time," she said, with a haughty lift of her chin. "I'm not interested in you or anything you might teach me."

His hot gaze roamed over her bare shoulders and the swell of her bosom. Uncomfortably aware of how much of her breasts the dress exposed, she crossed her arms and tried to shield herself from his hot eyes.

"How do you know if you don't give it a try?" he said in a cajoling tone. He reached out and fingered a lock of her hair. "A couple of hours with a hot little chili pepper like you'd probably give a man a danged heart attack. I ain't got no death wish, but I'd like to give it thirty minutes or so."

"You'd better be moving on, mister."

Howard! Eva could hardly believe that the cold, hard voice that delivered the warning belonged to her husband. She offered a grateful smile to the man standing on the other side of the cowpoke. He didn't smile back.

"Sez who?" the stranger asked.

"Says me."

The cowboy took Howard's measure for long seconds. "Why don't you run along, city boy?" he suggested, unimpressed with Howard's refined, clean-shaven looks and his glasses. The cowpoke's smile was condescending. "Go peddle your encyclopedias somewhere else and let a man tend to business." He turned his back on Howard and slid his arm around Eva's bare shoulders.

Repulsed, she gave a little squeal of dismay and ducked out of the man's grasp. As she was turning around, she heard the sound of flesh meeting flesh. The man went sprawling onto the sidewalk with a grunt of pain.

Eva's startled gaze shifted to her husband. Howard stood straight and proud, his hands curled into loose fists at his sides, a lethal gleam in his eyes. She blinked in surprise. Howard had decked the man! More surprising—he'd *enjoyed* it.

Wearing a stunned expression, the stranger wiggled his chin and raised himself to his elbows. Reaching up, he lifted a hand to the corner of his mouth, where a thin line of blood trickled onto his chin. Seeing the blood ignited his fury, and giving a mighty roar, he lunged to his feet, his hands clenched into fists.

"Come on, big time," Howard said, the recklessness a dangerous glitter in his blue eyes.

The man gave another bellow of anger and charged Howard, who sidestepped the rush with a graceful pirouette. Standing firm, his fists raised and ready, Howard offered the man a grim smile. "A word of warning, my friend. I was college boxing champ two years running. Ask anybody here."

Something in his voice or the confidence of his stance must have convinced the stranger that Howard was telling the truth. The cowboy dropped his hands to his sides with a suddenness that was farcical.

"Excellent choice," Howard said, doing the same.

The man wiped the corner of his mouth with the back of his hand and reached down to retrieve his hat from the sidewalk. He set it on his head and gave Howard a wary, slit-eyed look. "Who the hell are you?"

Howard extended his hand in a gesture of civility that shocked everyone watching. "Blake," he said, pumping the man's hand with his customary fervor. "Reverend Howard Blake."

WITH HER ARM gripped in the vise of Howard's fingers, Eva skipped alongside his long-legged gait as fast as her high heels would permit. Though it looked as if lunch at MacBride's was out, she was so relieved that Howard had come to her rescue, she didn't even mind.

Mercy! She couldn't believe he'd actually *slugged* that man, but she was thrilled at the way he'd stood up for her. How many men could pop a guy in the mouth, then introduce himself, apologize and invite the other person to church services? she wondered in genuine amazement.

"Get in the car."

"B-but I brought my car," she stammered, looking up at him in perplexity.

"We'll get it later."

"Where are we going?"

"Home, so you can change out of that dress."

"What's wrong with this dress?" she asked, her thankfulness over his rescue fading beneath the irritation she felt by his constant harping on her choice of clothes.

"It's too... revealing to be worn out in public."

What remained of her earlier indebtedness evaporated like a pot of water simmering on the stove. Even though she'd felt a twinge of shame in the dress just moments ago, tears of humiliation and anger burned beneath her eyelids. Would Howard ever find favor with anything she did?

"If I can't wear it in public, where will I wear it?" she demanded, louder than was necessary.

Noting the curious looks cast their way, Howard commanded, "Keep your voice down." He opened the passenger door of his car and almost pushed her inside. Eva jerked the door from his grasp and slammed it shut. Howard got in on his side and started the engine.

"Thou shalt keep your voice down," Eva said in a low, bitter parody. "Thou shalt not strike up any conversations with men. Thou shalt not laugh too loudly. Thou shalt study your Bible an hour a day."

"That's enough!" Howard said.

But Eva was just getting warmed up. "Don't get too friendly. Don't dress so gaudily. Don't do anything that might be construed as fun. Good grief, Howard! I can't even go to any dances, and I *love* to dance!"

Howard's jaw tightened. Neither spoke during the remainder of the drive to the house. As soon as Howard pulled the car to a stop, Eva wrenched open the door and leapt out.

"Change your clothes, and then we're going to have a talk."

"You don't talk. You lay down the law. The Ten Commandments according to Howard Blake. Well, I don't mind telling you that all of your 'thou shalts' and 'thou shalt nots' are about to drive me insane!"

She slammed the car door behind her in her haste to get away. Outrage carried her toward the front door. She was almost there when Howard grabbed her arm and whirled her around to face him. She jerked free, her breasts heaving with anger.

"You should have thought about all that before you agreed to marry me," he said, the muscle in his jaw knotting.

"You're right. I should have," she agreed. "But I didn't, and now we're both stuck in this marriage made in hell."

Howard looked as if she'd struck him. Eva felt his shock deep inside her bruised and aching heart. Shame for the unfairness of her outburst warred with the anger that bubbled inside her. Without a word, she turned and ran from his presence, praying that she would make it to the bedroom before she burst into tears.

She refused to come out of her room for dinner that night. Actually, Howard never even asked her to. She spent the time pacing in her room and trying to figure out how her marriage to Howard could work when they were two such different people with two entirely different approaches to life.

Her husband believed in walking the straight and narrow; she liked a broader path. Howard saw everything as black or white; she saw various shades of gray. He believed good would triumph over evil; she thought he was waging a losing battle. Howard was a straight arrow; she was a loose cannon. He was the good and faithful son; she was the prodigal. He was John to her doubting Thomas, Samson to her Delilah.

It was, she thought on a sigh of despair, hopeless.

HOWARD, TOO, was dismayed at how quickly things between him and Eva had deteriorated.

Previously they had had moments of peaceful cohabitation, times when they got along with no problem. He was pleased with her in so many ways. She kept a clean house and was a fantastic cook. She kept his clothes clean, his shirts starched. Though he knew chafed, she was always ready for services on Sunday and Wednesday nights. She joined him in Bible study and listened as he tried to explain things to her, even though he knew her defiance and weak faith kept her from absorbing the lessons he so desperately wanted her to learn.

She still wasn't as involved as he'd like in the activities of the church, but that, he supposed, would take time. And, other than the invitation to the McKineys', they still hadn't been invited to any of the members' homes. The situation was caused some-

what by stiff-necked pride on the part of the congre
gation, but also because Eva held back.

Howard didn't know what was going to happen t
them, especially now that she'd made her unhappi
ness so clear....

THE NEXT DAY, the first Saturday of June, was th
church's annual homecoming weekend. As was cus
tomary, members who'd moved away were invited
back for a day of fun and food at a local park. The
activities included an all-day barbecue, softball, bad
minton, croquet and other outdoor games. At nigh
songs around a bonfire were followed by homemade
ice cream, cakes and cookies. Howard had the fol
lowing day off, with the song-leading, prayers and
even the sermon handled by former members.

It was a weekend he'd always enjoyed, but because
of his marriage to Eva and the public spectacle he'd
made of himself in front of MacBride's the day be
fore, he had no idea what to expect this year. He'd al
ready taken a dressing-down or two from Paul Dunn
and Fred Graves.

At ten o'clock, Eva still hadn't come out of her
room. Howard, dressed in jeans, a white T-shirt and
old loafers for the occasion, was wondering whether
or not to leave by himself or go and drag her out of her
room, when she strolled through the kitchen door
way.

When he saw what she had on, his mouth fell open
in shock. Had his disapproval the day before meant so

ttle to her? Was she deliberately trying to drive him
razy?

Her shapely legs were bared by a pair of pink short
horts. A halter top—which obviously had nothing
eneath it—was tied around her neck and under the
ush fullness of her breasts. White sandals encased her
eet; wine-red polish tipped her finger and toe nails.

The same hue colored her lips and was echoed by
he cream rouge that highlighted her cheekbones. Her
yelids were dusted with blue eye shadow and lined
vith black eyeliner. The delicate curve of her brows
ad been enhanced with an auburn pencil, creating a
rame for her long, false lashes. Her hair was piled on
op of her head in an elaborate nest of curls.

Anger ascended. Forbearance fled. A red mist
ilmed Howard's eyes. He pointed to the door. "Go
nd take that—that *mess* off right now."

Shock and confusion filled Eva's eyes for an in-
tant. She raised her chin. "I will not."

"You're not going anywhere with me looking like
a—a streetwalker!"

Eva's mouth gaped. Tears filled her eyes.
"You...bastard!" she cried, launching herself at him
like a wild woman.

Howard deflected her blows easily, and just as easily, pinned her arms behind her back. Pushing her
ahead of him, he forced her down the hallway and into
the bathroom.

"What do you think you're doing?" Eva screeched
as he dug his fingers into a jar of cold cream.

"Trying to make you see reason!" He smeared the creamy concoction all over her face while she sputtered and swore at him, trying to free her hands. A well-aimed kick connected to his shin as he squeezed warm water from a washcloth. "Ouch! Stop it, Evie!"

"Go to hell!" she shrieked as he slapped the wet rag against her gooey face.

"I'm beginning to think I'm already there," Howard said in a grim voice. He began to scrub off the thick makeup with surprisingly gentle strokes. "It can't be any worse than living with a shrew for a wife."

She swore.

"And if you curse me again, I'll wash out your mouth with soap while I'm at it!"

"Oooh!" she screeched, turning her head this way and that to try to escape his ministrations. "How dare you treat me like a child!"

"If you don't want to be treated like one, then don't act like one," Howard retaliated, stripping off the false eyelashes and drawing the cloth over her closed eyes.

"Take that chip off your shoulder and stop defying me at every turn." He scoured at her cheeks. "We made a deal, Evie, and you went into this marriage with your eyes open. I can't help it if it's not what you expected or what you wanted."

His words took all the fight out of her. Her shoulders slumped in despair and frustration. "I don't know what I wanted," she whimpered, looking up at him with lost eyes.

The defeat in her posture robbed Howard of his outrage. He tossed the washcloth into the sink and began to work the bobby pins from her hair.

"I'll tell you what you wanted," he told her in a softer tone. "You wanted an easy way out of your predicament. Anyone would. But I've got news, sweetheart. There ain't no free lunches. And if you want to dance you have to pay the fiddler." He combed his fingers through the snarls of her hair, regarded his handiwork with a thoughtful expression and nodded. "There."

He took her by the shoulders and turned her toward the mirror. Her hair fell around her shoulders like waves in a fiery sea. Devoid of the thick makeup, her complexion was pale, almost translucent. Her blue eyes were fringed with long fair lashes, and her eyebrows arched in a natural curve. Her naked lips had a bow that Howard found irresistible.

Their eyes met in the mirror.

"You don't need all that paint," he told her. "You're just gilding the lily. Can't you see that you're beautiful without it? Not just beautiful. Stunning."

"I don't have any eyelashes," she said, her voice quavering a bit.

"Then use some mascara." Howard turned her to face him. Her shoulders were smooth and warm beneath his palms. "I'm not trying to be an ogre, Evie. I'm not trying to be a dictator. I'm not saying you can't wear makeup or sundresses or slinky nightgowns."

"Then what are you saying?" she asked, looking up at him with a limpid gaze.

"Moderation in all things," he quoted. "Modesty. Use what cosmetics you need to enhance your natural beauty. Don't draw undue attention to yourself by trying to look like a movie star. Be the prettiest Eva Blake you can be."

He cupped her cheek with his palm. "You're a warm, vibrant woman, and you should dress in a way that suits you as well as your station in life. Like it or not, Evie, you and I live under a microscope. It goes with the territory."

"I don't know if I can be what you want me to be," she said, her eyes filling with tears.

"I just want you to be yourself."

As Howard stared into her limpid blue gaze, he felt like a drowning man going down for the third time. Without thinking of the consequences ... without considering anything except how her lips would taste, he drew her into his arms and covered her mouth with his.

Her lips were softer than an angel's whisper, as alluring as a deal from the devil, as hot as the fiery furnace. She made a little sound in her throat and, taking it for acceptance, Howard deepened the kiss. Her lips parted beneath the pressure of his, and the softness of her breasts pressing against his chest ignited an undeniable passion.

Nectar, he thought, sipping from the sweetness of her lips again and again. He'd found the land of milk and honey.

Suddenly, she wrenched free and pushed him away. "Stop," she said in a voice that trembled.

Howard reached for her. "Evie..."

"Don't!" she said, backing away. "Just don't touch me." Tears pooled in her eyes. "You broke your promise."

"What?"

"You reneged on our deal. You said there would be no sex until I was ready." Her tone was accusatory.

Howard thought about pointing out that she'd responded to his kisses but thought better of it. There was no use stirring up more trouble.

"You're right," he said with a heavy sigh. "I did. I'm sorry." He stepped aside. "Go on and get ready. I'll wait for you."

"I'm not going to the picnic," she told him. "I never planned to, so all your worry about my embarrassing you was for nothing."

Howard nodded, unable to retaliate, unable to even think. "What will I tell everyone?"

"Just tell them the truth—that I couldn't stand to be whispered about behind my back anymore. If you don't want to do that, then lie and say I'm not feeling well."

Howard left her in the bathroom and took his car keys from his jeans pocket. He drove to the park, the taste of her mouth lingering on his lips, her scent lin-

gering in his nostrils, the memory of the way she felt
in his arms lingering in his mind. The next thirty or so
years loomed before him like an empty tomb.

Were his bride's kisses manna from heaven? he
wondered. Or were they temptations sent straight from
the devil to show him how weak the flesh really was?

WHEN EVA AND MAGGIE had returned to the hospital, Howard had left to take care of some pressing
church business. A steady stream of people stopped by
with get-well wishes and flowers, all eager to let Maggie know they were concerned about Rio.

Maggie found it heart-lifting to know that there
were so many people out there who cared. Elena, Jeremy and Tess had popped in several times, offering to
relieve Maggie, but she wasn't ready to leave Rio alone
again just yet.

Maggie and her mother had talked away the afternoon, and she found the soft, dulcet sounds of her
mother's voice as comforting as she found her story
uplifting...and surprising. She'd thought she knew her
parents well, but she'd had no idea that their marriage had gotten off to such a rocky start.

"Did you really scrub off Mama's makeup, Daddy?" Maggie asked her father when he returned later
that afternoon.

Howard's face turned beet-red. "Did she tell you
that?"

"Uh-huh."

"Well, it's true," he said, taking a seat in a battered vinyl chair. "What else did she tell you?"

"That you coldcocked a guy who made a pass at her."

"That's true, too, but I can't say I'm proud of it."

"I am," Eva said, rising from her chair and settling herself on his knee. She pressed a kiss to his forehead. "My hero."

"Behave yourself, woman," Howard admonished. "Someone might come in here and see you fooling around."

"Do you think I care?"

Howard grinned, and Maggie saw a glimpse of the young man he'd once been.

"You never did, did you?"

"Nope."

Howard looked at Maggie. "I guess your mother told you everything."

"Not everything," Maggie said. "We're just getting into the good stuff."

"And are you... all right?"

Maggie could see that he was really worried. She abandoned her teasing tone. "Do you mean do I love the two of you any less for finding out you made a few mistakes along the way? Of course I don't. I'm a woman, Dad, not a kid."

The worry in her father's eyes vanished. He blew out a relieved breath. "Good."

"There you are!" Maggie and her parents turned toward the sound of a masculine voice. Dr. Dekker stood in the doorway. "I figured you were in the hospital somewhere."

"Is something wrong?" Maggie asked, unable to hide her anxiety.

Sonny Dekker shook his head. "No. Believe it or not sometimes I have good news."

Maggie surged to her feet. "Rio—"

Dr. Dekker held up his hand and shook his dark head. "Your husband is the same. Dr. Purdy had an emergency appendectomy, and he asked me to stop by and give you the results of your lab work."

"Is everything okay?" she asked, unable to hide the new concern in her eyes.

"Everything is fine."

Maggie exhaled a deep sigh of relief. "Just a flu bug, huh?"

"No, Mrs. Langley, your dizzy spells have nothing to do with a virus."

"Then what is it?"

"You're pregnant."

Maggie sat down hard. "Pregnant? How can I be pregnant?"

Dr. Dekker smiled. "I figured a big-city girl like you knew how these things happened."

Maggie was too stunned to respond to his clumsy attempt at humor. She was going to have Rio's baby, and he wasn't able to share the joy of that good news. Where *was* the joy? she wondered.

Maggie felt Eva's arms go around her in a familiar embrace. "I think that's wonderful news, honey," she said. "Why don't you go tell Rio?"

"Tell Rio?" Maggie snapped. "He can't hear me."

"We might all be surprised at how much people in his condition hear, Mrs. Langley," Sonny Dekker said. "Go on in. He's stable. I've told the nurses in ICU to let you stay indefinitely."

"Thank you."

"I'm doing all I can, Mrs. Langley," the young doctor said. "And your husband looks like a tough hombre. Don't lose faith, okay?" He started to leave, turned and with a smile added, "Congratulations."

Maggie watched his retreating form. Congratulations! How could he offer her his congratulations? What was there to celebrate? Her world was tumbling in around her. First she had lost Greg. Now Rio had been shot, and she was expecting a baby he might never get to see . . . to hold. . . .

Maggie's troubled eyes found her mother's tender gaze. "How can I be happy about this? Why did I get pregnant *now?*"

"'All things work together for good,' Margaret. You've got to believe that," Howard said, answering for his wife. He held out an elbow to each of them. "I think that under the circumstances, we should go to the cafeteria and celebrate with a little something to eat."

"I'm not really hungry," Maggie said.

"You ought to eat something," Eva urged, going along with Howard. "At least have a piece of pie or something." She winked. "While we're there, I'll tell you about Grandma Blake taking me shopping."

CHAPTER SEVEN

June 1951

EVA SAT IN THE PEW next to her husband and pretended to listen to the visiting speaker's sermon, her gloved hands clenched in the lap of her navy-blue skirt.

Where was her backbone? Why had she let Howard humiliate her yesterday? How dared he force her into the bathroom and wash off her makeup? How dared he dictate how she should dress, how she should fix her hair and how much makeup she should wear? Why had she knuckled under and dragged out this god-awful skirt and blouse that her mother had bought her in high school?

And worse, how could she have let Howard kiss her that way?

As much as she hated to admit it, Eva knew her anger was directed as much at herself as at her husband. She sneaked a peek from the corner of her eye and caught him looking at her. She darted her glance away and tried to concentrate on the sermon, which was an impossibility when all she could really hear was the rapid beating of her heart, the same runaway rhythm she'd felt when Howard kissed her.

The memory of the way his mouth—so soft, so masterful—had claimed hers was indelibly imprinted in her mind. Even now, thinking about it, her breasts felt full and achy with the need to feel the touch of his hands. And even though she might want to, she couldn't deny the way her body had gone all hot and melting, the way it had with Denny.

No! she thought in dismay. There was no way this mind-boggling thing with Howard could be compared with what she'd experienced with Denny. Denny's kisses had been almost...innocent. Their lovemaking had been like an adventure. They'd set out to chart unexplored territory, to experience new and unsampled delights. Deep inside, she knew she'd been driven as much by curiosity and her desire to make Denny happy as she had been by any physical desire.

Though she had a sneaking suspicion Howard had never, well, *done* it, there was nothing innocent about the way he kissed or the frightening feelings his kisses invoked. Even more shocking was how quickly they'd flared up...like a prairie fire sparked by a bolt of lightning. One minute he and she had been mad and yelling; the next they'd been caught up in something that was beyond her ability to understand...or accept.

Face it, Eva. It isn't the way he kissed you. It's the way you responded that has you in a tizzy.

Eva clamped her teeth onto her bottom lip. Tears filled her eyes, and she shut them tightly, cursing her traitorous body for responding to Howard's kiss.

What kind of woman was she, to be carrying one man's child and still feel desire for another?

No doubt about it. The people of Crystal Creek were right. She *was* the kind of woman they thought she was. She had tried to convince herself that it wasn't her; it was the situation. It was impossible to live in the same house with an attractive man and share dozens of unforeseen intimacies without becoming aware of that person. Anyone would respond the way she had. She cursed the memory of Howard in his jeans and T-shirt, the muscles in his chest hard beneath her fingertips.

From the place next to her, the clean, masculine scent of Old Spice tantalized her with the recollection of the way his arms had held her with such tender assertiveness while his mouth devoured hers with a hot hunger.

Damn Howard Blake, anyway! He'd taken advantage of her. This was all his fault! First he'd demoralized her by denying her the armor she donned to face the world, and then when he'd caught her feeling unsure of herself, he'd used her vulnerable state to gain the upper hand.

To Eva's relief, the song-leader rose and announced the final hymn, ending her self-castigation. She stood with the rest of the congregation, determination in the set of her mouth, in the gleam of her eyes. There was nothing she could do about what had happened the day before, but she could darn well make sure it didn't happen again.

OVER THE NEXT FEW DAYS, things at the Blake house
were tense at best. Eva and Howard went through the
motions of being a happily wed young couple. She at-
tended a Tuesday morning meeting to discuss a wedding shower for one of the young ladies. She and
Howard went to church together on Wednesday night.
On Thursday, she accompanied him to a welcome-
home party for his parents, who had returned from
their extended vacation.

Several times throughout the course of the party,
Eva caught the Blakes regarding her and their only son
with some emotion that trod the uncertain line between sorrow and horror, but she had to give credit
where credit was due. The former minister and his wife
treated her in the same gentle manner she remembered from her many years of association with them.
In fact, the elder Blakes' kindness went a long way toward softening the resentment that had simmered inside her ever since the previous Saturday.

Eva's emotions had run the gamut the past week—
from anger to sorrow to self-pity. She didn't know
what she thought about her marriage to Howard anymore. But she knew she was raw inside. Raw and uncertain and miserable.

On Friday morning, she fixed Howard's breakfast
and left for an early appointment at the beauty par-
lor. She was greeted with a hesitant friendliness by the
owner of the shop, Nell Harrison, who, according to
gossip, had given birth to her two-year-old child out of
wedlock. In complete sympathy with her plight, Eva

gave Nell a friendly smile and complimented her on the photo of her daughter that sat on her vanity.

Keeping up a steady stream of chatter, Nell snipped and cut and rolled Eva's hair in pin curls. Sara Nelson, the beautician across the way, was giving someone a permanent, squirting foul-smelling solution onto each curl. The small room's single window was closed, and the offensive odor played havoc with Eva's stomach, which still acted up on occasion. She mopped at the perspiration beading her face and hoped she could control her nausea until Nell finished pinning up her hair. She couldn't.

"I think I'm going to be sick," she said, leaping from the chair and running toward the rest room at the back of the shop.

Inside the small area that doubled as a supply room, Eva found a clean washcloth and bathed her flushed face, reveling in the coolness of the water, not caring that she was ruining the elaborate makeup that she'd donned to please herself instead of Howard.

When he'd walked into the kitchen and seen that she'd gone against his wishes once more, he hadn't said a word, but his lips had tightened, and his eyes had narrowed in irritation. Eva hadn't been sure whether to be glad or sad. All she knew was that the minor victory was a hollow one.

Now she regarded her pale face in the mirror—the streaked mascara, the eyelashes gone askew, the splotchy powder. She looked horrible. It occurred to her that maybe Howard had given up on trying to reform her and had decided to just let God exact his own revenge, which he appeared to have done in spades.

She drew in a deep breath of the odor-free air and realized that her stomach had stopped doing cartwheels. There was no rhyme or reason to her bouts of sickness, which were certainly not confined to the mornings. She had the fleeting thought that maybe this was another of God's ways to get back at her.

Clutching the damp cloth in her hand, she opened the door and started back out to let Nell finish pincurling her hair. The sound of her mother's name stopped her at the doorway.

"Sally Carmichael is beside herself," Sara Nelson said in a low, but carrying voice.

"Well, she's not the only one," replied another. "The whole church is in a state of shock! Lucy and Thaddeus Blake are just *devastated.*"

Aware that she was eavesdropping, but unable to bring herself to step into the room and put an end to the gossip, Eva stood transfixed in the doorway.

"They're holding up well, though."

"They certainly are. I hate to think how I'd feel to know that my son knocked up some floozy and then had to marry her."

Eva's hand went to her lips to stifle a gasp of shock. Wanting—needing—to see who was spouting such venom, she peeked around the corner. She recognized the unidentified woman as Ginny Sloan, Sara's perm customer, who taught Sunday school. Eva noticed that Nell was busy straightening her vanity.

"Did you hear about Howard getting into a fist-fight with that man over at MacBride's last week?" Sara asked.

"Who hasn't?" Ginny said with a dismissive wave of her hand. "Robby said the board was considering asking for Howard's resignation again."

"Again!" Sara cried, aghast.

"Well, certainly. The deacons brought him up before the board when they found out about his marriage and the baby. The only thing that saved his hide was Calvin McKinney, but I'm here to tell you that they won't condone much more. I don't care how much influence the high-and-mighty McKinneys have."

"You can't blame the board," Sara said philosophically. "They do have a solemn duty to look out for the good of the congregation. It's a real shame, though. Howard Blake was such a nice young man."

"You know what they say about evil companions corrupting good morals, Sara," Ginny reminded her, meeting the beautician's eyes in the mirror. "The wrong kind of woman has led many a good man astray, and Eve Michaels apparently offered Howard a fruit he couldn't turn down."

Crushed beneath the sudden, startling realization of what their marriage had done to Howard's reputation, Eva didn't hear any more. Later, she would remember leaving the security of the bathroom and gathering her things, tossing some crumpled bills on the vanity and telling Nell she had to go, that she was deathly sick. Later, she would recall the smug look on Ginny Sloan's face and the concern she saw in Nell's eyes as she murmured a soft apology. But at that moment, all she could think of was getting away from the hurtful talebearers as fast as she could.

Eva didn't know how she got home without having a wreck. She let herself in the back door, sobbing for breath while tears of hurt and remorse chased one another down her cheeks.

She'd been so busy being miserable that she hadn't considered Howard's feelings at all. She'd been a—a *bitch* about almost everything, and, with the exception of their arguments over her clothes, he had accepted everything she'd thrown at him, including her ongoing wallow in self-pity. How could she have been so selfish, so self-centered as to think Howard was having an easy time of it?

It dawned on her that she hadn't given more than a cursory thought about how their marriage would affect him. Dear God, they had almost fired him—and still might—all because of her! The amazing thing was that he'd never said a word about it. She wondered what else he'd suffered.

He took the blame for what I did with Denny. Everyone—even his parents—thinks he's the father of my baby.

A low moan escaped her. When she'd made the deal with Howard about not telling about Denny, she'd been so thankful that she and her baby would be taken care of and that she could come home, that she'd given almost no thought to the fact that people would assume Howard was the baby's father. If the idea *had* crossed her mind, she supposed she'd believed that Howard's sterling reputation would hold him in good stead with the community. She'd never dreamed that the people who knew him so well would turn on him this way. Until she'd come back to Crystal Creek, she'd had no idea just how malicious some people could be.

Had Howard known what he was getting into when he offered to marry her? Had he suspected the town's reaction? And if he had, why had he sacrificed himself this way?

"I love you, Eva."

The softly uttered words drifted through her mind. Without a doubt, Howard had known exactly what he was getting into, but he'd done it anyway because he loved her and cared what happened to her. He hadn't wanted her to bear her burden alone. He wanted to share it. No. He wanted to take it from her, to bear it himself. She sobbed harder.

He'd given her everything he had—his name, his home, his support. And what had he got in return? Threats. Gossip. A smear against his good name. And a wife who taunted him and made his life miserable in so many trifling ways. A wife who was miserable herself because she was mixed-up and confused and had no idea what she wanted to do about the rest of her life.

Eva thought of her many small defiances over the past weeks—her refusal to tone down her makeup, her grudging attendance at church, her unwillingness to really listen to what Howard was trying to teach her about becoming a better person.

Eva buried her face in her pillow and cried. Buckets of tears. Oceans of tears. When she finished, she washed her face and made a cup of tea. Even though her eyes had been opened wide about the town's view of her marriage, she was still uncertain what to do with the knowledge.

She needed a friend to talk to... or maybe her mother. But Sally wanted nothing to do with her, and she had no friends, except maybe Emily McKinney. Swallowing what was left of her pride, Eva called Emily and asked if she could spare a few moments. Emily graciously said she'd put on a pot of coffee, and Eva drove out to the Double C Ranch, her heart overflowing with guilt and sadness.

AFTER THIRTY MINUTES of small talk, Emily invited Eva to lunch.

"Oh, I couldn't!"

"Why not?" Emily said. "Isn't this the day the deacons have their monthly lunch meeting?"

"I think it is," Eva said with a nod.

"Good, then. You'll stay."

They had cold cuts with fresh tomatoes and lettuce from the garden and a slice of coconut pie for dessert. When the table was cleared, Emily sat down and looked into Eva's troubled eyes.

"I can't give you any advice until I know what the problem is," she said.

"I know."

"Did someone say something to you?"

Shaking her head, Eva raised her tormented gaze to Emily's. "Not to me." She gave a faltering account of the conversation she'd heard at the beauty salon. By the time she finished, she was crying again.

"I don't care what they say about me," she said. "But they don't have any right to say those things about Howard. All he's ever done is try to help me."

"Howard is a big boy," said Emily. "It won't hurt for him to take his share of the blame."

"But he—" Eva stopped her confession just in time, remembering her promise not to disclose the truth about the baby's paternity.

"Just remember that the people who are saying all those terrible things about you and Howard aren't lily-white," Emily counseled. "It's been my experience that the people who are the worst sinners are the ones who seem so determined to drag everyone else through the mud. I don't know... maybe it makes them feel better about themselves."

She smiled at Eva. "Don't worry about Howard. In spite of this unfortunate incident, he's a fine man. His life will speak for itself."

Unfortunate incident! Eva's eyes flooded again, and she had to bite her tongue to keep from blurting out

the truth to clear Howard's name. She hoped Emily
was right. Before the scandal surrounding his marriage, Howard was respected and well liked. Maybe
with his all-but-flawless past, it would just be a matter of time before the people of Crystal Creek forgave
him.

She was a different matter. Even before the Hollywood move, there had been whispers about her and
the way she dressed, the way she behaved, her figure.
As if she could help that. She sighed. She wasn't a
Howard Blake.

"How can I change people's minds about me?" she
asked Emily, fearing that nothing she did would alter
the town's attitude. "I have to do something! I owe
Howard that much for marrying me."

Emily frowned. "You don't owe Howard for marrying you. He just took proper responsibility for his
actions."

Eva licked her lips. "I . . . I . . . all I meant was that
he could have put the blame on me the way everyone
else has . . . instead of . . . doing the right thing."

"Howard isn't the kind of man to shirk his duties," Emily said. "You should know that."

"I do." *Believe me, I do.*

"Respect is earned, Eva. If you want to change
people's opinions of you, you'll have to work at it. It
may take years. It may take your entire life. And there
will no doubt be a few who never forget or forgive. But
that's their problem, not yours."

"It sounds hopeless," Eva lamented.

"No, not hopeless. Just hard." Emily smiled. "But you're not afraid of tackling hard things. You tackled Hollywood."

Eva nodded. She'd tackled Hollywood, all right. And failed.

THAT EVENING when Eva confronted him about what she'd heard at the beauty shop, Howard sighed.

"I didn't say anything because I didn't want to worry you."

"But it isn't fair for your reputation to suffer because of something I did!"

"Don't be so hard on yourself," Howard told her. "I'm a big boy. I knew what I was getting into."

Eva laced her fingers together and raised her chin, determined to make him see reason. "I want to tell everyone the truth."

"No!"

"Howard, it's your career! You've wanted to be a minister all your life. You can't let my mistakes rob you of that. Think about your parents. I can see their disappointment every time they look at you...at us."

Howard paced to the window and back. Then he turned and met her troubled gaze. "We made a pact," he reminded her. "God knows the truth. That's all that matters."

"It *isn't* all that matters. What people think of you matters. Please," she begged. "I can never make up to you for all you've done for me, but—"

"I don't expect you to do anything," he interrupted. "I just want you to be happy."

Eva's eyes filled with more of those troubling, unwanted tears. "I don't know what will make me happy," she confessed, "but I want you to know that I'm sorry for being so insensitive, so selfish. I'm sorry for being so defensive and so hard to live with. I'm going to try to do better."

The troubled look in Howard's eyes softened to disbelief...and tentative pleasure. The furrows between his dark eyebrows disappeared.

"Living a good and helpful life isn't hard," he said. "It's just a matter of going the extra mile and putting other people's happiness and welfare above your own."

Which meant being nice when she didn't want to. Showing kindnesses to people who treated her badly. Biting her tongue and smiling instead of replying with a sharp retort. Turning the other cheek.

Eva sighed. Emily McKinney had warned that it wouldn't be a picnic, but Eva knew she had to try to do better for Howard's sake. She was obligated to him. She owed him and, as a Carmichael, she'd been taught never to be indebted to anyone.

"I'm going to try," she said, determination lacing her voice, "but I'm not sure where to start."

"Look around," Howard suggested. "See what people need, and give it to them. Whatever you give will be returned a hundredfold...pressed down and running over."

Still dubious, Eva nodded. "I'd like for you to do something for me."

"What?"

"Tell your mom and dad the truth. I don't care about mine, but don't break your parents' hearts this way."

Howard's frown was back. "I'll think about it."

She nodded. For the moment, it was the best she could do.

THE FOLLOWING DAY, Howard's mother arrived to take her new daughter-in-law shopping...at her son's request.

With her new insight and determination firmly in place, Eva went along without a fuss. She had no desire to hurt Lucy Blake, and under the circumstances, it was the least she could do.

Though Lucy was friendly, there was a shadow in her eyes when she looked at Eva and her burgeoning stomach that said without words that she was worried about her son's choice of a wife and disappointed in his apparent fall from grace.

But however she felt about Howard's sudden marriage, Lucy Blake was nothing but amiable toward her new daughter-in-law. Her genuine concern and willingness to do what she could to help made Eva feel even more guilty for her behavior *and* for accepting Howard's terms for the marriage.

All day, Lucy dutifully carried clothes—maternity clothes—back and forth to the dressing rooms of a

dozen stores, doing her best to pick things that sh
thought would be suitable for Eva's new role as mi
ister's wife while still looking young and stylish.

Without exception, Eva despised everything Luc
chose. But, dutiful wife and daughter-in-law that sh
was resolved to be, she gritted her teeth and selecte
two of the least offensive garments. When she tried t
pay for them with the money Howard had given he
Lucy would hear none of it. She whipped out h
checkbook, telling Eva to consider it a token of h
and Thaddeus's love.

The kindness and generosity of the gesture mad
Eva feel lower than a snake's belly. She sighed. Tha
too, was a small price to pay for her former selfisl
ness.

THE NEXT MORNING, Eva got up the instant the alar
went off. There would be no more lying abed on Su
days. No more cajoling from Howard. She dragged o
a terry-cloth robe and hurried to the kitchen to sta
the coffee. When Howard stepped into the kitchen te
minutes later, he was greeted by the mouth-waterin
aromas of frying bacon and fresh-brewed coffee.

The emotions that crossed his face were priceles
Surprise. Confusion. Pleasure. Eva felt another jolt c
that nagging shame. Getting up without a hassle o
the one day a week that mattered was a small gestu
to bring so much joy.

After breakfast, she cleaned up the kitchen and pu
a pot roast and vegetables in a slow oven so dinn

would be nearly ready when they got home. All she'd have to do was make gravy and warm up the fresh green beans she'd cooked the evening before. Maybe she'd see if Howard wanted to ask the Logans over for dinner. They lived way out in the country and it was hard for them financially to make the trip back to town for the evening service.

Howard was thrilled with the suggestion. Satisfied with her morning's work, Eva went to get dressed. She hated to start wearing maternity clothes, which would be more grist for the gossip mill, but there was no putting it off any longer. She'd just smile and pretend she didn't see the looks and nudges.

Taking a firm grip on her resolve, Eva put on the maternity suit Lucy Blake had paid an arm and a leg for. Made from a mouse-brown linen, that, according to Lucy, went so well with Eva's pretty hair, the plain suit had a straight skirt with a hole for her expanding tummy and a boxy jacket that left plenty of room for growth. A satin blouse with a tie at the throat—that could be worn without the jacket—and some sensible, low-heeled brown pumps completed the ensemble.

With her spirits on a definite downhill spiral, Eva donned her makeup—toned down for the benefit of the congregation—and twisted her hair back into a bun. In for a penny, in for a pound. As she looked in the mirror at the dowdy picture she made, her eyes filled with tears. A stranger stared back at her.

Only the knowledge that her actions would bring Howard pleasure gave her the courage to leave the bathroom. Lifting her chin, she blinked back her tear and entered the living room, where Howard wa looking over his sermon.

He looked up. His surprise was apparent. But th other emotion she saw in his eyes wasn't so easy t catalogue. For one heart-stopping moment, sh imagined she saw disappointment, but why would h be disappointed in an outfit his mother had chosen?

"That outfit is...very appropriate," he said at last.

"Your mother picked it out."

"I thought so." He cleared his throat. "You look very...nice."

"Thank you." She twisted the strap of her purs between her gloved fingers. "I suppose there will be lot of talk because I'm wearing a maternity outfit."

"I suppose so," he said, rising. "Are you ready?"

She nodded. Howard held out his arm in a charm ing, old-fashioned gesture. Though her heart wa heavy, Eva couldn't help feeling that by taking How ard's arm, she had somehow become allies with hin against the ugliness they were to face together.

Despite everything, it was a comforting thought.

MAGGIE SAT in a chair at Rio's bedside, clutching hi hand. Though she had no way of knowing if he' heard her, she'd just passed on the latest installmen of her parents' story to him, hoping that he would hea and respond to the sound of her voice.

"She went through a lot, Rio," Maggie said to her husband. "More than I ever imagined. I don't know how she came through it all with her faith intact. I haven't suffered nearly what she has, and I'm so weak." Her voice broke. "I know I'm a disappointment to Daddy, but I can't help it."

Tears started in her eyes. "Oh, I can see that Mama's faith was weak, too, but she's a gutsier woman than I am. I'm afraid that if I lose you, I won't have what it takes to pick up and go on the way she did."

She clung to his hand, squeezing it tightly. "You *have* to get well, because we're going to have a baby— a baby, Rio, just like Emily."

Her voice caught on a sob, and she leaned her forehead against the side of the bed. "Wake up, Rio. You've got to wake up."

Rio didn't answer. There was no sign that he heard her. The monitor registering his heartbeats in soft blips was the only sound in the room.

"Please, God," Maggie groaned, unaware that she was asking for divine help. "Please . . ."

CHAPTER EIGHT

July 1951

EVA BLOTTED her perspiring face on the baby-do[l]
sleeve of her maternity smock and bent to take an
other sheet from the basket of clothes she'd jus
washed for Mattie Hinesley. Mattie was an elderl[y]
widow who'd recently suffered a stroke and had so fa[r]
regained only partial use of her left side. Since she ha[d]
no family nearby, Eva had taken on the job of doin[g]
Mattie's weekly laundry. Eva, along with several othe[r]
ladies of the congregation, brought food on a dail[y]
basis, and took turns cleaning the widow's house.

Fighting the fatigue that plagued her constantly, Ev[a]
shoved straggling tendrils of hair from her face. Sh[e]
knew she must look a fright...the humidity and per
spiration had taken the starch out of not only he[r]
clothes but her spine as well. There were stains on he[r]
smock from the jam sandwiches she'd made for th[e]
Lamonte twins' lunch, and she smelled of sour mil[k]
where their baby brother had spit up on her.

She was hot and tired and her back ached. Sh[e]
longed for nothing more than to go home, cool off i[n]
a nice tub of lukewarm water and sit in front of the fa[n]

with her feet propped up while she sipped a glass of syrupy-sweet iced tea.

But there was no time for that in the near future, she thought, remembering the Bible passage about not growing weary in well-doing. She had to remember that, according to Galatians, if Christians didn't faint in doing good works, they would reap their reward. Eva hoped that if she kept helping in the community, they would forgive her for leading Howard astray. *That* would be her reward.

So, no matter how tired and hot she was, she still had to take a hamburger casserole to Ginny Sloan, whose teenage son had contracted polio just two weeks after the incident in the beauty shop.

It was ironic, Eva often mused, that even though Ginny had said such unkind things about Howard, he had been the first one she'd called when Grover Purdy had broken the bad news. Ginny and her husband had turned to Howard for comfort and support, both of which he'd given unstintingly. He hadn't left the boy's bedside the first forty-eight hours after his hospitalization.

Eva had done her part by keeping the younger children while Ginny was at the hospital. Though Ginny thanked her, not once had she offered an apology for the things she'd said. Eva refused to let that stop her. She remembered the Bible passage about heaping coals of fire on the head of your enemy. She would make Ginny Sloan feel guilty if it was the last thing she did!

Eva blew out a weary breath and reached into the bag of clothespins, stuffing a couple into her mouth while she wrestled with the heavy cotton sheet.

"Here. Let me help you."

Eva snatched the clothespins from her mouth and whirled toward the sound of Howard's voice. The sheet fell back into the woven basket, forgotten.

"Howard! What are you doing here?" she asked breathlessly, her hands going to her hair in an automatic, feminine gesture of vanity.

"I came to see how Mattie was doing and saw your car in the driveway." He reached out and touched her flushed cheek with his fingertips.

Eva felt the jolt of electricity from his touch all the way to her toes.

"You're too hot, and you've gotten a sunburn."

"This is the last load," she said, brushing a wisp of hair from her damp cheek with the back of her hand.

"It is for you. Go on inside. I stopped by the ice house and picked up a couple of cold Cokes." He winked. "Mattie loves Coke. You drink mine, and I'll hang out the rest of the clothes."

Eva thought about how cold the colas were from the ice house. So cold that ice crystals formed in them. Her mouth began to water. "Are you sure? That's a woman's job. What if someone sees you?"

The corners of Howard's eyes crinkled with his smile. "I think I'm secure enough in my masculinity to hang out a basket of clothes without any permanent damage to my ego. Besides," he said, his smile spreading wider, "I'm getting used to people talking about me."

Eva felt her face flame. "That isn't funny, Howard."

He reached out and put his forefinger beneath her chin, tipping back her head until he could look into her eyes. "You're going to have to develop a sense of humor, Evie, if you want to survive this old world."

"Rest would be a bigger help in survival," she grumbled.

Howard's smile faded. "You should slow down in this heat. You're doing way too much for a woman seven months pregnant."

"I'm fine," she said. "It's just so hot."

"Go on," he said, cocking his head toward the house. "I'll be in when I finish here."

Eva nodded and turned away. She'd taken no more than two strides when she took a misstep in a small depression and twisted her ankle. Howard was beside her in a heartbeat, throwing his arm out and catching her before she fell. Eva found her nose pressed against the starched front of his white shirt. The hand he'd snaked around her rested perilously near her breast.

"You okay?" he asked.

She clutched his biceps and nodded, reveling in the strength of the arms that held her so securely. Tears prickled beneath her eyelids. At that moment, she'd have liked nothing more than to stay in his arms forever.

"You smell good," he said, his breath a soft gust against the top of her head. "Like hot summer sunshine and strawberries."

The poetic words evoked a mental image of her and Howard on a blanket beneath some trees down by the Claro River, the bounty of a picnic basket spread around them while sunshine sparkled on the surface of the river meandering past. She could see Howard's smile as he dipped his head to take her lips in a kiss....

"You all right, Eva?" Mattie called in a thick voice from the back door.

The vision vanished. "I'm fine, Mrs. Hinesley," she called to the little woman who sat on the back porch.

Her pulse still racing, Eva drew away. "You must have been out in the sun too long, yourself," she said, indicating the stains on her smock. "I smell like baby vomit and jam sandwiches."

"What kind of jam?"

"Strawberry."

"See?" Howard said with a smile.

"You always find the good," she said, amazed as always at his positive outlook.

"If you look hard enough, you usually can," he told her. "Go on inside and visit with Mattie. I'll be there in a minute."

Confused, bemused, Eva did his bidding. She wondered if there would be a special place in heaven for Howard Blake and decided that if there wasn't there should be.

"THAT EVA BLAKE is a demon for hard work," Harriet Meyers said to Prudence Burns via the telephone. "She's still doing for Mattie Hinesley and the Lamontes, not to mention a dozen other people, and I saw her over to Ginny Sloan's again today."

"Humph."

"Ginny says Eva comes every day or two and reads to Brian and helps with his exercises."

Prudence Burns snorted again and peeked through the crack in the drapes at the Blakes' house. "She's just tryin' to worm her way into the good graces of this town. Doin' her good works to be seen of men."

"That's what Ginny says, but I don't see *her* turning away Mrs. Blake's help. Don't you think we should give the woman the benefit of the doubt?"

"A leopard doesn't change his spots, Harriet," Pru reminded in a sharp voice.

"I guess you're right," Harriet conceded. "She did make an overnight one-hundred-eighty-degree turnaround. Howard most likely put his foot down about her doing her Christian duties and the way she should behave and such."

"No doubt."

"Are you coming to the ice cream social tomorrow night?"

"Wouldn't miss it," Pru said. "See you there. And if you hear anything juicy, let me know, okay?"

"You know I will," Harriet singsonged.

"WHERE HAVE YOU BEEN?" Howard asked a week later as Eve came dragging through the front door at dusk. "It's almost nine o'clock."

"I know. I'm sorry," she said, rotating her shoulders. She looked up at him from eyes ringed with dark smudges of weariness. "Did you find your dinner?"

"Yes." Concern edged Howard's tone. Eva mistook it for impatience.

"I turned the oven as low as I could," she said, brushing past him. "I hope it didn't dry out."

He caught her by the shoulders and turned her around to face him. His worried gaze roamed his wife's haggard features. The heat and the hours she spent helping out in the community were taking their toll. She'd lost weight, and both her hair and her eyes had lost their luster.

"Dinner was fine," he assured her. "I wish I could say the same about you."

"I'm okay," she said. "I just need a bath."

Howard ran his hands from her drooping shoulders to her elbows and back again. "You need to rest," he said in a gentle tone. "You're doing too much."

Her smile was the barest twist of her lips. "There's a lot to do. Grover Purdy said another case of polio was diagnosed at Hillsboro. He asked if I could help him get word out about prevention, so I've been going around town cautioning mothers about letting their children play outside in the heat of the day, telling them not to let the children play in the water hoses or go swimming, to get enough rest, and—"

"I can't believe Grover asked you!" Howard said angrily. "You have enough to do. There are other women who can help. Let them."

Eva reached up and put her hand against his chest. He felt the soft touch all the way to the deepest part of his soul. "I have to do this, Howard. Please let me do this."

Her eyes blazed with a determined blue fire. Howard acquiesced with a sigh. "Do it, but slow down. For your sake. For the baby's sake. And for mine."

"Yours?" she asked in surprise.

"Mine," he said with a nod. "You don't know how much I worry about you."

She looked up at him, the confusion his confession evoked showing plainly in her eyes.

"Go on and take your bath," he said, his eyes alight with concern and tenderness.

Eva started to turn, but a pitiful whining stopped her. "What's that?"

A dull red stained Howard's face. "A dog."

"Another one?" Eva said. "Howard, we have two dogs already, and that cat you found."

Two weeks before, Howard had brought home a very expectant tabby who had promptly delivered five offspring. A passel of cats was the last thing Eva wanted to contend with, but with a pleading smile and a wheedling if-you-just-say-yes-I'll-give-you-anything tone, Howard had convinced her that he could find homes for all of them.

Finding it harder and harder to resist that
smile . . . finding it harder and harder to resist everything about her husband, Eva had fixed the family of
cats a box in the toolshed behind the parsonage.
Howard had dubbed the female Jezebel, since they
had no idea which of the neighborhood Toms the father might be.

"Someone dumped the dog out by the Logans'," he
said now, as if that explained it all. "He's really cute,
Eva, and I knew Ed couldn't afford to feed it." He
shrugged. "I didn't think you'd mind."

He was hopeless, she thought with a shake of her
head. His tender heart wouldn't let him leave any stray
loitering around town. "I don't mind. You take care
of them, but if you don't stop bringing home every
stray you find, we'll be in the poorhouse."

Howard smiled. "We've got a long way to go before we wind up in the poorhouse," he told her. "Besides, I think Ginny Sloan's boy was wanting a dog."

Eva shook her head. "You're a soft touch, Howard Blake."

"And you aren't?" he said. "What about that dress
you made for Ginny's little girl just because she
wanted a blue silk dress, and the doll clothes you
sewed for the Lamonte twins because Jewel couldn't
afford to buy them anything for their birthday?"

"That was different," Eva said.

"Really? How?"

Embarrassed by the approval in Howard's eyes, Eva
looked away. "I'm going to go take my bath."

"Take your time. I'll fix you a plate when you're finished."

"I'm too tired to eat," she said with a shake of her head.

"You have to eat," he said, "or you're going to dry up and blow away. That fried chicken you made is wonderful, and if I have to, I'll feed you myself."

THE NEXT EVENING when Howard got home, he found Eva on her hands and knees at the small opening that led to the crawl space under the house, brandishing a flashlight into the darkness.

"What in the name of heaven are you doing?"

She jumped, turning to face him. "Trying to find the kittens. Jezebel moved them from the shed."

"Don't worry about them. Mother cats move them all the time."

"Jezebel is dead."

"What!"

"Pru Burns left a note on the door and said a car ran over the cat this afternoon. I buried her before I went to the Sloans, but I didn't have time to look for the kittens. I know they're under the house, because I can hear them crying. They'll die if we don't bring them in and hand-feed them."

"Neither of us has time to mother a bunch of cats," Howard said in exasperation.

She glanced up at him with a look that seemed to imply that he should have thought of that before he brought Jezebel home. But all she said was, "We'll have to make time."

Howard nodded, knowing she was right. He went inside and changed into his jeans. Then he crawled under the house and brought out the mewling, hungry kittens two by two.

Her weariness forgotten for the moment, Eva cuddled them and exclaimed over their various physical attributes, giving each a name and depositing them in a newspaper-lined box.

"They have their eyes open, Howard," she called to him.

"That's great," he said, wriggling out from under the house on his belly and elbows. He rose to his knees and handed her a pearl-gray kitten with sea-green eyes. "Here's the last one."

"Oh, isn't it adorable!" she cried as the kitten's pink tongue rasped against her finger.

Howard brushed the powdery dust from his clothes. "Adorable," he agreed in a less-than-enthusiastic voice. "Where are we going to keep them?"

Smiling for the first time in hours—or maybe days—Eva rubbed her nose against the gray kitten's. "In the kitchen."

"Rags will love that."

Eva looked up in surprise. "Rags is only a dog, Howard. He doesn't control our household."

"You know how jealous he is," Howard said, leaning over her shoulder to get a better look at the kitten.

"He'll have to adjust," Eva said with a shrug. The scent of something light and flowery drifted up to his nose. She turned and pinned him with a challenging look. "And while we're on the subject, might I remind you that you're the one who keeps bringing home all the strays."

Howard shifted from one loafer-shod foot to the other. "You're right," he said with a nod. "Rags will adjust. We'll all adjust. How are we going to feed them?"

"With an eyedropper, I guess."

He rolled his eyes. "Wonderful. That shouldn't take out four or five hours a day."

Eva laughed. Howard sobered.

"What?" she said, looking uncomfortable suddenly.

"I haven't heard you laugh in a long time," he said. "It's a shame. I wish you were—" he shrugged "—happier."

It was Eva's turn to feel uncomfortable. "I'm happy enough, Howard. I'm just pregnant and tired."

He regarded her solemnly for a moment, and then, to his surprise, she reached out and brushed at his cheek with her fingertips.

"Dirt," she explained.

Howard caught her wrist in a gentle grip. The eyes that probed hers were serious. "Promise me you'll take it easier."

"I'll try," she replied in a husky voice.

He pressed a kiss to the pulse that beat in the deli
cate blue vein of her wrist and let her go. Startled b
the intimacy of the gesture, she sucked in a shar
breath. Their eyes met for long moments, hers fille
with confusion, Howard's full of the concern he fel
for her. He wanted to do more, wanted to take her i
his arms and make her listen to reason, but he'd fig
ured out that there was no forcing his bride into any
thing. He had to give her time and space enough t
figure things out for herself. With a soft brush of hi
thumb against her wrist, he let her go.

A WEEK LATER, Eva let herself in the front door
turned on the fan and plopped down right in front o
it. She'd gone as far as she could go. She was used u
and burned out. Dead-dog tired. Down for the count
as Howard often said.

If possible, the early August days were hotter an
more miserable than July. Five more cases of poli
had been recorded in Claro county, and the sheriff ha
shot two rabid dogs as well as a skunk. There were th
usual births, deaths and illnesses that required visits
food and sympathy. There were church services thre
times weekly—thank God ladies' class was out for th
summer—not to mention visits to the shut-ins and th
backsliders.

Being the perfect minister's wife involved a lot mor
than she'd ever imagined, but she knew that eve
though Howard cautioned her about overwork, he wa
proud of her. For the most part, she could see littl

:hange in the way people treated her, but she imag-
ned she could see a lessening in the animosity di-
ected at him. As tired as she was, the knowledge that
Howard was regaining his standing in the community
1elped ease her burden of guilt.

Arching her spine against the nagging backache that
1ad been her companion for the past two days, she
went into the kitchen. The baby must be tired, too, she
:hought, smoothing her palms over her distended ab-
lomen, which tightened with a sudden cramp. She
:ouldn't remember the last time she'd felt it move. She
was low-down, downright miserable. She couldn't
imagine getting any bigger than she was, though she
1ad six or seven more weeks to go before the baby was
due.

In the kitchen, she turned on another fan to circu-
late the stale air. She was taking a pitcher of tea from
the refrigerator when the phone rang. She shuffled
into the living room to answer it.

"Mrs. Blake?"

"Yes."

"This is Natalie Jordan."

The corners of Eva's mouth turned down. Natalie
Jordan was Prudence Burns's daughter. And the very
thought of Pru Burns was like taking a bite from a
green persimmon. The woman was unfriendly, ob-
noxious and an inveterate gossip. Like Pru and Al,
Natalie and her family were church members, but in-
consistent in their attendance. If Eva remembered

correctly, the young woman resembled her mother in both looks and actions.

"Is Reverend Blake there?" Natalie asked.

"I'm sorry, Natalie, but he hasn't come in yet. Did you try the building?"

"He isn't there either."

To Eva's surprise, the woman began to sob. Contrition filled Eva's heart. No matter what she and her mother might be, Natalie Jordan was a very upset woman.

"Is there something I can do?" The question came automatically.

"It's Gary—my son." She sobbed again. "He's only six, and he's took real sick this morning. Doc Purdy's afraid it could be polio. Jerry and I...well, we all wanted the reverend to come to the hospital and...and pray with us."

The image of a cute blond boy with a face full of freckles and a gap-toothed grin flashed into Eva's mind. Gary Jordan. Her heart twisted in empathetic pain.

"I'm so sorry," she said. "Howard is probably out visiting someone, but he gets home for dinner about five-thirty, and I'll be sure and tell him you called."

"Thank you," the woman said in a choked voice and hung up.

With a frown furrowing her brow, Eva took her tea into the bathroom and drew a cool bath. She stripped and sank into the soothing depths of the water, trying hard not to be upset by the stretch marks on her abdomen.

Vanity of vanities. All is vanity. The quotation that popped into her mind brought a lethargic smile. With so many real problems in the world—in Crystal Creek—concern over a few red streaks on her stomach seemed like the height of narcissism.

Eva washed her hair and shaved her legs with the razor Howard had bought for her after she'd borrowed his razor and he'd cut himself with blades she'd used. While she performed her ablutions, her mind replayed the terror in Natalie Jordan's voice and conjured pictures of Gary Jordan's impish smile. Eva was toweling her hair dry and trying to decide whether to have cold cuts or tuna sandwiches for supper when the phone rang again. It was Howard.

"Where are you?" Eva asked, rubbing absently at her stomach.

"Out near the McKinney ranch. I had to come see the Dobsons."

The Dobsons were a family—more of Howard's strays—that he had taken under his wing.

"Oh, I forgot."

"I wanted to let you know that it's going to be an hour or so before I get home. My fuel pump went out and Cal's trying to help me fix it."

"Oh, no!" she cried in dismay.

"What's wrong?"

When Eva told him about the call from Natalie Jordan, Howard gave a harsh sigh. "There's nothing

I can do. I'll drive straight to the hospital when I get the bomb running again. Don't worry about cooking anything for supper. I'll eat a bowl of Shredded Wheat when I get in. In the meantime, I want you to put your feet up and take it easy, okay?''

"Okay."

When Howard said goodbye, Eva recradled the black plastic receiver. She supposed she should call the hospital and relay the message of Howard's car problem to the Jordans. Picking up the receiver again, she was greeted with Polly Rafferty's nasally intoned "Operator."

"Hi, Polly. Connect me with the hospital, please."

"Sure thing, Mrs. Blake."

While Eva waited for the connection to go through, she thought of Natalie and her husband sitting by their child's side, possibly alone. Pru might be a witch in disguise, but she was Natalie's mother, and mothers could be a blessing in times of sickness. Eva knew too well what it was like to need, and not have, a mother's support. Unfortunately, the Burnses were out of town for the week, gone to visit relatives somewhere in Louisiana.

Without giving herself time to consider the wisdom of what she was doing, Eva slammed down the receiver and scribbled a note to let Howard know where she'd gone. In the bedroom, she pulled on a clean skirt and smock and combed her damp hair into a loose knot at her nape. There was no time to worry about makeup, she thought, recalling again the sound of

Natalie Jordan's panicky voice. Grabbing her purse, Eva headed for the front door. Maybe Natalie wouldn't mind if she came instead of Howard.

WHEN EVA STEPPED into the hospital room where Gary lay, the Jordans looked up in surprise. Natalie was a slight, nervous type; Jerry, who rose as Eva entered the room, was a big, hulking man with a shock of blond hair and a timid demeanor. Their eyes were red-rimmed from crying.

Jerry was the first to find his voice. "Mrs. Blake!"

Eva clutched her handbag to her breasts. "Howard called. He's stuck in the country with car problems. I knew your mother was out of town, and I thought...well, that maybe you might like some company."

Natalie didn't speak, but her face turned red.

"We appreciate your concern, ma'am, we truly do," Jerry said, speaking for his wife. He gestured toward the chair he'd just vacated. "Have a seat."

Eva took the chair Jerry offered. Gary, his face flushed with fever, lay still against the pristine whiteness of the sheets. Too still. He should have been up and running around and giving his parents fits. She looked from Natalie to Jerry.

"How is he?"

"Doc says it ain't polio," Jerry said. "It's scarlet fever. He thought it was polio at first 'cause Gary was complainin' about his muscles hurtin'."

Scarlet fever. Since the disease was highly infectious, Eva's first impulse was to leave. But the Jordans looked so tired, and she was already there, already exposed. Besides, she'd heard that children were more susceptible to the condition than adults.

"If you'd like to go and get something to eat, I'll be glad to sit with Gary," she offered.

Jerry looked at his wife, whose glance moved from Eva to Gary. She nodded sharply. "I could use something to drink." Jerry helped her up and she followed him from the room.

As the door swished shut behind them, Eva heard Natalie say, "I can't believe she had the gall to come."

"Well, I sure don't see any of your so-called friends offering to help."

Eva was too tired to care what they said about her. She leaned her head against the chair's high back and closed her eyes. She should pray. Howard would.

She sighed instead. Ever since Denny's death, she'd questioned whether God answered prayers—hers, anyway. So what was the use of wasting her time and his? She could just sit here in case Gary needed her, and try to will away the ache in her back.

The child in the bed thrashed, fighting the covers. Uttering soothing words, Eva stood, walked to the bed and held him until his movements stilled. She touched his forehead. He was burning up.

Frowning, Eva tried to remember what she knew about the disease that had invaded the child's body. She'd read an article that said penicillin helped. She

new that the danger was that if it wasn't treated, it
ould cause heart or kidney problems.

"Dear God, please let him be okay."

The words that fell softly from her lips came as
omething of a surprise. Had she just uttered a prayer?
Of course she had. There must be some part of her
hat believed God would hear her, especially since she
vas asking for a child, a precious little boy whose life
iad hardly begun, and not for herself.

Eva reached out and touched Gary's hand with a
oft caress. Such a small hand ... so helpless. ...

As she stood gazing down at him with tenderness
ind sorrow, Gary opened fever-bright eyes. "Mama,"
ie rasped, reaching his thin arms out to her. "Hold
ne."

The simple request brought tears to Eva's eyes. She
new that the fever had addled his thinking. He
hought she was Natalie. Knowing he wouldn't un-
lerstand that his mother was gone for a few minutes,
Eva perched on the edge of the bed and lifted him into
ier arms.

When Howard, the Jordans and Pru and Al Burns
walked through the doors a few moments later, they
found Gary cradled against the mound of Eva's stomach while she rocked him back and forth. Unaware
that she had an audience, she smoothed the hair from
his forehead with loving tenderness and brushed her
tears from his face while the comforting strains of
"Jesus Loves Me" fell from her trembling lips in a

pure sweet soprano that would have done the angel proud.

EVA WAS SO TIRED and so emotionally drained by the time Howard arrived that she made no objection when, after he'd said a prayer for Gary's improved health, he announced to the group that she needed to go home. The Burnses regarded her with a shuttered gaze; Jerry Jordan was profuse in his thanks. Natalie was quiet, contemplative.

Howard and Eva said their goodbyes and, as they started down the hallway, Howard draped his arm around her shoulders and drew her to his side, dropping a kiss to the top of her head.

"What am I going to do with you?" he asked in a gruff voice.

"Put me to bed, I hope," she said, leaning heavily against his hard body.

"I certainly intend to do that. I thought I told you to take it easy. Why on earth did you go to the hospital?"

"Natalie was so distraught. I knew Pru was out of town, and I thought that maybe she and Jerry needed someone just to—I don't know, just to be there with them."

Howard nodded. "You're a good person, Eva Blake."

The praise embarrassed her, and brought a resurgence of her guilt. "No, I'm not. Not really. You're a good person."

"Spoken like a dutiful wife," Howard said with a smile as he pushed through the front door of the hospital. "You wait here. I'll bring the car around."

Eva nodded. She just hoped she didn't fall asleep standing there.

Ten minutes later, Howard pulled into the driveway of their house.

Ten minutes after that, Eva was fast asleep in her solitary bed.

Three hours later, she awakened Howard with the unbelievable statement that she thought the baby was coming even though it was too early.

An hour later, Grover Purdy delivered the child she'd conceived with Denny Talbot. It was a perfectly formed, stillborn boy, who had the umbilical cord wrapped around his neck.

EVEN THOUGH more than forty years had passed, the sorrow in Eva's eyes was undeniable. "That baby wasn't planned or wanted, Maggie, but when I lost him, it was like someone ripped out my heart. Babies seldom come at optimum times in people's lives. You be glad about this baby you're expecting. Be glad you have a piece of Rio."

The story of her mother's loss made Maggie ashamed of her own lack of enthusiasm about having Rio's baby. She was about to say as much when she heard a light tapping on the doorframe and Wayne Jackson poked in his head.

The weary smile that crossed the sheriff's rugged
weather-beaten face allayed the flutter of fear that
scampered through Maggie. "Hi, Maggie," he said
as he strode into the room, carrying his hat in his hand
with typical Texas correctness.

"Hi, Wayne," Maggie said with a wan smile.
"How's Jessica?"

At the mention of the country and western singer/
songwriter who'd stolen Wayne's heart, his smile
deepened. "She's fine, thanks. Lorrie Morgan is
looking at one of her songs."

"That's great!" Maggie said, pleased for them.
"Tell her I wish her luck."

"I will." He took a chair next to Eva and put his hat
on it, crown down, in the acceptable cowboy fashion.
"How's Rio?"

"He's holding his own."

Wayne nodded. "I came because I wanted to tell
you what's going on with Rick."

Maggie looked at him, a question in her eyes.

"He's really shook up, Maggie. I like to have never
got him to open up and talk to me, but he finally did,
and..." Wayne rubbed at his furrowed forehead in
perplexity and pinned Maggie with a steady look. "He
says he didn't do it, and I have to tell you, I'm in-
clined to believe him."

Disbelief swept through Maggie—who else could it
have been?—but there was another, lesser emotion
pulsing through her. Relief. "I don't want to believe

it, but I saw him with the gun, Wayne, and I heard him
say he was sorry."

"I know. But his story makes sense, and it jibes with
what Jeremy told me."

"What *is* his story?"

"Rick said that he and Rio *did* have an argument
over Babydoll, just like Jeremy said, but Rick claims
they got things squared away. He said Rio found out
his dad had beaten him, and that when Rio drove him
home, he insisted on going in and having a talk with
Bull. They had a few words and Bull said he'd shoot
Rio if he ever came on his place again. Rick knows
Bull is crazy enough to try it, so Rio agreed to pick up
Rick on the road the next day. Did Rio mention any of
this to you when he got home?"

"No," Maggie said, her face growing hot at the
memory of the lovemaking that had driven conversation from their minds the night before. "Rio doesn't
usually bring his ranch problems into the house."

Wayne nodded in understanding. "Rick claims he
was out in the barn trying to stay out of Bull's way after Rio left. About dark, he saw Bull carrying his pis-
tol out to his pickup. When he drove off, Rick went
inside and asked Ada what was going on. She was
crying and told him Bull said he was going to kill Rio.
Rick panicked. He told Ada to call the Sheriff and Rio
to warn him. Then he got in his mom's car and followed Bull to your place. He said he tried to get to Bull
before he pulled the trigger, but he was just a few seconds too late. That's what he keeps apologizing for."

"Dear God!" Maggie said, her face ashen.

"Rick told me that Bull looked like he'd sobered up pretty good when he saw Rio lying there. When Rick grabbed the gun away from him, Bull didn't try to argue. He just took off."

"And you believe Rick?"

Wayne nodded again. "We found a few footprints in the grass—inconclusive in themselves—but the kicker is that Bull's truck and Ada's car were both out front of your house."

In the commotion, Maggie hadn't noticed.

"Ada confirms Rick's story," Wayne continued. "She said that at first she didn't believe Bull would really do anything to Rio, so she didn't call. But then she realized that Bull might do something to Rick, so she called the office and your place. She said no one answered."

Maggie thought about the phone call that had come while she and Rio were in the bathtub. "There was a call, but they...hung up before we got it. It might have been Ada."

"What happened next?"

Maggie related what she could remember about the few minutes after she'd heard the gunshot.

"That pretty much jells with Rick's and Jeremy's statement," Wayne said.

"What about Bull?"

"No one knows where he is, but the fact that he seems to have fallen off the face of the earth says a lot about his part in all this. We've got an APB out on him through local and state peace officers. We'll find him, and when we do, we'll get a confession out of him."

Wayne reached for his Stetson and rose. "I'd like for you to come down to the station and give Peggy your statement whenever it's convenient, Maggie."

"I will."

He held out his hand and shook Maggie's firmly. "We'll be thinking about Rio."

"Thanks."

"What do you think?" Maggie asked her mother after the sheriff left.

"It makes sense. Rick doesn't seem like the kind of kid to shoot someone . . . or even a dog."

"I know. He claims he's innocent of that, too. He was there, and he didn't try to stop the other boys, but he swears he didn't do it."

Eva pursed her lips in a familiar gesture of thoughtfulness. "Considering his vehemence on both counts and the information Sheriff Jackson has turned up, maybe we should give Rick the benefit of the doubt."

"You don't know how much I'd like to."

"Oh, I think I do," Eva said with a smile. She reached out and took one of Maggie's hands in hers. "See? The good things you and Rio did made an impression on him. He'll come through this a stronger young man."

Maggie looked unconvinced. "Maybe. But why do Rio and I have to suffer so Rick can be stronger?"

CHAPTER NINE

August 1951

"THINGS LIKE THIS just happen," Grover Purdy said to Howard. His weathered face reflected the collected sorrow of a hundred such tragedies as Eva's dead baby. "No one knows how or why."

"My mother said it was probably from stretching her arms up over her head."

"Listen to me carefully, Howard," the physician said, his pale blue eyes stern and unyielding. "No one knows why, and it's futile to second-guess or to try and lay the blame on anyone's doorstep. I know it's traumatic, and it tears you up inside, but you're both young and healthy. You can have a dozen babies together. From past experience, I'd say the sooner the better."

Howard didn't respond, and Grover Purdy took the silence for thoughtfulness.

"The important thing is that physically, Eva is doing fine, but I should warn you that emotionally she's got some tough times ahead of her."

"I know. What can I do to help?"

"Do what you do best, son," Grover said with an exhausted smile. "Pray."

HOWARD PUSHED the mower across the back lawn. The blades he'd just sharpened whirred round and round, making short work of the sere grass. The lawn didn't really need mowing, but he needed something to occupy the long hours of the evening.

Summer was almost spent. The dog days of August were drawing to an end, and despite his usual optimism, he couldn't shake the premonition that another end was coming....

Even though Grover Purdy maintained that the loss of the baby was no one's fault, Howard blamed himself for allowing Eva to do too much in the community.

Telling himself that he'd cautioned her about overwork and reminding himself that she'd begged him to let her do it didn't assuage his guilt. He should have insisted that she slow down. After all, it was his duty to take care of her.

The only good thing to come from Eva's losing the baby was that the incident had brought Sally and Pete Carmichael to their senses. When Howard called and told them the news about the baby, Pete broke down and cried.

The Carmichaels had shown up at the hospital, their other two girls with them. Through tears of contrition, they'd expressed their regret to Howard for the way they'd treated Eva, but claimed that, after behaving so badly, they weren't sure Eva would forgive them. Howard suggested that the only way they would know was to ask.

Eva had listened to her parents' confession of self-ishness and wrongdoing and cried more of those heartrending sobs that tore at Howard's heart. She had embraced them, told them it was all right, but in spite of their daily visits, she had continued her downward spiral into a quiet, uncommunicative mel-ancholy. Howard found himself wishing someone could stimulate her emotions enough to make her cry. The tears he'd found so unsettling were far easier to cope with than her withdrawal.

As he strode past the back porch, the lawn mower whirring, he cast a glance at his beautiful, ethereal-looking bride, who was shelling beans with an au-tomatism that was frightening. The look on her too-thin face was absent, vacant. Her depression was rob-bing her of every spark of life. She was wasting away before his very eyes.

He wondered what was going on behind her bland facade. He wondered if her mind was as blank as her countenance. And he wondered, with a sharp and shameful jab of jealousy, if her thoughts were filled with Denny Talbot and his baby.

Guilt for his uncharitable thoughts swept through him. In one way or another, that emotion was a ma-jor player in his and Eva's lives. Somehow, during the course of their brief marriage, she had gotten past blaming God for the sorrows in her life. Howard would have considered this a step in the right direc-tion if she hadn't proceeded to transfer the blame to herself.

She was now convinced that the tragedies in her life were her fault. She had done wrong, and nothing she did could make up for her transgressions. She embraced the notion that God considered the taking of Denny and their baby as a just punishment.

Howard had counseled her for hours, trying his best to reassure her that God didn't operate that way, doing all he could to convince her that no one could know the plan an omniscient deity had for their lives. "'All things work together for good to those who love God,'" he reminded her.

He never let on that, at the moment, he was having a hard time believing what he said himself. In fact, he wasn't sure when his own faith had been at such a low ebb.

He had asked himself a hundred times what possible reason God could have for taking the two most important people in Eva's life, and how losing her baby son could translate into a good thing.

His blasphemous thoughts always left him with a soul-deep guilt. What kind of minister was he to entertain such ungodly thinking? How could he be an example to the congregation when he was so weak?

Since his marriage, he'd seen the worst come out in the people he was expected to lead. The majority of his flock were unforgiving and stiff-necked. Though Eva had worked as hard as—if not harder than—anyone in the congregation the past couple of months, only a handful of members had come to visit her when she lost the baby, a fact that angered Howard as much as it saddened him.

He wheeled the mower into the toolshed and wiped his perspiring face on his handkerchief. For the past three weeks, he had entertained the possibility that the congregation's actions and attitudes might be a reflection of his own flaws and weaknesses. How could they get to heaven with a defective compass to guide them?

No less than a hundred times over the past few days, he had contemplated resigning. He honestly didn't know what was stopping him.

He cast another look at Eva, and his heart throbbed with a painful ache. The prospect that she might want to end their marriage now that she no longer needed a husband caused him even more sleepless nights than his distress over his faltering leadership. His self-absorption over the worldly concerns added to his growing burden of shame, but he couldn't seem to help himself. What would he do if she left him? And, dear, sweet God, he loved her so much, how could he ever let her go?

SHE COULDN'T GO ON this way any longer, Eva thought, letting the cold tea trickle down her aching throat. It wasn't fair to Howard. Ever since the baby died, he'd lost his smile, the spring in his step, his optimistic outlook. She knew he was blaming himself for what had happened; he'd said as much on more than one occasion.

In his darkest mood, his angriest moments, she'd heard him berating not only himself but the people of Crystal Creek—especially the church members who continued to treat her like a pariah. She knew that Howard was questioning his beliefs and his impact on the community...and all because of her. The idea that he'd done anything wrong was ridiculous. All he'd ever done was try to help her, and all she'd done in return was bring him misery and trouble.

He didn't blame her, of course. Howard Blake was too kind, too noble, to place the blame on anyone but himself. She had learned that her husband was that rare creature—a gentleman. A gentle man. A man whose strength came from his intelligence and sensitivity as much as it did his from physical endowments. A man who was generous with his time, his money, his belief. A man too good for the likes of her. And since she couldn't stand seeing him miserable any longer, there was nothing to do but leave before the situation worsened.

When she had awakened the morning after losing the baby and seen him kneeling beside her bed, his head bowed in prayer, she'd realized that she loved him. The knowledge came to her on the silence of an angel's wings, filling her with a great joy and a greater sorrow.

Howard hadn't spoken of his love for her since the day in Dallas he had asked her to marry him. Eva imagined her negative attitudes and worldly ways had killed whatever feelings he might have had for her, a punishment she accepted without question. The truth was, she didn't deserve Howard's generosity or his goodness, and she didn't want to be responsible for any more of his unhappiness.

She could go to her mother's. The thought of her reunion with her parents brought a feeling of thankfulness to her heart. All it had taken was the sight of their tears and the feel of their arms around her to make her realize just how strong the ties of blood were. All it had taken was their faltering apology to underscore the biblical truism that love did indeed cover a multitude of sins.

Looking back, Eva could see that she had been headstrong and impatient, determined to do what she wanted whether her parents liked it or not ... whether they worried or not. Now, with the lessons life had taught her resting heavily on her shoulders, it was clear that the blame for their estrangement was as much her fault as theirs.

It had been comforting to talk to her mother about the loss of the baby. Sally had pooh-poohed Eva's notions about her sins invoking God's wrath and, with her usual philosophical attitude, said that it was far more likely that stretching up to hang clothes on the line or getting down on her hands and knees to scrub floors had caused the cord to wrap around the baby's neck.

Eva had given her mother's idea a lot of thought—and even though she wasn't wholly convinced, Sally's pragmatic attitude helped ease the pain that gnawed at her heart.

Her worries over Howard were just as excruciating, but she couldn't share them with her mother without telling about Denny. Eva knew she wasn't up to that. Besides, she'd promised Howard she would never tell, and making him happy was her newest priority.

"I'M GOING to my mother's tomorrow," Eva said at supper that evening. Too tired to eat, she massaged the tight, aching muscles in the back of her neck.

Howard smiled his beautiful smile and her heart contracted in pain.

"That's great. I'm glad you finally feel like getting out."

Eva shook her head, even though the slight movement was painful. "I'm not going to visit, Howard. I'm . . . leaving."

Howard's smile faded. He laid his fork onto his plate. "Leaving?"

You can have back your life, Howard. And your faith. You won't have to put up with me and my contrariness anymore. "Under the circumstances, I think it's the best thing for both of us."

"Now that there isn't a baby, you mean?"

She raised her chin a millimeter. "Yes."

"What if I asked you to stay?"

Eva couldn't hide her surprise, but then she realized that he hadn't said he *wanted* her to stay. "I can't."

He exhaled a harsh sigh, tossed his napkin to the table, stood. Plunging his hands into his pockets, he strode the length of the kitchen and back, stopping beside her chair.

"I can't say that I blame you. Our marriage hasn't been a bed of roses."

She didn't answer. It hadn't been easy, but it was as much her fault as his.

"The people in town haven't made you feel very welcome, have they?"

"My decision has nothing to do with the town's treatment of me, Howard." *But I can't stand the way they're treating you. Talking about you behind your back and then expecting you to give and give and give....* "I thought it might be good for you to have your old life back."

"I was just getting used to this one," he said with a half smile that held not one smidgen of humor.

Was she imagining the hint of despair in his voice? *Tell me you love me, Howard. Beg me to stay.*

But he didn't. He just stood there looking at her with those impenetrable blue eyes, which was just as well, because even if he told her he loved her, even if he begged her to stay, she would have to find the courage to say no... for his sake.

"What will you do?"

She shrugged. "I'm not sure. Get a job, I guess." She, too, tried to smile and failed. "Maybe I'll take some college classes and make my parents proud of me."

"They're already proud of you," he told her. "So am I."

Tears constricted her throat. "Thank you."

"Will you . . . file for an annulment?"

The lump in her throat doubled in size. "Yes," she croaked.

"Do me a favor?"

Anything. She nodded.

"Don't rush it. Give yourself some time to heal. Maybe . . . maybe when you get a new perspective on things, you'll change your mind."

In spite of her resolution, her heart gave a leap. She shook her head again.

"We took a vow before God and man, Evie . . . 'till death us do part.' There are thousands of satisfying marriages based on mutual respect."

Eva's fragile dream of hearing Howard say he cared died a swift, merciful death. "Respect isn't enough for me." *I want your love. Your passion. Your heart.* "It shouldn't be enough for you, either, Howard. You deserve the best—a wife who is worthy of you, someone the town will look up to and respect as much as they do you."

"I'd rather have a wife who loved me," he told her. "Failing that, I'd rather have you."

EVA TOSSED CLOTHES into the yawning suitcase willy-nilly. The conversation from the night before echoed through her mind like a voice bouncing off some canyon wall. She should have known it wasn't love for her that prompted Howard's desire to keep their marriage intact. It was his innate need to do the right thing.

As much as she'd come to love him, as tempting as his offer was, she wouldn't settle for second best. She couldn't. She wanted everything he was and all he had to give. Since she couldn't have that, she'd rather have her few, but precious, memories.

She looked at the contents of the luggage. She should have packed more of her clothes—not that she'd probably wear any of them—but she'd been feeling feverish and achy all over since the evening before. Besides, now that she'd broken the news to Howard, she wanted to put as much distance between her and the mess she'd made of his life as fast as possible.

She slammed the suitcase shut and grabbed the handle. She was so weak, it was all she could do to lift the suitcase to the floor. By the time she got to the living room, her arms were trembling with fatigue. She set the piece of luggage beside the carryall that held the mewling gray kitten. It was the only thing she was taking to remind her of her time with Howard.

She glanced around the silent living room with a heavy heart. Leaving while he was at the church building was taking the coward's way out, but after last night, she couldn't bear saying goodbye face-to-face.

She had left a casserole in the oven and a note on the kitchen counter, telling him that she appreciated all he had done, urging him to take good care of himself, letting him know she'd fed Rags and the kittens and saying she would send her dad for the rest of her things.

As she bent over to pick up her suitcase and the kitten, sharp pains pricked the calves of her legs, and a wave of dizziness swept over her. She leaned a hand against the door frame to steady herself, straightening slowly.

Her image—the circles under her eyes, the hollows in her flushed cheeks, her limp hair—wavered before her in the mirror over the sofa. Her lips twisted in a bittersweet smile. No wonder Howard hadn't made any undying confessions of love. Taking a deep breath, she stepped through the door and started toward her car.

In defiance of the approaching autumn, the early September sunshine beat down with all the potency of its August predecessor. The few short yards to the car seemed the length of a football field as Eva struggled to put one foot in front of the other. Halfway there, she set down the suitcase and wiped a shaky hand down her hot face.

Sunlight bounced off the chrome of the car, blinding her and sending a shaft of agony through her eyes. Her stomach clenched in sudden nausea. The ground whirled, dipped and dropped out from under her. Eva's legs gave way and, with a startled cry, she fell into the yawning black void that waited to swallow her up.

PRU BURNS, who was pulling nut grass from her dahlias, looked out from under the wide brim of her poke bonnet. "What in the Sam Hill is that woman doing now?" she muttered to herself as she watched Eva's struggle with her belongings. But the suitcase and cat carryall spoke for themselves. Eva Blake was leaving her husband.

Pru squinted against the brightness of the sunshine and wondered what had brought this on. She'd heard—from Sara and Ginny and half the town—that Eva was depressed over the loss of her child, and understandably so. Truth to tell, the reverend didn't look too swell these days, either. Pru couldn't imagine them splitting up, though. Hard times were what made a marriage stronger.

The thought had no more than crossed her mind when she saw Eva crumple to the ground. For a moment, Pru was too shocked to do anything but sit back on her heels with her mouth hanging open.

She looked up and down the street, to see if anyone else had witnessed Eva's collapse. It was almost noon, and only the most stouthearted braved the heat . . . or, as Al said, the most stupid. Pru chewed the inside of her lip and wondered what she should do. Call the ambulance? Call the church? Go help? Or wait for someone else to find her?

Shame, fierce and painful, squeezed her hardened heart. As it had often the past month, a picture of Eva Blake holding Gary in a loving embrace filled Pru's mind. Eva, holding a child she hardly knew, singing

"Jesus Loves Me" while she cried. At that moment, Pru had known that whatever else the minister's wife was, she was a tenderhearted, caring soul.

Pru pushed herself to her feet. She had to do something. She couldn't just let the woman lie there and bake in the sun. Drawing off her gardening gloves, she raced across the street and knelt by Eva's prostrate body. She lay on her side, one leg bent back under her at an awkward angle. Uncertain what to do, Pru took Eva's limp wrist and felt for a pulse. It was weak and rapid. Pru looked up and down the street again, and wished Al were there. He was always so calm in a crisis.

Certain that time was of the essence, she got to her feet and hurried back across the street and into the relative coolness of her darkened house. She picked up the telephone receiver with shaking hands.

"Operator."

"Get me the Baptist Church, Polly. And hurry."

"What's the matter, Pru?" Polly Rafferty asked.

"Eva Blake just fainted in her front yard, and I don't have time to jaw with you. Now get me the church and then call the hospital and have them send out an ambulance."

"My, aren't we the concerned neighbor?" Polly said with syrupy sarcasm. "When did you and the reverend's wife become such good friends?"

"Just do your job." Pru snapped. "I've got to get over there and see about her."

"Okeydoke."

Pru listened to the ringing at the other end of the line. "Baptist Church," the secretary singsonged.

"Mabel, this is Prudence Burns. I need to speak with Reverend Blake. It's an emergency."

"Howard is counseling someone right now, Pru. Can I help you?"

"Go tell him that his wife just collapsed in the front yard. You call for the ambulance—pronto. I'm fixin' to go over and see what I can do for her until they get here. I thought he'd want to know."

Without waiting for the secretary's response, Pru hung up and clutched her head, trying to think of what she should do next. Should she try to move Eva into the shade? What would she need? A wet washcloth? Smelling salts? An umbrella to keep the sun out of Eva's face?

Going as fast as her skinny legs would carry her, Pru set about gathering the items she thought she'd need and raced back across the street.

Kneeling, she opened the umbrella and set it so it would shield Eva's face from the blistering sun. Then she straightened Eva's leg. Finally, she eased the younger woman onto her back and wiped at her flushed face with the cool washcloth.

"Mrs. Blake. It's Pru Burns. Come now, dear, wake up. The reverend will be here any minute." When there was no response from Eva, Pru's heart fluttered in apprehension. She lifted Eva's head and rested it on her bent knees. She was just taking the bottle of ammonia from her pocket when she heard the sound of a siren in the distance. Thank God! Help was on the way.

Howard Blake's car pulled into the driveway just seconds ahead of the ambulance. Pru noticed that his face was almost as white as his shirt. Without any thought for his nicely pressed slacks, he dropped to his knees in the grass and eased Eva from Pru's lap into his arms.

"Evie!" he cried, his voice thick with emotion. "Evie, sweetheart, it's Howard. C'mon, love, open your eyes."

"Excuse me, Reverend," one of the ambulance workers said, "but we need to get her on the stretcher."

Howard nodded and moved out of the medical personnel's way. He stuffed his hands into his pockets, as if, Pru thought, doing so was the only way he could keep from holding on to her. His eyes were bleak as he watched them carry her to the ambulance.

Pru knew pain when she saw it, and Howard Blake was hurting as much as anyone she'd ever seen. He was a good man, she thought, surprised to realize that she was just now seeing it.

All the ugly things she'd said about Eva and Howard Blake surfaced on a wave of guilt, a sentiment she hadn't experienced in years. She'd slept with Al before they got married. The only difference was that she hadn't got caught, so who'd set her up to be judge and jury?

Again, that giant fist clutched her heart. Her mama used to say that everyone was allowed at least one mistake in this old life. And if Eva Carmichael was Howard's, that was the way it was. Any fool could see he was nuts about the woman, and in the end, that was the important thing.

"Reverend!" she called, as Howard started to climb into the back of the vehicle.

"Pru!" He looked at her as if he just noticed her presence, as indeed he probably had. "Thanks for calling and . . . everything."

"Is there anything else I can do?"

"Pray."

Pru swallowed. And nodded. She'd be glad to. If she hadn't forgotten how.

"I'M NINETY-NINE PERCENT sure it's polio, Howard," Grover Purdy said.

"Dear God, no!" Howard cried, spinning away on his heel and clutching his head as Prudence Burns had the day before.

"The lab in Austin is running some tests. We'll know what type it is shortly."

"What can you give her to make her well?"

"There is no known drug that can kill the virus or stop its spread. All we can do is watch the fever and see to it that she gets a lot of rest. It's commonly held that fatigue makes it worse."

Though Eva had gotten plenty of rest since losing the baby, she wasn't in the peak of good health.

"She's having some trouble breathing, and we don't have an iron lung. I'm moving her to Austin."

Howard turned and looked at the doctor who'd brought a goodly portion of Crystal Creek into the world. Torment raged in his blue eyes. "Do what you have to do," he told the doctor in a quaking voice, "but please don't let her die."

THERE WAS GOOD NEWS and bad news in Austin. Eva's tests showed that she had contracted spinal paralytic poliomyelitis, the most common type.

It was some consolation to Howard to learn that most victims of the crippling disease were confined to the iron lung only temporarily. Length of stay depended on just how well the patient fought off the disease and how much damage it did to the lungs. He didn't know whether to rejoice or cry when he learned that, depending on the severity of the paralysis, most people were able to resume their normal activities.

Paralysis. The very idea of Eva being paralyzed sent fear into the deepest corners of Howard's being. It was impossible to imagine her confined to bed, or a wheelchair, or even braces, but if God let her live, Howard would do his best to make her happy, however the disease left her.

When he expressed those fears to doctor in Austin, the physician said that the best thing to do was to start fighting the paralysis the instant the fever subsided and Eva was able to leave the iron lung.

"How?" Howard asked.

"Well, first," the doctor said, "you should use moist, hot bandages to help ease the pain of the muscle spasms. You can move her limbs so that the muscles don't tighten up and cause deformities. Go easy at first, but later, when you're building strength and start retraining the muscles, you can step up the exercises."

"How long will it take?" Howard asked, a glimmer of hope in his eyes.

"As long as it takes."

Howard took encouragement from the doctors' optimism that the fever was manageable, and, determined to stay by her side until she recovered, he got a room at the YMCA. It would be a place to stash his things and clean up, which was the only thing he would leave her side to do. Thaddeus consented to take over the pulpit until Eva was out of the woods.

Armed with hope and his prayers, Howard took his vigil beside the iron lung, where Eva lay sleeping the deep sleep of the very ill. For the first time in his life, he began to understand what the Bible meant when it spoke of praying without ceasing.

He not only prayed, he begged. Pleaded. Bargained. Even though he'd been taught from boyhood that there was no haggling with God, Howard did his best to negotiate a deal. If the Almighty would just let Eva live—not just live, but be able to walk and have a happy, useful life, Howard would give her the freedom she wanted so badly. He would devote his life to doing the best for the congregation.

God wasn't the only one he pleaded with. He begged Eva to fight the illness that was robbing her of her strength and vitality. He tried to get through to her any way he could—from reading the Bible, to talking to her about everything he could think of while he smoothed her bright hair away from her pale face. By telling her stories from his childhood. Jokes. As far as he was able to discern, she didn't hear a word he said.

When he had been at her side for more than thirty hours, Eva opened her fever-glazed eyes for the first time. Howard thought it was the most beautiful sight he'd ever seen. A prayer of thanksgiving darted through his mind.

"Hi," he said with a weary but happy smile.

"I'm sick, Howard," she said, as if he didn't know.

Tears prickled behind his eyelids. "I know."

"What's wrong with me?"

He swallowed thickly. "Polio."

She just nodded, as if she'd expected the news to be bad. "I'm tired of fighting God, Howard. I'm so tired."

"I know, sweetheart. I know."

"Will you do something for me?"

"Anything."

"Go home and let me die."

The tears Howard had fought so hard to control slipped in tortured silence down his cheeks. He clenched his teeth until his jaw knotted. "Never!"

"Please," she said, her own tears running down her temples. "Please..."

"Never," he said again, a zealous light burning in his eyes. "Not as long as there's breath in me...."

HOWARD'S VOICE, gruff with the tears of a painful memory, trailed away in the silence of the waiting room. At Eva's request, he'd taken up the story of their past while she went home to rest for a few hours.

"I had no idea," Maggie said, her own voice hushed. "I knew Mama had polio when she was young, but I never knew it was so bad. She always made light of her limp."

"That's your mother," Howard said. "She's not a complainer."

Maggie blew out a deep breath. Her troubled eyes bored into her father's. "I can't believe the two of you went through all this and everything turned out so well."

"It's been a great forty-three years," Howard agreed, "but the worst was yet to come."

Maggie's mouth fell open. "How could things have gotten any worse?"

"Your mother left me anyway," Howard said, rising. "I'm going down to the cafeteria. I saw some coconut pie that looked mighty tasty."

"Daddy!" Maggie said, grabbing his arm. "You can't say something like that and just leave."

"Watch me," he said, his blue eyes twinkling behind his glasses. He nodded toward the door. Cal and Serena McKinney stood there, as if they were afraid of intruding. "Looks like you have company." He winked. "I'll fill you in when I get back."

He held out his hand to Cal and hugged Serena.

"I'm glad you two came," he said. "Margaret will have someone to keep her company while I grab a bite to eat."

"Go right ahead, sir," Cal said. "We'll be glad to stay."

Howard nodded and left the room.

Cal and Serena hugged Maggie tightly. "I'm sorry I couldn't be here sooner," Cal said, his usually teasing eyes solemn with regret.

"It's okay. I know you'd have been here if you could."

"How is he?"

"Worse at the moment." Maggie explained as best as she could about the coma.

"He'll pull through," Cal said, a fierce determination etched into his features. "He's too damned ornery to die. Besides, the son of a buck owes me money."

Cal's comment brought a smile to Maggie's lips, just as he hoped.

"I've heard something that'll make you happy," he said.

"What's that?"

"I hadn't eaten all day, so Serena and I grabbed a bite of supper at the Longhorn before we came over. Wayne Jackson was there. He said the state troopers in Tarrant County picked up Bull Farmer a couple of hours ago.''

Maggie's relief was so profound she felt light-headed. "Thank God! Did he confess?"

"Wayne said Bull was so shook up over the whole thing that he was a blithering idiot. The last Wayne heard Bull was singin' like a tweety bird.''

BECAUSE SHE KNEW it was so important to him, Maggie let Cal take the next available time in ICU. Maybe a pithy comment from Rio's old rodeo buddy could jog him into coming round. Most likely, Maggie mused, Cal would just outright demand that Rio wake up.

At the moment, she was too disheartened to spend any more time with him, a comment she made to her father when he returned.

"That's not a very good attitude, Margaret," Howard told her. "I thought you'd come back to Crystal Creek with a new outlook on life."

"What do you mean?"

"I mean that I know you're tired, and I know you're discouraged, but I can't believe you're giving up so easily," Howard chastised her. "I thought Maggie Langley was a fighter."

"I'm like Mama. I'm tired of fighting God," she said, using the same phrase her mother had so many years before. "If it's his will that Rio dies—"

"You don't fight God," Howard said. "You have faith, and you bow to his superior wisdom."

"Faith." She shook her head. "You sound like Mama. But it's hard to have faith when the person you love more than anything in the world is lying near death's door."

Howard's steady blue gaze locked with hers. "Believe me, sweetheart, I know."

Her father's simple statement made Maggie feel small, mean-spirited . . . selfish. Hadn't she just heard the tribulations her parents had suffered? If anyone had any idea of what she was going through, they did, yet they'd both come through the crises in their lives stronger than ever.

"You don't fight God, Maggie," Howard said again. "You just have the faith of a mustard seed. I truly believe that so many times when our prayers aren't answered, it's because we don't ask in the right way, and we don't really believe we'll get what we want."

Maggie thought about that for a moment, and knew her father was right. How many times had she prayed for something, even though her heart told her that what she wanted was an impossibility? "Okay," she said reluctantly. "I'll admit to that."

"Good," Howard said with a smile. He patted the cushion beside him. "Sit down, sweetheart, and I'll tell you about your mother leaving me. Then I want you to get in there and give Rio the courage to fight this thing."

CHAPTER TEN

October 1951

WHEN EVA HAD BEEN home from the hospital for a couple of weeks, she came to the conclusion that Howard was going to kill her and himself. His dedication to getting her up and on her feet was second only to his dedication to doing his best for his congregation.

While she was in the hospital, he'd spent hours sitting at her side, talking, praying, begging her to get better. Though the pain was excruciating, and the will to do anything but sink into blessed oblivion was almost zero, it seemed churlish not to respond.

The image of his face when she'd begged him to let her die—haggard, weary, with tears running down his cheeks—would stay with her for as long as she lived. It was only for Howard that she'd fought her way up through the thick quagmire of unconsciousness and forced herself to swallow the food he put in her mouth.

Since that day, his eyes had gleamed with a fanatical light as he imposed the very strength of his considerable will on her. Once the fever abated, he'd spent days wrapping her limbs in hot, wet towels, flexing

and moving her arms and legs so that they wouldn't
grow stiff and atrophy. As soon as she was able to
come home, he had stepped up her workout, adding
strength-building exercises to her daily regimen, sup-
porting her as she tried to put one foot in front of the
other, cajoling her time and again into doing "just one
more."

It was all she could do sometimes not to cry out in
pain when the muscle spasms in her limbs became
more than she thought she could bear. It was even
harder not to give in to tears as she witnessed the strain
her illness was putting on Howard. Worry and weight
loss had added five years to his looks. They were both
exhausted to the point of collapse, but he kept pushing them both.

Eva had taken about all she could. Of the exercises. Of the pain. Of being the cause of Howard's
misery. The added responsibility and burden of her
illness only added to the guilt she felt for the problems she'd caused Howard from the outset of their
marriage.

She knew he was devoted to making her well and
making a go of their marriage because he felt that was
the right, the Christian thing to do, but his determination only added to Eva's growing depression and
remorse. She begged him daily to take her to her
mother's and forget she existed. She didn't want
Howard's allegiance to be to their marriage promises;
she wanted it to be to her.

The disturbing thoughts chased themselves through her mind with a relentlessness matched only by Howard's tenacity. But when she happened to catch a glimpse of herself in the mirror, she realized just how futile her wishes and dreams were.

How could Howard love her now? The polio had taken its toll on her looks as well as her arms and legs, which were rail-thin and kitten-weak. Her figure had lost its curvy voluptuousness. There was no spark of life in her eyes, no healthy shine to her hair.

The ugly orthopedic shoes and the heavy braces on her legs were hardly the height of fashion. The possibility that she might never be able to walk without them, that she might never be pretty and graceful and *independent* again was like a thorn festering deep inside her soul. The last thing she wanted was to be an albatross around Howard's neck. He deserved better. She had to try harder to make him let her go....

"COME ON, sweetheart," Howard said that afternoon, "just a few more steps. That's it. Come on. One more. Good. Another."

Eva stopped in her tracks, unable to pick up her foot one more time, even though Howard's arms supported the bulk of her weight.

"I can't." Two tears slid down her cheeks.

"I know you're tired," he said in a gentle tone, "but let's just go to the kitchen door and back."

"Dammit, I can't!" Eva cried, her voice trailing away on a sob. "I can't...."

Without another word, Howard swung her up into his arms and carried her back to the master bedroom, which had been equipped with all sorts of things to help her regain her strength and keep her occupied. A bar on a chain was suspended from the ceiling: he made her grab the bar and pull herself up several times a day to strengthen her arms. Two-pound dumbbells sat on the bedside table next to a small radio, a stack of books and a pitcher of water.

It was a sickroom, not a bedroom, Eva thought as Howard deposited her in the middle of the bed and began to unbuckle her braces.

"I'm sorry," he said, contrition lacing his voice. "I'm an insensitive slave driver. I don't mean to push so hard."

"Then stop," she said, falling back against the pillows and throwing her forearm over her face.

"But we're gaining progress. I can—"

"Please, Howard." Eva lowered her arm and looked at him with haunted eyes. "Please. I don't want to be beholden to you any more than I already am."

Howard's hands stilled. "What are you talking about? Beholden to me? This is what marriage is all about. You know—for richer for poorer, for better for worse, in sickness and health—"

"Till death us do part," she interrupted on a wave of anger and impatience. "I know. But you've done so much for me, I'll never be able to repay you."

"Repay me?" Howard's eyes registered his shock. "What do you mean?"

Unable to bear the look in his eyes, Eva plucked at the sheet with her fingertips. "It took me a long time to come to realize how much you sacrificed by marrying me," she told him. "You risked losing the job you'd wanted all your life. You've borne the brunt of gossip that was brought on by my behavior."

Howard stilled her hand by covering it with his. "I never thought of it as a risk or something to be borne, Evie," he said in a thoughtful voice. "I thought of marriage to you as an honor. Once you settled in, you've been the perfect minister's wife. Helpful, dedicated to doing good—"

"But it wasn't enough!" she cried, breaking in again.

"Enough for what?" he asked, his lack of understanding making him irritable.

"To change the way people felt about me. So I wouldn't be an embarrassment to you."

"Embarrassment! How could you ever think you were an embarrassment?"

"How could I not be?" she wailed. "Everyone in town thought that I was the original Eve incarnate. I'd offered you the forbidden fruit and you took a big bite. I didn't dress right, and I wore too much makeup. I was conspicuously the wrong wife for you."

"But you stopped all that."

"Yes, I did. But do you know why, Howard? I did it for you, so the people in the congregation would like me, so they *couldn't* say I wasn't a good wife for you."

Tears glistened in her eyes, and her shoulders lifted in a helpless shrug. "It doesn't matter, I guess, because it's obvious that no one appreciated anything I did. Not Ginny Sloan or Pru Burns or Natalie Jordan. None of them."

"Maybe no one appreciated it because you did it for the wrong reason," Howard suggested.

"What do you mean?"

"You did it to be seen of men. Don't you remember that our good works are to glorify God—not ourselves?"

He rubbed her thin fingers with his. "If you did all those things so that people would think better of you, if you weren't motivated by genuine love and concern for them, you did it all for nothing."

Eva looked at him for long, agonizing moments. There was desolation in her eyes and a quiver in her voice when she finally spoke. "I can't do this anymore, Howard. God knows I've tried. You've tried. This marriage won't work. Not now. Not ever. I'm not the right kind of woman for a man like you."

"Evie . . ."

"No!" she cried, jerking her hand from his. "Don't say any more. Just take me to my mother's."

Howard looked into her unflinching gaze for long moments. Then, without another word, he rose and began to pack her things.

A FEW "Amens" of total agreement sounded from the audience.

"In chapter 2 of First Peter, we're told to love the brotherhood." Howard waved his arm to indicate the entire audience. This was his first sermon since taking Eva to her parents' house and he had decided that the congregation was long overdue to hear about forgiveness and love. "The brotherhood. Our brothers and sisters. We're also commanded to love our neighbor. This is *not* a suggestion, brethren. It's a command."

More nods of agreement and looks of interest.

"But all too often, we let the devil convince us that judging our neighbors and gossiping about them is all right. Yet in Romans 13, the Bible says that love works no ill, and in Proverbs 3 it says that we're not to devise any evil against our neighbor."

Howard thought he saw a few uncomfortable souls glance away.

"Another commandment is to love our enemies, but how can we love our enemies when we can't even find it in our hearts to love our neighbors and our brothers?" he asked in a quiet voice that was all the more condemning for its softness.

More throat clearing and foot shuffling rose and fell throughout the assemblage.

"There are those who are too anxious to cast stones at another person when they need to be worried about getting the sin out of their own lives. The problem with this congregation is that it lacks love," he said. "First

Peter 4, verse 8 says, 'charity shall cover the multitude of sins....' "

For twenty more minutes, Howard extolled the virtues of love and harped on the consequences of judging others and not showing love and compassion to one's fellow man. There was not a person in the audience who didn't feel that the sermon had been preached directly at him.

For days, the sermon was the talk of Crystal Creek, shaming the congregation into taking a careful look at itself collectively and individually. Howard's tearful apology for his own shortcomings after the sermon endeared him to his flock. When he said that he and Eva had parted company because she didn't want to be a burden to him and asked for prayers for them both, his apparent love and devotion to his wife was the talk of the town—a true inspiration....

There were subtle changes in attitude that only the most unobservant could have missed. There was a sudden rash of calls to the Carmichael residence concerning Eva's welfare that trickled down to a steady, concerned stream. There were bouquets of garden flowers delivered almost daily. Casseroles and entire dinners were delivered to both residences just to "help out."

"Whatever the circumstances of their marriage, can't nobody deny that he loves her," Ginny said to Pru the Sunday afternoon of Howard's sermon.

"That's for sure," Ginny concurred.

The whole town seemed to be of the same mind ... everyone but Eva.

THE OCTOBER DAYS grew shorter, and autumn came to the Hill Country, bringing cool nights and glorious sunny days. Howard, who dabbled in wildlife water color painting when time permitted, was so miserable that not even the sightings of several white-tailed deer and two flocks of wild turkey were able to arouse more than minimal interest. His mind wasn't on painting. It was on Eva.

Eva's mind was on him, too.

Her mother said he called every day without fail, and even though Eva refused to talk to him, the calls always turned her thoughts to the time she'd been Howard's wife; there was little else to occupy her mind.

She thought about what Howard had said about her motivation for her good deeds. She spent hours poring over her Bible, reading the things God wanted his people to be known for. She came to the conclusion that Christianity was a serious thing. It was far more than a role to be played out for others. It was a way of life. A life of service.

Howard had been wrong about one thing, though. She had gained some good from the things she had done. Gary Jordan called her every day to see how she was doing, and Pru Burns had shown up a few days ago with an apple cake and an apology, tears in her eyes.

"I don't deserve your forgiveness," she said to an astonished Eva, "but I want you to know that I'm sorry for everything I've said about you and the reverend."

Taken aback by the apology, Eva could think of nothing to say except, "It's all right, Mrs. Burns."

"It's not all right," Pru objected, blowing her nose noisily into her hankie. "Once you say things, they're always out there to hurt other people, but I want you to know that I'll do my best to stop any gossip I hear from here on in."

In spite of herself, Eva was touched by the gesture. "Thank you."

"I'll never forget what you did for our Gary," Pru said between sniffles. "And you in labor and all. It was an act of pure unselfishness."

"Oh, no!" Eva denied, embarrassed by the praise. "I just—

"No!" Pru interrupted. "Don't make light of it. You were worn-out and in pain, but you were still there for Natalie and Jerry. I'll never forget that."

Eva could think of no ready reply. Looking back, she could say in all honesty that when she'd gone to the hospital to be with the Jordans, she'd been prompted by nothing but a desire to be there for them in case they needed her. Maybe that was why it had resulted in good.

Pru's thin lips quirked upward at the corners. "Do you know what little Gary told his mother and me?"

Eva shook her head.

"He said that when he woke up and saw you sittin
by his bed singin' 'Jesus Loves Me,' he thought yo
were an angel."

An angel. A lump came to Eva's throat. The child'
comparison was touching, but she was hardly a can
didate for the heavenly host.

"That's sweet," she said to Pru, "but I'm no an
gel, I assure you. Besides, if there's any thanking to b
done, it's I who should be thanking you for calling th
ambulance and watching over me until it arrived."

"Oh, pshaw!" Pru said, waving aside Eva's thank
with a bony hand. "It was nothing any neighbo
wouldn't do for another. I'm just glad I was outsid
and saw you, otherwise no tellin' how long you migh
have laid there in that hot sun."

The picture Pru's words brought to mind were un
settling at best. Eva held out her hand in a gesture o
friendship. Startled, Pru looked from Eva's hand int
her eyes. Then, slowly, she extended her own hand
The two women smiled at each other through a shee
of tears.

"If I can ever do anything else for you, you be sur
and let me know," Pru said. "And I mean it."

"I will."

EVA'S MOODS RANGED from unabashed self-pity t
self-righteous anger. From hating Howard to lovin
him. From feeling happiness and forgiveness for th
people who came to visit, their condolences and apo
ogies on their lips, to thinking that their misery wa

good enough for them . . . Until Ginny Sloan came calling.

Ginny was accompanied by her son, whom Eva had sat with for days. The boy had recovered from his bout of polio with nothing but a slight limp. As Ginny stumbled through an apology for all her bad thoughts and everything she'd said about the Blakes and their marriage, Eva was reminded of her attitude while she'd sat with Brian, Ginny's son.

Though she had felt genuinely sorry for him, she recalled her smug attitude and her determination to wring an apology from Ginny Sloan someday. Unlike the Jordans, the help she'd given to the Sloans hadn't been for the right reasons. Eva had wanted to make Ginny ashamed, to see her crawl. And now that she was, Eva wished with all her heart that she could take back all the terrible thoughts she'd harbored against Ginny Sloan.

Though she wasn't quite brave enough to spill it all, she did tell Ginny she was sorry, too, and later, when the Sloans had gone, she cried and begged God's forgiveness for her spiteful, arrogant attitude.

She wondered what Howard would think of her behavior and decided that his disappointment would be tempered with his usual loving forgiveness. Dear Lord, how she missed him!

She was feeling particularly sorry for herself one afternoon about ten days after she'd moved to her parents', when Emily McKinney came to call.

"You're looking better," Emily said.

"Sure," Eva said in a pensive voice.

"Feeling a little sorry for ourselves, are we?" Em ily rolled Eva's wheelchair out onto the back patic where the sun shone brightly. "What's the matter Missing Howard?"

"How did you know?" Eva asked with a shar glance.

"It's a natural assumption, since I know you'r crazy about the man."

"What makes you say that?"

Emily shrugged. Smiled. "Maybe I'm psychic." Sh poured Eva a glass of iced tea and handed it to he "This self-imposed exile of yours is ridiculous, yo know," she said with a thoughtful pursing of her lips "All you're doing is making both of you miserable."

"Both of us?"

"Yes, both of you." Emily's voice was firm. A cusatory. "Why on earth did you leave him, Eva? know you love him."

"That's why."

Emily's forehead puckered in a frown. "Do yo mind explaining? I must be missing something here."

Eliminating any reference to Denny, Eva reveale how she felt her marriage to Howard had affected hi standing in the community.

"I just couldn't stay any longer, Emily. I felt as if was just another good deed to Howard, another of hi strays to be looked after. Something he'd made commitment to and would take care of no matte what."

"You think you're just another of Howard's strays?" Emily asked with a disbelieving shake of her head. "Well, if you are, you're an ostrich who's been sticking her head in the sand. Surely you haven't been so blinded by guilt that you don't know how much Howard Blake loves you?"

The flicker of hope in Eva's heart was dashed by a dose of reality. "What makes you say that?"

"Because it's true. I've known Howard since he was a child. He may be a do-gooder, but he isn't a masochist, and he isn't stupid. He'd never tie himself to a woman he didn't love. Good Lord!" Emily went on. "Hasn't he proved how much he cares? He's stuck by you through thick and thin."

Though she was afraid to believe, Eva thought about Emily's theory for long moments.

"If I were you, I'd think seriously about packing my things and moving back home to the man I loved."

"I don't want to be a burden on him," Eva said in a harsh whisper.

"Then don't be."

"But how do I know if I'll ever walk or be self-sufficient again? How do I know I won't have to rely on him for everything for the rest of my life?"

"You *don't* know that. But even if you never get out of that wheelchair or walk without the help of those braces, it doesn't mean you have to be a burden. It doesn't mean you can't be a joy and a help to Howard—does it?"

EVA THOUGHT A LOT about what Emily had told her
the next few days. Comprehension came in slow degrees. Once again, she suffered under the burden of a
terrible shame. It was time she stopped being so selfish and started putting others ahead of herself, the way
Howard did.

Howard Blake was a man who lived what he taught.
There was no hypocrisy in him, no guile. His concern
for people wasn't acting. His concern for her wasn't
based on his need to do the right thing. It was based
on his love for her.

How could she not have known he still loved her?
Why had she assumed his feelings had changed just
because she hadn't heard him say the words? Hadn't
he told her how much he cared every day they'd spent
together—with everything he'd done from taking out
the trash to helping dust the furniture?

Even his occasional burst of anger had been motivated by his desire to make her see that the changes he
asked for were in her best interest.

She realized something else. That even though she'd
felt guilty for wanting Howard to show interest in her,
she'd been peeved from time to time that he
hadn't...especially after he kissed her.

Living with Howard had taught her something else.
It had taught her that what she had felt for Denny was
nothing in comparison to real love. Her feelings for
Denny were those sweet passionate yearnings of two
young people as much in love with love as they were
with each other. Though her time with Denny would

always be special, what she'd learned to feel for Howard was far deeper.

Real love was so much more than the quick flaring of passion and common ideals. It was bad times, hard times. The pain of a dozen disappointments. The frequent discord that accompanied the subtle meshing of two disparate lives. Sharing. Learning. Quiet walks in the woods. Studying and praying together. Dragging a passel of orphaned kittens out from under the house and keeping each other awake while the kittens were fed with an eyedropper.

It was caring for someone in spite of his faults— maybe even because of them.

Exhilarated by her new understanding, Eva reached for the telephone and asked Polly to put her through to Pru Burns.

HOWARD SPENT a harrowing Halloween, greeting hosts of goblins at the door, passing out handfuls of candy and wondering if Eva was as miserable as he.

Thanksgiving was spent at his parents, who, though they hadn't approved of Eva, had learned to care for her, despite her penchant for diving headlong into life and flouting conventions. It was as easy to see that her heart was good as it was to see that Howard was lost without her.

Howard ate his mother's traditional dinner, but there was no joy in his heart without Eva at his side.

November dovetailed into December with relative ease. The weather remained the same. Howard's life held a monotony that grated on his nerves, and his misery level was as high as Mattie Hinesley's blood pressure. He longed for a good rousing argument so he'd know he was still alive.

The choir was working on its Christmas cantata, and sounding pretty bad—according to Thaddeus— since Eddie Marshall had moved his family and his wife's gorgeous soprano to El Paso. Though it was supposed to be a joyous time of year, Howard couldn't dredge up much goodwill toward his fellow man.

Two short days before Christmas, he was in Austin buying gifts for his parents, when he saw a deep forest-green suit and cape in a department store window. Something about the ensemble caught his eye, and after studying it for several minutes, he decided that the outfit looked like something Eva might like, even though its classic style didn't call attention to itself. Probably wishful thinking.

Before he could talk himself out of it, he bought the suit, had it gift-wrapped and made arrangements for it to be sent to Eva at the Carmichael's home as soon as possible.

He walked out of the store certain that he'd just blown a month's wages—not that it mattered. Even if Eva accepted the gift, he'd never see her wear it.

HOWARD LEFT the church building on Christmas Eve amid a chorus of Merry Christmases and Happy Holidays. The cantata, such as it was, had gone off with only a few minor glitches, and the potluck get-together before the presentation had been filled with excitement and laughter and a bounty of good food.

Howard drove to the house, glad that it was over. If he could just get through the following day, he could make it to the new year. If he could make it to the new year, he had hopes of making it until spring, when hopefully, the time of new beginnings would jolt him from his doldrums.

Howard pulled into the driveway, got out of the car and let himself in. The soft glow of a lamp in the living room stopped him just inside the doorway. Hadn't he turned off all the lights when he left?

Curiosity drew him through the arched doorway, where the sight he beheld stopped him in his tracks. Eva sat in the wingback chair his parents had left. She was wearing the green suit he'd bought for her.

The soft, draped collar of the suit dipped low—but not scandalously so—and was held together off-center by a dozen or so small, covered buttons. Because she was sitting, the skirt, long and slightly flared, brushed her ankles...ankles wrapped with slender leather straps of gray suede high heels. A felt fedora was tilted over her eye at a rakish angle, and held in place with a long wisp of black chiffon that crossed beneath her chin and trailed down over her back. The matching cape lay draped over the arm of the chair.

Her hair was curled under in a chic pageboy and gleamed in the soft glow of the lamp. Her makeup was artfully applied to enhance her natural beauty. She'd gained some weight, he thought. Thank God.

"I came to thank you for the gift," she said, breaking the growing silence.

Howard shrugged. "I wasn't sure you'd like it, but I thought it had a dramatic look without being..."

"Ostentatious?" she supplied when his voice trailed away. He nodded. "I love it," she said.

"I'm glad."

"How was the cantata?"

"I've heard better. We need a soprano now that Patricia Marshall has moved."

"Maybe I can try out next year," Eva suggested. As Howard watched, she grabbed the arms of the chair and levered herself upward.

Howard sucked in a great gulp of air. She was standing.

"I came to give you your Christmas present, Howard," she said, taking the cane resting beside the chair and moving toward him with unsteady but determined steps. She stopped directly in front of him.

Howard was so stunned and bemused that he could do nothing but look into her blue eyes and wait to see what else she had in store for him. Blood pounded throughout his body. He'd felt more alive for the two minutes that he'd been in Eva's presence than he had since he'd deposited her in her parents' living room.

"What is it?" he asked, afraid—so afraid—he might be misreading the situation.

She undid the ends of the scarf and, pulling the hat from her head, sent it sailing across the room to land on the sofa. The cane clattered to the floor. "Me."

The instant the word left her lips, the first glimmer of uncertainty entered her eyes. Howard's heart thundered in his chest. Reaching out with trembling hands, he took her shoulders and, leaning forward, took her lips in a gentle kiss.

Eva flowed into his embrace, her curves melting against the hard planes of his body like warm butter conforming to a mold. She smelled of Halo shampoo and Tabu cologne. She tasted like the nectar of the gods. Felt like heaven.

Her mouth parted beneath his, deepening the kiss, kicking his libido into high gear. For an instant, he worried whether he could please her the way Denny had, but then Eva moaned in her throat and dug her fingers through his short hair while she ground her mouth against his.

He was lost. Adrift on a sea of pure sensation... the way her breath caressed his wet lips between kisses... the little gasp his touch elicited when he unfastened the dozen buttons of her jacket and slid it from her shoulders to the floor... the way his skin tingled wherever her fingers touched... the way her kisses burned.

He had no idea how long they stood in the middle of the living room and kissed, but unable to wait any longer, Howard swung her up into his arms and carried her to the bedroom.

He had wondered all his life what Eden was. That night, he learned.

"OH, DADDY," Maggie said with a shake of her head. "What a perfectly wonderful ending. I can only imagine how miserable you must have been without Mama."

"And I'm still driving the man crazy," Eva said from the doorway of the waiting room.

"Hello, sweetheart," Howard said. "Did you get some rest?"

"I did." Eva sat down beside him and pressed a kiss to his cheek. "Now it's your turn."

"I think you should both go home," Maggie said. "Rio seems stable, and a lot of people are stopping by to keep me company."

"She has a point, honey," Eva said.

Howard nodded, rose and stretched. "We'll go in a little while. Right now, I'll settle for a cup of coffee. Do you girls want anything?"

"Nothing for me, Daddy, thanks," Maggie said. "Mama?"

Eva shook her head. Eva and Maggie watched Howard leave the room, fond looks on both their faces. Eva turned to her daughter with a twinkle in her blue eyes.

"Do you know what *I* found out that night, Margaret?"

Maggie shook her head.

Eva cast another glance at Howard's retreating figure. "I found out that being a preacher doesn't diminish a man's sexuality one tiny little bit."

"Mama!" Maggie said, scandalized.

"Oh, please, Margaret. You're a modern woman, and I know you talk about these things."

"Not with my mother, I don't."

Eva giggled girlishly. "Well, your mother isn't like most mothers. And your father isn't your garden-variety minister. He's a wonderful man, a superb father and he's a fantastic lover—not necessarily in that order."

This time Maggie couldn't help joining Eva in her laughter. Sobering, Eva said, "You know, there's that poem about the best-laid plans of mice and men going astray? Well, that's exactly what happened in my life. I had my dreams and my goals, and I worked and prayed so hard to make them come true. What I didn't do was pray for God's will to be done... and it always is." Her lips tipped upward at the corners in a smile of supreme happiness, supreme beauty.

"Daddy said you called Pru Burns," Maggie said at last. "Why?"

"Well, once I started thinking about what Emily McKinney told me, I realized that she was right. I could be a positive part of your father's life, even if I did have to spend the rest of my life in braces or a wheelchair. But I didn't want to be in a wheelchair, so I called Pru to see if she'd come over and help me with my exercises. She did, and voilà!" Eva did a quick little tap routine that brought an indulgent smile to her daughter's eyes.

"That easy, huh?" Maggie asked.

Eva shook her head. "No. Not that easy. Admitting you're wrong and that you've behaved badly is never easy. And taking that first step in putting things right is even harder. I have to hand it to Pru. If she hadn't come to apologize, I don't know how long it would have taken for me to gather up the courage to get on with my life."

COURAGE. Maggie thought about her mother's words long after she'd convinced her parents to go home. Courage was one quality she had given little thought to. Courage was something super heroes had in abundance, but after hearing the story of her parents' first year of marriage, she realized that it took courage just to get through each day.

It had taken courage for Rio to get up every day knowing he would be thought of as a bastard, a half-breed. It had taken courage for Serena to trust Cal's love enough to marry him. It had taken courage for Jeremy—who'd been born with the proverbial silver spoon in his mouth—to make the break with a father who had lied to him, and to take on a wife and child at nineteen. It had taken courage for Rick to follow Bull and try to stop him from hurting Rio.

Basically, it took courage to take what life offered you without whining and complaining about the cards you were dealt or placing the blame on those around you—or God.

Facing the possibility of a future without Rio was more than Maggie thought she could bear. Yet she knew that if it was God's will that Rio not survive Bull Farmer's attack, she would pick up the pieces and go on with her life, just the way her mother had.

With a sigh of acceptance, Maggie started for Rio's room in ICU. After hearing her parents' story, she knew that she would never take life or happiness for granted again, but she knew something else, too: she wasn't going to give Rio up without a fight.

RIO LAY STILL, his wide chest rising and falling with every breath he took. Maggie went to stand beside him, taking his hand in both of hers. She closed her eyes and begged God again to spare his life. And then, she added the words she had not been able to say before, "Not my will, Father, but yours."

A strange peace stole over her, and clutching Rio's hand to her breasts, she let her mind go back to their wedding night and the promises they had made to each other after the ceremony, after they had gone home.

"I love you," she had whispered. *"Completely. Forever."* Her eyes brimmed with the sweet sorrow of the memory and she whispered the words into the silence of the hospital room.

"And I'll love you just as much, just as long," Rio had replied. He had kissed her then, as if, she'd thought, he had been waiting to kiss her that way all his life. With a hunger and need that had been as exhilarating as it was frightening. The same way he'd kissed her—was it just two nights ago?

"You promised to love me forever, Rio Langley,'
she said in a tear-roughened voice. "And forever isn'
nearly over yet. Don't you dare think about leaving m
here by myself, because I'm not through loving yo
yet, cowboy. And I'm not raising this baby of our
alone. *Do you hear me?*"

Her voice broke and she laid her head on the edg
of the bed and let the scalding tears fall. She didn'
know how long she cried before she heard a soft
whispery something pass from Rio's lips that sounded
remarkably like "yeah."

Bolting upright, Maggie stared down at him
stunned. His eyes were still closed, and his face wa
still pale. "Rio?" she said, her voice faltering. "D-did
you say something?"

"I said . . . I . . . hear you."

CHAPTER ELEVEN

MAGGIE REPORTED Rio's response to the nurse in charge, who called Nate Purdy and Sonny Dekker. It seemed that both arrived before Maggie could do more than shower Rio's face with kisses and offer up a prayer of thanksgiving.

Confirming her hope that his speaking was a positive sign, Nate ushered Maggie out of the room with instructions to call her folks and break the good news to them. Not only did she call her parents, she called Tess and Jeremy and Cal and Ken. They could spread the news from there.

Thirty minutes later, Maggie was assured by both doctors that Rio had indeed come out of the coma and that things were looking up. They said he needed to get some sleep—some real sleep—and advised her to go home and come back in the morning.

Maggie didn't like leaving him, but since the strain of the past two days was starting to get to her, she decided that, for the baby's sake as well as her own, going home for a few hours was a good idea.

Jeremy flagged her down as she pulled into the lane and announced that Tess had supper ready. Anxiety had robbed Maggie of her appetite the past couple of days, but she realized suddenly that she was starving.

She pulled to a stop next to Jeremy's battered Mustang. When she got out of the car, Rio's baby brother took her in a bear hug and swung her off the ground.

Maggie squealed with surprise and laughter. "Put me down before I heave on you," she said, only half joking.

Jeremy set her to her feet with comical abruptness. Off balance, Maggie grabbed his arm to keep from falling. She gave him a quelling look, but couldn't squelch the half smile that claimed her lips when she saw the unabashed joy in his eyes. "Isn't it great about Rio!" she cried, giving him a big hug in return.

"Better than that."

Maggie looped her arm though Jeremy's, and they started up the steps to the trailer together. Jeremy opened the door and the smell of something spicy assaulted Maggie's nostrils.

"Tacos?" she asked hopefully.

"And beans and rice and guacamole," Tess said, greeting Maggie with a smile and another hug. "I hope you're hungry. I made enough for an army."

"I'm *starving*. Where's Emily?"

"I banished her to her playpen while I finished supper. You can spring her if you want."

"Of course I want," Maggie said, negotiating the narrow hallway that led to the bedrooms.

The trailer house Elena was letting Jeremy and Tess rent was old, but with a little paint, wallpaper and ew good flea market finds, Tess had made the place nto a dollhouse. No, Maggie thought, going into the small room that was Emily's. She'd made it into a home.

Six-month-old Emily was sitting in her playpen chewing on the foot of a rubber giraffe when she spied Maggie. With an excited squeal and wide smile that revealed her two new front teeth, she tossed the toy aside and began to wave her arms.

"You little charmer." Maggie picked up the baby and buried her face in Emily's neck, breathing in the delicious smells of talcum and baby lotion. "I love you, punkin'," she said, heading back to the kitchen. "Yes, I do."

Emily chortled with glee.

Maggie was putting the baby in her high chair when the phone rang. "Can you get that?" Tess said. "I'm elbow deep in tortillas, and Jeremy went to feed Babydoll."

"Sure." Maggie handed Emily a rubber spoon and picked up the receiver. "Westlake residence."

"Tess?"

The voice at the other end of the line belonged to a man. An older man, if Maggie was any judge. Probably Tess's father. "No, this is Maggie."

"Maggie? Rio's wife?"

"Yes," Maggie said, a frown drawing her eyebrows together. "May I ask who's calling?"

"This is John Hardin Westlake. I'm —"

Rio's father. "I know who you are, Mr. West lake," Maggie said, the warmth in her voice plum meting several degrees.

Across the room, Tess dropped the tongs she wa using to turn the hot tortillas.

The man on the other end of the line cleared hi throat. "Yes," he said, "I guess you do. I suppos Jeremy told you he called and told me abou the...shooting."

"Yes."

"Yes, well, I was calling to see how Rio is doing."

Maggie's first reaction was anger. How dared John Hardin Westlake call when he'd denied Rio's very ex istence until a few months ago? Maggie wanted t slam down the receiver. She wanted to give Rio's fa ther a piece of her mind, to tell him he had no busi ness calling either of his sons, but from somewhere i the back of her mind came her father's gentle re minder, followed by her mother's comment just tw days ago.

"Love suffers long and is kind...." Howard woul say.

Your father was born good. I have to work at it, Ev had said.

No doubt about it, Howard Blake was a hard act t follow, and she was definitely her mother's daughter Maggie sighed.

"He's much better this afternoon, Mr. Westlake," she said, striving for civility, since friendliness was ou of the question. "He came out of the coma an hour or so ago."

For a moment, Rio's father said nothing. Then she heard him say softly, "Thank God."

"Yes. Thank God."

"Is there . . . anything I can do?" Westlake asked. "Do you need money or more doctors' opinions?"

He doesn't need your money or your doctors. He's needed your love all these years. "No. We don't need any money, and the doctors here are excellent, thank you. You might keep praying, though," Maggie said. Assuming he had been, of course.

"I will. How is Jeremy? And his . . . family?"

"Fine. Wonderful, actually. Jeremy is outside feeding Rio's dog, and Tess is busy with supper. Did you know Emily has two new teeth?" Maggie asked perversely. Maybe if there was one tiny corner of John Westlake's heart that hadn't been hardened through the years, he would realize just what he was missing by alienating himself from his family.

"No, I didn't."

"Children grow up so fast," Maggie said. "One day they're cutting their first teeth, and before you know it, they've graduated from high school."

"That's very true."

Was that a hint of remorse in Westlake's voice? The urge to tell him about the baby she and Rio were expecting was strong, but a sense of loyalty forbade it. It didn't seem right for him to know before Rio.

"Jeremy told me earlier that they caught the man who shot Rio."

"Yes."

"That's good." Neither spoke for several seconds. Finally, Rio's father sighed, as if he realized he had exhausted every topic of conversation, whether he was finished talking or not. "I'll let you get to your dinner, Maggie. When you see Rio again, you might tell him I called."

"I will."

"Goodbye."

"Goodbye." Maggie recradled the receiver.

"Who was that?" Jeremy asked, as he shut the door behind him.

"Your dad."

Jeremy's eyebrows rose and he shook his head slowly from side to side. "I have to give the devil his due. He's been calling several times a day ever since I told him about the shooting."

Tess looked from Maggie to Jeremy and back again. She shrugged. "Maybe he's discovering he has a heart after all."

MAGGIE WAS LYING in bed, reliving the moment Rio had spoken to her and trying to contain her excitement over his improvement, when a memory of John Westlake's hesitant voice intruded. She heard Tess's comment about the possibility of Westlake discovering he had a heart and realized that her own treatment of Rio's father had crossed the boundary into downright rudeness. After all, he had cared enough about Rio's condition to call.

Admitting you're wrong and that you've behaved badly is never easy. And taking that first step in putting things right is even harder.

Her mother was right, Maggie thought, as shame coursed through her. John Hardin Westlake might have treated his sons despicably, but he was a human being whose heart could obviously still be touched. Whatever mistakes he had made in his past, whatever he had done to Jeremy and Rio, judging him was not her place.

The realization brought a measure of peace. The next time Rio's father called, she would apologize for her shortness. She would be nice. Genuinely nice... and heap those coals of fire on him that the Bible spoke of.

Rio and Jeremy would have to work through their feelings about their father themselves.

MAGGIE SLEPT like the dead and didn't awaken until midmorning the following day. Fearful that something might have happened during the night, she called the hospital and was told that Rio was doing fine. Thankfulness washed through her on a giant wave. She knew he had a long way to go before he'd be his usual active self, but at least he was out of the woods.

She spent the next thirty minutes fixing her hair and putting on her makeup, so that her pale face and the dark circles beneath her eyes wouldn't scare him into

a relapse. Then she drove to the hospital and found to
her surprise and pleasure that Nate had moved Rio
from ICU into a private room.

As she searched for the room number, Maggie saw
a middle-aged man with a paunch and thinning gray
hair pacing the hallway a few feet past Rio's door.
With her usual friendliness, she smiled. The quick
humorless lift of the man's lips held no real emotion.
Probably worried over someone, she thought, turning the knob and letting herself into Rio's room.

"Hello...gorgeous."

Maggie thought the two softly spoken words were
the most beautiful she'd ever heard, and that they'd
been uttered by the most beautiful man in the world.
Her eyes filled as she drank in the sight of Rio, who
was looking at her with eyes glazed with pain and the
effects of the medication he was on.

"Hello gorgeous, yourself," she said, crossing to
him and pressing a kiss to his dry lips. "How are
you?"

His smile resembled a grimace. "Don't think
I'm...up to any...bareback riding...just yet."

"I don't think so either," Maggie said with a tender
smile. "But I'm just glad you're back from wherever
it was you went."

"It would have been...easy just to...keep sleeping. I...dreamed a lot."

"Good dreams, I hope."

Another of those pitiful smiles claimed his mouth.
"Dreamed me and Slats at this bar...doin' the two-

step with some...good-lookin' dollies. Me and Cal...gettin' stomped by bulls. Was Flash here?" Rio asked. "Or was I...dreamin'? Thought...I heard him...a time or two."

Maggie smiled at Rio's nickname for Cal McKinney. "He was. He, Ken and Elena have spent almost as much time here as my parents and I have."

Rio made another attempt at a smile. "They're good...people." The look in his eyes grew grave. "I almost...died...didn't I?"

Maggie gripped his hand. "It was nip and tuck there for a while."

He tried to nod. "I was hurtin' real bad, Maggie. I kept wantin' to just...let this...dark place...pull me under, but...you guys wouldn't let me go. You kept...telling me to...come back. You *made* me...come back."

"How?" Maggie asked, wondering if he'd experienced one of those controversial life after death experiences.

"Everyone kept tellin' me...not to...give up. You. Slats. Could...swear Cal kept...sayin' I couldn't die, 'cause I owed him money...and we had a deal. He sounded like...he'd been...cryin'. And I heard...you say you weren't...finished lovin' me yet."

"I'm not," Maggie told him, smoothing back his black hair.

"What happened, anyway?"

"You don't remember?"

Rio's head moved in a slight negative motion "Slats...tried to tell me a while ago...but I...flaked out...on him."

"I'll tell you, if you just shut up and listen. You're talking too much."

"Yes...ma'am."

Maggie told him what had happened after he'd answered the summons of the phone. She explained how she and Jeremy had found Rick standing over him holding the revolver, and how helpless she'd been.

"Rick...didn't...do it." Conviction laced his voice.

"I know." She told him what Rick had told Wayne Jackson, and how, when the state troopers had picked up Bull, he had confessed to pulling the trigger.

"Then you went and scared me to death by slipping off into a coma."

"I'm sorry," he said in all seriousness.

Maggie gave him a loving smile. "Just make sure you don't ever do it again," she told him.

"Do my best."

There was a soft rapping at the door and a nurse poked in her head. "I've got some more flowers." She unpinned the card and handed it to Maggie, and then set the bouquet of roses on a nearby table and left the room.

Maggie opened the small, rectangular envelope. The card read: *I'm more sorry than I can say. Hope you're soon on your feet. John Hardin Westlake.*

"They're from your father," Maggie said, reading the inscription to Rio. Instead of replying, Rio closed his eyes. In a matter of minutes, he had fallen asleep. Maggie sighed. Smiled. Pulled the sheet higher in a loving gesture. She hadn't even told him about the baby yet.

VISITING HOURS that afternoon brought an influx of visitors, but the nurses were like watchdogs—determined that the people who visited their patient stayed only for short periods of time. Wayne Jackson came, saying that he knew there was no way to pry Maggie away from Rio's bedside long enough to get her statement, so he'd come to take it himself. He'd get Rio's when he was stronger.

Jeremy and Tess came that night, leaving Elena to watch Emily. The genuine love in Jeremy's eyes as he stood looking down at his big brother brought tears to Maggie's eyes. Would she ever get over being so weepy? she wondered.

Jeremy spent thirty minutes telling Rio what was going on at the ranch, what Cal had accomplished in Calgary, and bragging about Emily's newest accomplishments. Mostly, Rio listened. Talking sapped his small reserves of energy.

"What about that fence over in the...north pasture?" Rio asked.

"I've been really shorthanded without Rick," Jeremy said. "I had to put it off."

Rio nodded.

"I went to see Rick this afternoon," Jeremy said almost fearfully. The only emotion in Rio's eyes was curiosity, and Jeremy relaxed. "I wanted to tell him I was sorry for jumping on him that night. I was way outta line to just place the blame on him like that. Being scared is no excuse."

"Maybe not," Maggie consoled, "but it's understandable."

"He's been really worried about you, and he'd like to come and see you, but he isn't sure you want to see him," Jeremy said to Rio.

"What Bull did doesn't affect...how I feel...about Rick," Rio said.

"I thought you might say that," Jeremy said with a half smile. "He's in the waiting room. I'll go get him."

Maggie couldn't help recalling what her mother had said about courage. While Jeremy's apology to Rick might not have taken courage, it *was* proof that he was growing up. Facing Rio was courageous of Rick, too. It would have been easy for him to assume that the relationship he shared with Rio had been made null and void by Bull's act of violence.

Rick returned with Jeremy a few minutes later and stood near the door with his head bowed. Maggie had the impression that he might take flight at any moment. Tess and Jeremy slipped from the room.

"Hi," Rio said, his voice still weak and breathless.

Rick refused to meet Rio's eyes. "Hi."

"I'm sorry...about what happened."

Surprise and wariness brought Rick's head up. "What are you sorry for?"

"That... Sheriff Jackson took you in... that you had to go through all... that booking stuff. Jail. Must have been... hard."

Rick shrugged. "I only spent one night there. It wasn't so bad." He took a step nearer the bed. "I'm the one who's sorry. I just wanted you to know."

"No need to be," Rio said with a hint of a smile.

Maggie suspected the gleam in Rick's eyes was tears. She saw him swallow.

"Bull's screwed up my whole life. I been trying to live down his reputation for as long as I can remember, but I never thought I had a chance of being anything until you and Ms. Langley came along." Rick's voice cracked with emotion. "All you ever did was try to help me, and now Bull's messed that up, too."

"How's... that?"

"I like to never found a job after that deal with the dog. Who's gonna hire me now?"

"I thought you... had a job," Rio said. "Jeremy said that fence... in the north pasture is still down."

"You still want me to work for you after what Bull's done?" Rick asked, unable to hide his shock.

"Way I... see it, one has... nothing to do... with the other."

It took Rick a moment to digest that. As he stood there, his face crumpled like a hurt child's. "Thank you," he mumbled and bolted from the room. Maggie was the only witness to the tears wetting his cheeks.

She put her hand on Rio's shoulder. "That was a good thing you did."

"He's a good . . . kid."

"I'm glad we agree on that."

"We agree on . . . most things—except what we're gonna . . . name our baby."

"Who told you about the baby?" Maggie wailed, unable to believe that the doctor or her parents had let the cat out of the bag before she had a chance to break the news.

"Simmer down...sweet...Maggie," Rio said. "You told me."

"Me?" The only time she'd said anything was when he was in the coma. "Are you saying that you could hear me?"

He nodded. "It's taken me a while to . . . piece together what was dreams and . . . what I really heard, but . . . I'm pretty sure . . . I heard you saying that we were going to . . . have a baby, and you had . . . no intention of . . . raising it alone. You were pretty . . . emphatic about that. Mad."

A blush stained Maggie's cheeks. "I was upset," she said, defending her anger. "I was mad at everyone— Bull for shooting you, you for answering the door. God."

"Wasn't his fault."

"I know," she said, tracing a finger down the groove in his lean cheek. "I just wanted you to get better."

"I will. I am. And I have no intention of . . . letting you raise our child alone."

"Good."

He smiled, the closest thing to a real smile he'd been able to muster. "I think we should name the boy... Jacob Cain... and call him Jake."

"Boy?" Maggie said in mock surprise. "I'm having a daughter. Evalyn Delora Elena Langley."

There was a pleased expression in Rio's dark eyes. "That's quite a mouthful... for a kid. Jake's easier."

Pretending not to hear, Maggie said, "We'll call her Delora. No, Eve." She frowned. "Do you think Elena's feelings will be hurt?"

Rio shook his head. "Not Elena. I have an idea. That'll... solve everything."

"What's that?"

"Let's just have three girls... and a boy, and you won't have to worry about... hurting anyone's feelings."

"If you really sweet-talk me, I might take that into consideration, but for now, I have a better idea."

"What's that?"

"Let's just get this first baby here all healthy and safe—no matter what we call *her.*"

Rio's lips twitched. "For God's sake, don't...make me laugh."

"Oh!" she cried, leaning over him with genuine contrition. "I'm sorry."

Rio got control of his laughter and reached up a heavy hand to touch her cheek.

"I love you."

"I love you too, cowboy."

Rio's fingers trailed to her mouth. "Bull Farmer taught me . . . some valuable lessons, Maggie. Revenge . . . isn't worth a damn. Life is . . . too short to be miserable . . . and too uncertain to . . . hold grudges."

"What are you trying to say, Rio?"

"That when I'm able, I'm going to go to Austin and do my best to make peace with my father."

CHAPTER TWELVE

RIO WAS HOME by mid-December. Howard said that it was as if, once he'd made up his mind to get well, there was no stopping him. Bull Farmer was formally charged with the shooting and remanded to the Claro County jail to await trial. Knowing there would be no retribution from Bull, Ada took her courage in hand and filed for a divorce. Rick said Bull didn't plan to contest it.

With Christmas just ten days away, there was a lot to be done to get the Langley place ready for the holidays. Not only was Maggie behind at work, she still had her decorating, shopping and baking to do. Rio said to forget it; she told him "no way." It was their first Christmas together, and she intended for it to be memorable.

"So there!" Elena added, her hands planted firmly on her hips.

No sooner did Maggie get Rio home from the hospital than she turned around, took the pickup and headed back into town. She came home with the bed filled by a gorgeous tree that she, Tess and Elena proceeded to decorate with clear lights and red orna-

ments of every size and shape, while Elvis Presley san
about a blue Christmas.

The next day, the trio started the Christmas bak
ing. Emily, who'd had a rough night cutting teeth, wa
ensconced in her high chair—albeit unwillingly—an
Rio, who was sick of bed and already complainin
about being bored, joined them in the kitchen. Mag
gie gave him an arch look and set several small bowl
of colored frosting and a platter of cutout suga
cookies in front of him with the instructions to ge
busy. Muttering under his breath, Rio began to slap
icing onto the cookies.

Five minutes later, the muttering stopped from botl
Emily and Rio. Rio was munching on cookies and en
grossed in making the Christmas tree he was decorat
ing a work of art; Emily was chomping on a teethin
biscuit, and soggy crumbs covered her from ear to ear

Maggie smiled. She was sure Delora had made Rio'
Christmases the best she could, but there was no de
nying that he had been forced to grow up too fast
Thank God there was still enough little boy in him tha
he could enjoy the simple things life offered.

Maggie was measuring flour for her fruitcake wher
the front doorbell rang.

"Can you get that, Maggie?" Elena asked. "I have
candied pineapple stuck to every finger."

"Sure." Maggie popped a green cherry into her
mouth and headed for the living room. The womar
standing with her back to Maggie turned with the
opening of the door.

Ada Farmer, Maggie thought in surprise. The last person she expected to see on her doorstep. Why would Bull Farmer's wife come to see her? Though Ada was clean and neat as usual, she looked as uncomfortable as Maggie felt. The older woman didn't speak. She just stood there, twisting the strap of her shoulder bag.

"Ada!" Maggie said, finding her voice at last. "Won't you come in?"

Ada stepped over the threshold. "Thank you."

"How are you?" Maggie asked, indicating a chair for her guest.

"I'm fine, Miz Langley." Ada lifted her chin a notch and sat down. "Actually, I haven't been this good in a long while. Not since before I said 'I do' to Bull eighteen years ago."

Maggie perched on the edge of Rio's worn recliner and laced her fingers together. "Rick said you filed for divorce."

Ada's bravado deserted her, and the haunted look reappeared. "I should have done it long ago. I'd have saved me and my kids a lot of misery and heartache."

"Making a decision like that is always hard," Maggie told her.

"Don't I know it!" Ada took a tissue from her purse and dabbed at the corners of her eyes. "I was afraid of him, Miz Langley. And afraid to be out on my own with three young'uns to feed and no schoolin' to fall back on."

"There are ways, programs that can help—"

"I know. I'm finding out about more every day. I'v
been out looking for cleaning jobs. It'll be hard, bu
me and the kids can make it."

"I'm sure you can," Maggie said gently.

Ada's gaze shifted from Maggie's, and she drew
deep breath. "I come for two reasons. First off, I wan
to thank you and your mother and—and your man fo
all you done for my boy."

Maggie shook her head. "All we did was give Ric
a chance."

"That's more'n most would have done." A tenta
tive smile of pleasure glowed in Ada's dark eyes. "Mi
Blake just called and told me that Rick got that schol
arship she helped him apply for."

"Oh, Ada, that's wonderful!" Maggie cried, gen
uinely pleased.

"It won't cover everything, but it's a beginning. A
least he'll have a shot at getting a college education."

"He'll do more than that. He'll get his diploma. Ric
and I will help all we can."

"Why would you do that?" Ada asked point-blank
the bewilderment back in her eyes.

"Why?" Maggie echoed.

Ada nodded. "Why would you want to help a kic
whose old man shot your husband? Why would you
husband want to help Rick?"

"Because Rio knows what it's like to have to live
down your heritage. Because we both see something in
Rick worth saving. And because it's our duty as

Christians to forgive one another and to gladly help those who need help."

Ada's eyes filled with tears. She nodded, as if the answer satisfied her. "I wanted to say that I'm sorry for that day in the grocery store when Fran Dunbarr was talking about you and Mr. Langley."

Ada gripped her purse so tightly her knuckles turned white. "I didn't hold with what she was sayin' but I didn't try to stop the gossip either, and that makes me a party to it, same's if I'd said those things myself. I want you to know that I'm real sorry, ma'am."

"Thank you, Ada," Maggie said, controlling her emotions through sheer force of will. "That means a lot to me."

Ada rose to leave.

"Would you like to stay for coffee and cookies?"

"No, thank you. I need to get home and start supper. Janice has choir practice tonight."

"I didn't know Janice sang in the choir," Maggie said.

"She didn't until your mother heard the glee club sing for the kids at the hospital the other day. Miz Eva says she's the best alto she's heard in ages. She's singing a duet with your mother in the cantata." The gleam of pride and pleasure was back in Ada's eyes.

Thank you, Mama! Maggie smiled. "Mama has an ear for talent, and she's an excellent teacher. Tell Janice I wish her luck."

"I will."

Maggie ushered her guest to the door. As Ada stepped off the porch and onto the sidewalk, Maggie called, "Merry Christmas, Ada."

"Same to you, ma'am."

"Yoohoo! Reinforcements have arrived!"

Maggie, who was stealing a kiss or two while Rio shaved, groaned. "Mama. I forgot she was coming to help me fix some things to take to the church get-together tonight."

With Rio unable to attend, Maggie had wanted to skip the church's annual Christmas party, but her husband would have none of it. She needed to get out for a while, and he was certainly well enough to sit in front of the television for a couple of hours alone. Besides, Elena could "baby-sit," if Maggie thought it was necessary.

"It's high time she got here," Rio said with a smile that bordered on grim. "You keep that stuff up, and I'll be right back in the hospital—cardiac arrest this time."

Maggie pressed a kiss above the bandage that still swathed his broad chest. "You know just what to say to make a girl feel good about herself, don't you?"

"Just bein' truthful, sweet Maggie."

Maggie smiled. "I want you to finish shaving and go back to bed. I think you're doing too much too fast."

"Not nearly fast enough for me," Rio said. Seeing the stern look in her eyes, he nodded. "I hear you.

Now go out there and start makin' some more goodies."

"Slave driver," she said, but she smiled.

"If I take my nap, can I get up for lunch?" Rio asked with false humility.

Maggie coaxed her features into a reproachful look. "Do you promise to eat all your broccoli?"

"Oh, yes, ma'am," Rio said, making an *X* over his heart.

"Then I'll think about it."

His rich chuckle followed Maggie from the room.

Maggie found Eva in the kitchen, already assembling the ingredients for peanut brittle. She brushed her mother's soft-scented cheek with a kiss. "'Morning, Mama."

"'Morning, dear. How's Rio?"

"Good, but not half as good as he thinks he is."

"Aren't men the absolute worst patients you've ever encountered?" Eva asked with a shake of her head.

"The worst," Maggie agreed.

"I hope I didn't interrupt anything, barging in like that," Eva said with a sly, sideways look.

"Only a kiss and lot of wishful thinking," Maggie told her with a sigh.

Eva laughed. "'This, too, shall pass,'" she quoted. "and how's our little mother-to-be?"

"I'm great, with the exception of a queasy stomach every now and then."

"You lucky dog. I heaved for months with my pregnancies."

It was Maggie's turn to smile.

"I had a bit of good news yesterday," Eva said. "Rick Farmer got the Claro County Businessmen's Scholarship."

"I know. Ada told me."

"Ada? Where did you see her?"

"She came by yesterday to apologize for talking about me and Rio and to thank us for helping Rick."

"That was big of her."

Maggie nodded.

"If she and those kids want to, they can turn this all around. In time, people will forget," Eva said.

"Like they did with you and Daddy?"

"Yes."

"What did you do? I mean, after you and Daddy got together, what made people change their minds about you?"

"Well, I worked hard," Eva said. "I started taking courses at the community college over in Hillsboro so I could get my teaching certificate in Drama and Speech." She smiled. "As you're well aware, I taught for thirty years. I became my husband's helpmeet. I'd like to think I became a better person along the way."

"You're a wonderful person," Maggie said.

"Thanks, honey. But to answer your question, I guess what I'm trying to say is that I believe people are willing to give you the benefit of the doubt if they see you making a sincere attempt to change. I think that's what they'll do with Ada and her family."

"I hope so."

"Me, too. So," Eva said, changing the subject to something more upbeat, "have you decided what you're going to wear tonight?"

"I'm still thinking about it," Maggie said.

"That's what I like about you, honey," Eva said, pouring the sack of raw peanuts into the boiling mixture. "You're such a decisive person."

THOUGH IT WOULD HAVE hurt Maggie to the bone to know it, Rio was glad for the time to himself. He'd turned off most of the lights and the TV. The leaping and dancing of the flames in the grate was all the entertainment he needed. He'd been a loner for too many years to take all this maternal clucking in stride. Hell, he hadn't had so many women fluttering around him since the year Cal had won Best All-Round Cowboy and Rio had gone with him to Billy Bob's over in Fort Worth.

Rio smiled at the memory. Flash had been in rare form that night. Come to think about it, so had he. But he wouldn't change a second of his life with Maggie for all the girls in Billy Bob's. In all of Texas, for that matter.

Rio stared at the fire, his face a study in thought. Bull Farmer's brand of retaliation had shown Rio that he had taken his life too much for granted. Riding in the rodeo, he'd been busted up more times than he could count. The possibility that one day a nasty critter might kick in his head was always in the back of his mind, but the thought that he might not live to a ripe old age had never seriously bothered him until now. The idea that he might have checked out, leaving Maggie with a child to raise alone, made him break out in a cold sweat.

Rio drew a deep breath and wished he hadn't. He still hurt like hell. He shook out a pain pill and took it with a sip of the tepid hot chocolate Maggie had fixed before she left.

Maggie. Was there another woman like her on the face of the earth? Though there had never been any doubt about his feelings for her, Rio was more aware of how special that love was now than he had been a few short weeks ago.

The sound of a car in the lane caught his attention. Maggie had probably forgotten something, or it was Elena coming to check on him. He listened intently, but the car's engine didn't sound familiar. Rio's forehead puckered, and he levered himself to his feet. He heard the slamming of a car door and someone walking on the porch. It wasn't Maggie. It wasn't a woman.

A heavy hand knocked on the door. Automatically, Rio started to go open it. Stopped. Memories of the last time he'd opened that front door swept through him in vivid, shocking detail. Despite himself, he felt a fine sheen of perspiration break out on his upper lip.

The knock came again. Moving cautiously, Rio went to the window and peeked out. A silver Mercedes sat in the driveway. Surely someone who drove a Mercedes wasn't out to do violence. Calling himself

en kinds of fool, Rio opened the door and encountered a masculine hand raised and ready to knock.

His gaze moved to the visitor's face, and his eyes
widened in surprise. The man standing in the doorway was John Hardin Westlake. His father. The man
Rio had vowed he would try to make peace with as
soon as he was physically able.

Surprise mingled with a residual anger and resentment. A generous dollop of pain rubbed elbows with
his new sense of duty and determination to do the right
thing. Trying to make peace had seemed like a good
idea a couple of weeks ago, the right thing to do to get
his life on track. But now, with the man who was responsible for his existence standing before him, Rio
had no idea what to say or do.

If possible, Westlake looked even older now than he
had three short months ago, when Rio had gone to his
mansion in Austin and confronted him about Jeremy... and Delora. Older and beaten. As if life had
reared back and kicked him in the gut.

"Hello, Rio," his father said, breaking the long,
uncomfortable silence that stretched between them.

Rio gave a short nod of acknowledgment.

"May I come in?"

Rio stepped aside.

His father entered the living room and looked
around. "Nice place."

"Mom did it, mostly," Rio said, deliberately men-
tioning the woman John Westlake had used and dis-
carded.

Westlake turned and met Rio's steady gaze. "She was always a talented woman."

Rio's surprise was surpassed only by his curiosit about what Westlake had in mind. "What can I do fo you?"

"I came to see how you were doing."

Again, Rio was torn between his feeling that hi father's concern was overdue and pleasure that he'd cared enough to make the drive from Austin. "I'n fine, thanks."

"I'm glad," Westlake said with a nod. "May I si down?"

"Sure."

John Westlake took a seat on the sofa. "I'd hoped to see Jeremy and . . . his family while I was here."

"They went to Hillsboro to visit some friends."

"I see. And your wife? Maggie, isn't it?"

Rio nodded. "Yeah. She's at a Christmas party a the church."

Westlake accepted the news with another nod. " came, Rio, because. . ." His voice trailed away as if he were having trouble finding the right words. He stared at the hands clasped between his knees. Finally, he looked up. "I came to try and resolve the hard feel ings between us . . . if possible."

Rio was too stunned to comment. He couldn't have thought of a reply if his life had depended on it. Fi nally, he said, "My mother loved you, and you kicked her out of your life. You don't know what she wen through trying to bring up her half-breed bastard."

Westlake flinched at Rio's choice of words. "I don't deny that I've committed my share of sins and made my share of mistakes," he said. "I've put success and my quest for money and things ahead of the people in my life. I've hurt my share of people and made a lot of enemies. But I got that success I wanted. I made the money. I have three houses in the States, one in Athens. I have several cars and servants and clothes and more *things* than I know what to do with."

Rio had a sneaking suspicion that a big "but" was coming on.

"But I don't have a family. I don't have any love. My son—neither of my sons has any use or respect for me." His mouth twitched in a humorless smile. "It's a pitiful story, isn't it? Poor old rich man. Everyone should be so miserable."

The hell of it was, it was a pitiful story. John Westlake *was* a poor old rich man. Three weeks ago, Rio would have said that John Hardin Westlake was only reaping what he'd sowed, that he deserved everything he got, but staring down death had given Rio a new perspective. He hadn't been put on earth to judge his father's mistakes or to cheer because he was down. He was here to offer what compassion and help he could. He was here to forgive.

"A few weeks ago, I'd have kicked you out on your butt and told you to take your pathetic story straight to hell," Rio said.

"And now?"

"Maggie and her family have taught me a lot abou tolerance and sacrifice and good old-fashioned guts Almost dying taught me that life is too short to b miserable or to add to another person's misery. I go my own sins to worry about, my own mistakes to cor rect. I'm not in any position to cast stones."

"That's more than I'd hoped for from you." West lake's voice was rough with emotion. He rose to leave

Rio did the same. He supposed it was okay... for beginning.

His father was at the door when Rio spoke. "Yo say you don't have a family. You're wrong. You hav a family. But having their love and respect is som. thing else. Love is a mutual feeling. If you don't giv it, you don't get it back. Respect is earned."

"I know what you're saying, and I appreciate wher you're coming from," Westlake said. "Maybe in time I can at least earn your and Jeremy's respect. And fo whatever it's worth, I loved and respected Delor Langley. I just didn't love her enough."

The confession brought a sharp stab of pain to Rio' heart. He drew himself up straighter. That was quit an admission for a man like Westlake.

"Will you tell Jeremy that I'm glad he called to tel me about your accident and that I came by to se him?"

"Sure."

Westlake was at the door when it burst open an Maggie, who looked like a million dollars in a blac sweater dress, barreled in.

"Now don't start fussing at me," she said, shaking her finger at Rio. "I couldn't stand it without you. Whose car is that out in—?"

Her sentence came to an abrupt halt when she came face-to-face with Rio's father. For a moment, she was too stunned to speak. Confusion darkened her eyes. "I saw you at the hospital," she blurted out. "Outside Rio's room."

Rio moved to Maggie's side and closed the door. "This is Maggie, my wife," he said. "Maggie, this is John Hardin Westlake. My father."

HOWARD FLIPPED through the stations, looking for something to watch while he waited for Eva to get off the phone. He started to call out and see what she wanted to watch, but she was obviously engrossed in her conversation. They'd hardly stepped through the door from the party when the phone had rung. At first he'd feared it was one of the congregation with a problem, but if it was, Eva must be handling it herself. He smiled. Was there another woman like her in the world?

He stopped the channel selector at a station that specialized in country and western dancing. "Club Country" was in full swing, with couples in matching outfits doing the Cotton-eyed Joe.

"That was Maggie," Eva said, kicking off her high heels and coming into the living room.

"Is everything okay? Rio's all right?"

"Rio is fine—she thinks."

Howard rolled his eyes. "And what is that sup
posed to mean?"

Eva took off her earrings. "Rio had a visitor whil
we were at the party."

"Oh?"

"His father," Eva said, sitting down next to How
ard on the sofa.

"Westlake?" Howard wiggled his eyebrows an
drew Eva into a close embrace. "The plot thicken
What did he want?"

"To make his peace with Rio and try to straighte
things out with Jeremy."

"Mmm. Makes sense. He's getting older. He has n
one but Jeremy and Rio left, and he's probably lonely
A lot of people want to make their peace with th
world—and God—when they know their time is lim
ited. What else did she say?"

"To set another place for Christmas dinner. Sinc
Mr. Westlake made the first move, she thought
might be nice to invite him over, too, since Jeremy
Tess and Emily will be here."

Howard chuckled. "That sounds like Maggie. Doe
she think Rio was really okay with his dad?"

"She says he is." Eva drew back and looked up a
Howard. She smoothed a rose-tipped finger over hi
eyebrow. "I know you didn't want me to tell anyon
about what had happened between us all those year
ago, but I honestly think it did Maggie and Rio a l
of good to know that their situation wasn't unique."

"What can I say? Once again I bow to your superior wisdom."

"Flatterer." She drew a deep, determined breath. "You know, Howard, I feel better for telling it, too. Whoever said confession is good for the soul knew what he was talking about."

The driving rhythm of "Achy, Breaky Heart" filled the room, and the people of "Club Country" lined up and began to do the steps to the popular line dance with enviable precision.

"Oh, look!" Eva cried, her eyes alight with pleasure. "They're doing the Achy Breaky."

"So they are." For several minutes, he watched her watching the dancers. "Evie..." he said at last.

"Hmm?" she asked, completely engrossed.

"Do you have anything else you want to confess?"

She turned to face him, wide-eyed with surprise. "What could I possibly be keeping from you?" she asked.

A devilish light gleamed in Howard's blue eyes. "Come on, now. You just said confession was good for the soul."

Eva felt her face flame. "Oh, you!" She reached out and pinched him hard on the arm. "All right, all right. I cannot tell a lie. Sometimes while you're at the office I do country and western dancing here in the living room. I'm a wicked, evil woman. Burn me at the stake."

"I have a better idea," Howard said, his mouth curved in a tender smile.

"What's that?"

"Dance with me."

As if on cue, the fast song ended and Garth Brooks's tender "Unanswered Prayers" sent couples into each other's arms. Eva stood and moved into Howard's embrace. Her head rested against his chest over his heart.

The tender melody was no more tender than the feel of Howard's arms around her as they moved around the room in a sweet synchronization of their own, the synchronization that comes from being with each other through good and bad, from taking the time to learn each other's likes and dislikes, the sweet synchronization of love.

"Not bad for a guy who never dances," she said drawing back to look up at him.

"Who says I never dance?" he replied.

"Howard..."

His smile was unrepentant. "You know the night you go to visit at the hospital?"

"Ye-e-e-s," she said with raised eyebrows. "Howard, what are you saying?"

Howard jerked her close and draped her over his arm in a dramatic dip. "Don't play the dumb blonde with me, Eve. You do the redheaded seductress much better."

"Oh, really?" she said as he pulled her upright.

He brushed a lock of auburn hair away from her cheek. "Don't you still have that gown you wore on our wedding night?"

"The one with the ostrich feather peignoir you made me take off?"

"Uh-huh."

"Yes, why?"

Howard's smile was slow and every bit as naughty as that of a man thirty years younger. "I thought if you put it on, I'd make you take it off again."

"Animal," Eva said with a soft giggle.

As she led Howard toward the bedroom, she drew a deep breath of happiness and satisfaction. The song was right. Sometimes the greatest gifts of all came from unanswered prayers.